# NOTHING DENY

## SCARLETT FINN

# Also by Scarlett Finn

# ONE

"THIS IS CRAZY," Freya Dere said.

Without any hesitation, her cousin, Holly, tugged her along the sidewalk and through the glass doors of a building right in the heart of the city.

How could it be so central? So unashamed?

No, Freya, not the right mindset. She didn't judge, as such, it was just a surprise the agency wasn't in some seedy corner of town. Hidden, not so… public. Was Squires in the directory? Surely not.

Calm. Different businesses rented out floor space. No one would know what went on in every corner, would they? God, what was she doing? Their intention was to do something illegal. Illegal!

What the hell was wrong with her? Most people worried about falling victim to peer pressure when they were teens. She was most definitely not a teen, so why, at her age, was she embarking on a criminal career for the first time? Family, that's why. Oh, family.

Looked like she was about to get an answer to her question. Holly stopped to check the building directory. Her? No, she couldn't look. Plausible deniability. Seeing was believing… and culpability. This was taking too long. They were loitering where people could see them. Hadn't her cousin claimed to know where she was going? Why the stop?

"You know what would be crazy?" Holly asked. "Us, putting up with Kelly's nonsense without backup."

She and her cousins were raised close. Relatively close. Close… ish. Okay, maybe not so close. Still, they kept in touch, not a lot of families even did that. Holly and Kelly Piven were the daughters of Gerry and Brenda Piven. The two sisters had a brother as well, Alan, and the three siblings grew up in a picture-perfect life with their parents.

To be fair, hers hadn't been far from perfect either. Except, obviously, the glaring blight on her upbringing: the loss of her parents. Okay, admittedly, most wouldn't call that perfect. Their deaths left her under the care of her paternal grandfather, Truman Dere, a man richer than God and more ruthless than Lucifer. So other people said. That hadn't been her experience, but as his only living blood relative, her position was unique.

Her grandfather should be the last man on her mind while waiting for an elevator to a place he'd despise her visiting.

The metal doors whooshed open and whoa, boy… this was happening, it was actually happening… New year, new adventure. Was that the idea?

Holly grabbed her hand to pull her into the carriage and stabbed a button, wearing a gleeful grin.

"An escort agency," she muttered, watching the numbers light as they ascended. "This is a bad idea."

Holly huffed. "Seriously, Frey, I mean, seriously? You've heard Kelly, right? Heard how she's so loved up, so adored, so perfect? Aren't you sick of it?"

"Hearing how amazing Nickson is twenty-four, seven? Yes, I am sick of that. Very sick of it. But I am also tired of listening to how amazing your fictitious boyfriend is."

Holly had reason to be upset about the state of her love life. When the woman started talking about new boyfriend, "Paul," Freya assumed things were looking up. That false picture lasted right up until she learned "Paul" was nothing but a figment of Holly's imagination. What a tangled web…

"This is going to make it all okay," Holly said, looping an arm through hers and lifting her chin. "Loretta recommended this place. Loretta knows everything."

Loretta being Holly's boss. The two had been friends for years. To say that Holly idolized the older woman would be an understatement. For the most part, the relationship was healthy… not that she knew a lot about it. What she did know? Loretta was more daring than anyone in their family. And right then, Loretta could be their undoing.

They arrived on the agency's floor. Still reluctant, her heavy feet would only move with Holly's effort dragging her out. The beautiful lobby looked more like an expensive apartment than an office. Good, okay, the environment put her at ease.

Wait, was that good?

No orgies or mandatory nudity, those were good. Couches, warm colors, perfect lighting, it seduced her like a sailor to a siren, probably exactly the decorator's aim.

Freya dug her heels in and stopped, backing them up to the wall. "Please, Hol, you know I can't—"

"Yes, you can," Holly said, letting go of her arm to cup both hands around her face. "You are allowed to have fun, Frey. You're even allowed to have sex."

According to who? Not her grandfather.

"Truman will build me a dungeon," she said, certain in the widening of her eyes. "An actual dungeon, if he finds out about this."

"You thought he'd cut you off when you went out on your own," Holly said. "You said he wouldn't like you getting an apartment or building the foundation."

Like it or not, her grandfather hadn't stood in the way of her creating Children's Connection, ChilConn, her now-thriving charity. Truman Dere excelled at supporting her… usually.

"This isn't exactly the same thing."

"It will be fine."

If only she could have the same confidence. "Hol—"

"It's no big deal," Holly said, straightening up, exaggerating her grin. "This is a fun adventure. We're being daring. Don't you want to be daring?" When Freya tried to shake her head, Holly tightened her grip to clamp it still. "Men do this all the time. All over the world. Every day. And this place has the good stuff, we're not curb-crawling. It's elite. Top secret. No one will know what we've done. All we need is a couple of men to be loved up and devoted, just like Nickson. It's the only thing that will make our lives bearable. Don't you want a bearable life?"

"A bearable life?" Freya muttered. "Yes, I do, but—"

"My sister is marrying a man who proposed after two months of dating. Two! They're getting married, talking about houses and kids. And what are we doing? Nothing. We're losers, love losers."

Hmm, she couldn't argue against that.

"But—"

"My father is forcing us to go away with them to get to know this man who came from completely nowhere. Do you know how many social functions we're going to have until this damn wedding? Days, maybe weeks, at some resort with my sister and her adoring fiancé, a private engagement party, a public engagement party. We have the bridal shower, bachelorette parties—"

"I don't see how fake boyfriends will help us with that."

Stepping back, Holly thrust her fists to her hips. "You don't want to be the only loser singleton at a bachelorette party. Trust me, that's announcing eternal spinsterhood." Whoa, wow. "Besides, we can send *our* men to the bachelor party, make sure this Nickson doesn't do anything that might hurt Kelly."

Great idea. Maybe. Her nerves jangled. There was no one around, yet it felt like they were being watched.

Paranoia didn't usually shake her. "This just seems… complicated."

"It's not complicated. Squires is the premier male escort agency in the country. Probably in the world. The men here are vetted to the hilt; they're not crazy perverts. They're discreet and will offer any service we want. Any service…" Her cousin's suggestive tone didn't allay her anxiety. "It's tailored to what the client wants, that's us. We're the clients!" She grinned again. "Can you imagine having a guy who actually does what he's told?"

"I don't think—"

"Come on, Frey, we agreed to do this together." Did they? When did she say yes? Had agreement ever left her lips? The situation was snowballing out of control. "We have to support each other. This way, we can back each other up and talk, 'cause we'll know everything."

"I can know everything without having to participate," she said. "Seriously, Hol—"

"It's a man," Holly said and tilted her head. "One you're going to pay to treat you the way you want to be treated… the way you deserve to be treated." Obviously Holly could tell her argument wasn't convincing because she huffed again. "Either you control your own choice or I pick a guy for you." Crooking a brow, the threat was clear. Her cousin was aware of everything she'd hate in a partner… and how she hated to be out of control. "Bodybuilder, right? Low IQ… maybe someone who slurps his soup… you like messy eaters, right?"

Restraining her irritation at the attempted tease, she breathed out, resigned this was going to happen whether she wanted it to or not. Somehow this felt like a prime, "*What would Roxie do*?" moment. An adage some of her newest friends swore by.

"You're going to owe me big time for this."

Clapping once, Holly squealed. "I will. I love you. Thank you!"

Grabbing her hand, Holly led them across the large, curved space filled with couches and armchairs so soft they might consume a person. The carpet was thick. A warm beige color, it complemented the elegant gold pinstripe on the walls.

"You'd think they'd be more particular about security," Holly said, stopping at the far wall, looking left to right down the corridors running the length of the full-height windows.

Broad spiral stairs led away from the seating area. Were they supposed to go up there? Either way, there should be a more defined reception. The corridors were long, no labels or signs, which way should they go?

Holly spun around and planted her by the window. "You wait here; I'm going to find someone."

Without giving her a chance to respond, Holly stalked off, a woman on a mission. She wouldn't chase after her. If her cousin found someone, so be it. If not, oh, well, she wouldn't lose sleep over Squires not meeting Holly's expectations.

Breathing in and then out, she checked out the bustling street below. There were offices on the opposite side of the street, bullpens and private boardrooms with people in suits hustling. A typical work environment. Not like this one.

Something drew her eye toward the corridor opposite. Terrible at standing still doing nothing, she wandered that way. Not really going anywhere just… wandering. At the mouth of the corridor an archway to an enclosed circular space, maybe ten feet in diameter, prompted her on.

Headshots of men lined the walls from hip height to a couple of feet above her head. All kinds of men, men of different ages, races, builds, every demographic. Someone for everyone.

This was a menu. She shivered, unimpressed by the idea the men were lined up to be sampled and selected like caviar or wine.

All the men were attractive. Some more her type than others. How did the positioning work? There had to be some sort of system. Alternatively, the men were added and removed as they started and stopped working for the agency. Gaps would have to be filled. Could be scattershot. Maybe there was no pattern.

She wrapped her arms around herself, scanning the pictures as she would in a museum installation. One distinguished gentleman was familiar, hadn't she met him at one of her grandfather's functions? Maybe it was just that he looked like so many others. He could certainly fit in with her grandfather's crowd. Many of these men could.

Despite their appearance of sophistication, something drove these men into this line of work. Sure, Squires seemed upmarket, and the conditions were impeccable, so far, but no one chose sex work because they wanted to share themselves with the masses. It was a necessity.

She backed out of the gallery. This wasn't right. She had to find Holly and remind her these were real people, not meat meant to make their lives easier. Hurrying down the corridor, on the hunt, she went deeper into the complex and rushed smack, bang into the side of a guy who materialized from a perpendicular hallway.

"Whoa, hey," he said, whoever he was, and opened his arms to cocoon her without actually making contact.

Stumbling back, her heel wobbled and her ankle gave out, but the stranger caught her arm. Thank you. Good. She didn't fall on her butt. What a first impression that would make. None of these words came out. On instinct, her arm rose to push his down. And, heart racing, it didn't settle her any to see the dazzling white smile emerge on his lips. The warmth in his brown eyes stunned her into silence; words, all words, were lost.

"Second thoughts?" he asked. Somehow the deep growl of his voice intimidated and soothed at the same time. Still, she had nothing. "I recognize the look... Married?"

Her vocal cords had clenched shut. Relax. Relax. Progress was made in a shallow headshake. The act must have shaken something loose, though it wasn't sense, as proved by what did come out of her mouth.

"Are... are you a hooker?"

His practiced smile quirked to something much broader and more genuine. She hadn't thought the last one was false until she saw the light of a laugh in his eyes.

"If you're asking do I work here? Yes. I do work here."

Squeezing her eyes closed, she shook her head. "Oh, that was so offensive. I'm sorry. God, I'm so sorry."

"Baer will do just fine," he said and offered her a hand. Confused, she narrowed her eyes and tilted her head. "You don't have to call me God." Had she? No. That hadn't been what she meant, he was kidding, that was kidding... maybe. "Now, let me guess... You didn't come here alone."

"No," she said and pointed back over her shoulder. "I—"

"No, don't tell me... You said you weren't married." Glancing down, he stole a look at her hand. "No fiancée... So a girlfriend brought you... or a relative?"

"Cousin."

Bobbing his head, he slipped his hands into his slacks pockets. "It's an event."

"Something like that," she said. "I'm sorry I called you a hooker."

"It's okay. I've been called worse... You got all the way here, now you want to back out...? What changed your mind?"

Licking her lips, honesty was a good start. "Your gallery."

One side of his mouth curled high enough that a hint of a dimple showed. "Yeah, some of those guys should be hung by the neck not by picture hooks... You're skittish, aren't you?" Taking a backward step, he opened his arm toward the corridor he'd emerged from. "Would you do me the honor of a chance to change your mind?"

# TWO

FLOODED WITH GLORIOUS light, the wider hallway led all the way to the other side of the building.

"I... I haven't shaved my legs today..." she stuttered. "Are we going to have sex?"

Discernment crossed his expression. "I don't know... You got a major credit card?" Why did she keep saying insane things? Insane and insanely rude things? As she begged the ground to open and eat her, he released a laugh and smiled. "No sex, Little Skit... Let's start with coffee."

Going down the corridor, he stole several glances back, probably checking she hadn't fled. Getting the hell out of there would be the smart course. Worth consideration—whoa, he had an ass on him. What the— where did that come from? She was not one of those people. God, she made herself sick.

After a few more feet, he stopped and gestured for her to go ahead of him up a set of stairs.

"Am I allowed upstairs?" she asked as they ascended.

He came to her side. "How else will we get to the bedrooms?"

The smile on his face suggested he hadn't been offended by her stupid mouth. Could be he was a good actor. With her being a potential client, he probably couldn't tell her even if she had.

"I'm sorry I propositioned you."

"It's my job to be propositioned," he said. "If I'm not being propositioned, I'm not getting paid."

Good point. "Still, you're a human being."

"Not a piece of meat?" he asked, opening a door when they got to the top of the stairs. "Women have put up with that a lot longer than men."

He allowed her through first. This space wasn't as fancy as the lower floor. Carpet was gray, walls white. Further down, he funneled her into a breakroom. With vending machines, a corner of kitchen units around a small island, and a dining table, this room wasn't meant for entertaining clients.

Block couches and armchairs without arms were the only choice for sitting. The floor was a gray vinyl that must've been chosen for its functionality rather than its beauty.

"How do you take your coffee?" She hadn't seen him move past her, but he was in the kitchen, poking at a huge shiny machine in the far corner. "It's supposed to make lattes and cappuccinos, whatever you want."

He didn't sound confident he could get it to produce one, but he had his back to her, so she felt okay about smiling.

"Americano would be great," she said, heading toward the island.

Twisting to peek over his shoulder at her, his eyes were narrow like that meant nothing to him.

She laughed and put a hand on one of the high stools to boost herself onto it. "Black," she said. "Boring old black coffee works just fine."

Relief crossed his face before he turned back to the machine. "Ah, a girl after my own heart," he said, retrieving cups from an overhead cabinet. "That I can do."

"Not confident in the kitchen?"

"I am confident everywhere."

After he pressed a button, the machine sputtered to life. While it did its thing, he opened more cabinets, searching for something. Less than a minute later, the coffee dripped through. Once it was done, he switched out the cups, putting a second one in the first's place.

He served her coffee first, then went back to fetch his own. He didn't drink any, just put it on the island near hers without sitting down.

"What can you cook?" she asked, turning her cup to lift it by its handle while her other fingertips rested on the opposite rim. He raised his brows in question, she smiled. "You said you were confident in the kitchen, I wondered what you could cook."

"Not a damn thing," he said, slipping a hand into his pocket to pull out a bunch of coins. "But I'm good at faking it."

His attention switched between his coins and the vending machine, so he missed the smile she couldn't hide.

"I imagine you'd have to be," she said, amusement bleeding into her tone. "In your line of work."

Doing a double take her way, his mind caught up with his words, or hers. When his eyes stayed put, she laughed.

Clearing his throat didn't disguise his smirk. "That's not what I meant, Little Skit."

"I think it is," she said, sipping her coffee. "Unless you're telling me you've been genuinely involved with every client you've ever had."

"Of course I'm genuinely involved."

Setting her cup aside, she sealed her lips. "Mm, of course you are." Hopping off her stool, she opened her hand to him. "May I?" Glancing from his closed fist to her open palm, he turned his over to let the warm coins fall into her hand. "I never get to do this."

"Do what?" he asked, watching her go to the vending machine.

"What number do you want?"

Simple things like vending machines were everyday to other people. To her, they were toys she'd never been allowed to play with as a child... or as a grown up. Whenever she could, she made up for that lost time.

"Uh..." he said, coming up behind her, so close she could feel his body heat against her back.

But he wasn't done. Leaning over, he put a hand on top of the vending machine to peruse what was inside. Sandwiched between him and the machine, there wasn't much room to move. Yet the narrow space wasn't uncomfortable.

Odd.

Topping out at five two herself, she'd never been the tallest anywhere in her life. This guy had to be six three, maybe even six four. His height dwarfed her. And while he wasn't built like a quarterback, there was breadth in his shoulders and a strength in his form that betrayed he took care of his physique.

In his line of work, he was probably required to stay in shape. Imagining what may be beneath his black slacks and gray shirt felt like a violation, so she fought to clear her mind, or more aptly, clean her mind.

"B6," he said.

Having been so busy chastising herself for thinking about what was under his clothes, she almost forgot the task at hand. Blinking from her daze, she checked the price and scraped through the coins in her palm before slotting the right ones in and pressing the buttons.

Returning the remaining change to his hand without looking at him, the machine did its thing. The potato chips dropped into the well at the bottom. Delighted as a child, she dropped to a crouch to retrieve them, twisting while still down there to hold them up to him.

Her delight waned to something much more intense when their eyes met again. He didn't move to take the chips, instead he searched her gaze for a few seconds before his attention slithered to her mouth.

"Tell me something about yourself, Little Skit," he murmured, in that deep, intimate drawl he was so good at. "When was the last time you tasted a man?"

If any other person was so forward or indiscreet, she'd be offended, embarrassed even. Instead of her face flaming or her anger flaring, a different kind of heat seeped through her. From the depths of her gut, it simmered up within her, tormenting her curiosity and arousing her in a way she couldn't recall experiencing in the past.

Before she could answer, he opened his hand to her. "Forgive me, that was crude."

Sliding her hand into his, she let him draw her to her feet. Their hands stayed linked as he took hold of the chips.

Except Freya didn't let them go. "Baer—"

"Coffee's getting cold," he said and turned around, forcing her to let go of the chips and him.

Being attracted to someone wasn't a crime. True, it wasn't usually her first thought on meeting someone

new, but she did notice when a man was good-looking…
though not usually on such an instinctive level.

"I should find my cousin," she said, wishing she
could use the vending machine for support.

Shame her breeding wouldn't let her slump.

"To tell her you've changed your mind?" he
asked, tossing the chips toward the couch that had its
back to the kitchen. "Would you join me on the couch?"

Picking up both coffees from the island, he
carried them across to where he'd tossed the chips and
put them on the coffee table. Standing in front of the
couch, he gestured to the seat.

"You're polite," she said, leaving the vending
machine to go to him. "Respectful of women."

"And you're wondering if that's upbringing or
training," he said. "Maybe it's a little of both."

Only once she was sitting did he do the same. He
was quick to retrieve her coffee and put it in her hand.

"Is it against the rules to ask personal questions?"

"You can ask anything you like," he said. "Just as
I can… Our role is to make clients feel good… whatever
that takes… whatever you need…" His arm rested along
the low back of the couch; he raised a finger to brush the
tip against her sleeve. "What is your name, Little Skit?"

"Freya," she said. "Freya Dere."

"This event that brought you and your cousin
here. Will you tell me something about it?" he asked.
Without answering, she examined him closer. He flashed
another smile. "It's talking. Just talking. No charge."

This man could have a wife and kids, or a
girlfriend… he could have a boyfriend… maybe he had
several of each. Had she ever been so curious about a
person and their life? His avoidance of her query about
personal questions was practiced. This wasn't the first
time a client tried to get into his private life. She'd bet he
made a point to keep the two separate.

It made sense. He had to date dozens, maybe hundreds of people a year. Some of them probably spent more time with him than others. Women, in general, liked to talk and bond more than men. A lot of his dates probably valued conversation. From what she'd seen so far, he was good at it. How many women fell for him while he was just doing his job?

Despite liking him, being attracted to him, this wasn't real. It wasn't a genuine interaction. Romance didn't exist there. It was a business transaction.

Opening her mouth, she filled her lungs with air. "My cousin announced her engagement to a man the family don't know and have never met. Her father, my uncle Ger, was ready to veto the whole thing and refuse his permission until Kelly, that's the potential bride, convinced everyone to go away together. So we're supposed to pack up and go on vacation to get to know this Nickson who wants to marry Kelly."

"And you need a plus one."

Gulping her coffee, she shook her head and made a noise of rejection. "Me? No, I don't need a plus one. I do just fine without a man in my life… But, Holly, Kelly's sister, she was with her fiancé for several years before she found out he'd been cheating on her… After the relationship ended, she…"

Stop talking.

She couldn't, shouldn't, reveal too much to a man who may have to play Holly's love interest.

"Holly was embarrassed," he said. "She was in an established relationship with her life on a certain course. She thought she was secure. And this man, the ex, he took it away from her… Then Kelly shows up with true love, the future Holly was supposed to have… What did Holly do? Make up a boyfriend?" Surprised, she blinked and her mouth fell open. He had to catch her coffee cup when her hand relaxed. "This is what I do, Little Skit… And, believe me, I've heard it all."

She could believe it. Already she was beginning to trust him and they'd only known each other a few minutes. After a date with him, or two, or five, there wouldn't be much a woman would keep to themselves.

"You do seem to know what you're talking about. You must have been doing this for a long time… Downstairs, you sized me up in a minute." He combined a humble shrug with putting her cup back on the table. "How did you know so much about me?"

"You told me you weren't married," he said. "The rest was just experience."

"Experience?" she said, twisting more of herself toward him. "Don't hold out on me. I'm a nervous client, remember? It's not personal to tell me how you do your job."

Ah, that glimmer of the dimple.

"Husbands invite other men into their wives' beds for a number of reasons. Fiancés do it because they want to. Even if they say it's for their future wife, it's usually for them. Either because they want to enjoy the other man too or to see the other man enjoy their wife."

"That happens?" she asked, restraining a squirm. "Other men ask you to…"

He nodded. "It has."

"You didn't ask if I had a boyfriend."

"Boyfriends don't hook their girlfriends up with escorts… If they want a threesome, they find a friend… probably wouldn't occur to them to look for a male hooker."

Something about his smile betrayed his memory.

"I'm really very sorry I called you that." Mortified more like, devastated. "I'm not usually so rude. Quite the opposite."

Though his experience wouldn't jive with that claim.

"I'm not offended, Freya. You call things like you see them, I respect that. I don't need someone to…"

This time when he trailed off, she sensed there was something more behind what he'd been about to say.

"What?" she asked, reaching over to curl her fingers around his hand. "What were you going to say?"

"Something else crude," he said and exhaled a rough breath, driving his fingers into his hair. "Don't know what's wrong with me. I'm supposed to get the prep sheet before I cross lines like that with a client."

Squeezing his hand, she pulled it just an inch down his thigh toward her. "Have you never worked without a prep sheet?"

His gaze grew heavier. "Sounds like you're asking if I've ever seduced a woman."

"No, just wondering if you would."

"With a client? I wouldn't. With a woman…"

On a smile, she lowered her chin. "Except I'm not a woman…" she said. His eyelid twitched in curiosity. "Not one you're interested in pursuing…" Saying it aloud shifted her perspective. "Maybe this is a good idea… I've had so much trouble with men over the years… Maybe it's time to face the reality that I can't make relationships work. I've been with men, amazing men, some more amazing than others… It always ends the same, no matter how great or terrible they are…"

Shh, stop talking. Damming her streaming thoughts, she closed her mouth.

"There's nothing you can't get from Squires," he said. "Anything at all that you want, you can get it here… You don't have to worry about typical relationship issues. You'll have a boyfriend trained to fulfill your needs and have none of his own."

How unappealing. For a real relationship, which this wasn't. Damnit, Freya. Why was it so difficult for her to remember that? Probably because she'd never interacted with a man in this kind of situation before.

"You never fight with clients?" she asked.

"I fight with clients."

"About what?"

"Whatever they want."

He fought with the clients who wanted him to fight with them, who paid him to fight with them. If women could request anything they wanted, they could ask him to be rough and tough and dominant. They could request him to be gentle and tender, to ridicule or praise them. No doubt he had the ability to be whatever a "prep sheet" told him to be.

Baer, if that was his real name, was whatever his clients requested. Who he truly was, both in himself and with women he really cared about, would remain a mystery to them all.

His smile, his mouth, the smooth line of his square jaw, fascinated her. She wanted to put her fingers on his cheek and run her thumb across his lips before leaning in and—

Leaping to her feet, electrified by audacity, she wanted to kiss him. She'd been thinking… This man she'd just met. This man who wasn't here by choice. This man she knew nothing about.

"Freya," he said, his fingers grazing hers as he rose to stand beside her. "What's wrong? Did I say something to upset you? When I said fight—"

"You didn't upset me," she said. "I upset myself… I'm sorry, I have to leave."

Before she could turn away, he caught her elbow and scooped a hand around her face. "Little Skit, what spooked you?" he asked, trying to bring her attention up though she resisted. "Look at me."

Sensing he wouldn't let her go, her gaze drifted to his. "We just met."

"Yeah, and everything was going great. We were just talking. No harm in talking... What changed?"

"I was wondering what it would be like to... kiss you," she said, disappointed in herself.

It was disrespectful, impudent, to build such a visceral fantasy so quickly.

The concern in his expression loosened.

After a couple of seconds, a smile curved his lips. "Only one way to find out," he said, strengthening his hold. "May I?"

She might have nodded or made a sound of agreement. Honestly? She wasn't sure. When he bowed, tipping her head back, and brushed his mouth over hers, everything else blanked.

After testing the texture of her lips, urgency grew in the gentle press. Asking for more, his insistence increased, the growing pressure begged her to open for him. Instinct demanded her jaw relax until his tongue touched hers and—then he was gone.

# THREE

"OH… Looks like someone started without me."

Holly's voice whipped her around. Freya hadn't heard the door open, or anyone come in, but her cousin was there with a tall, handsome man behind her.

"Holly," she said. "I didn't—"

"I assumed you had second thoughts and ditched me," Holly said, coming deeper into the breakroom. "I like this way better. Who's your friend?"

Her cousin smiled at Baer, a coy sort of flirtatious look that made her uncomfortable. That said, nothing about the situation was particularly comfortable. Before the new arrivals joined them, she'd thought things were as mortifying as they could get. Apparently, the universe took that as a challenge.

The man behind Holly answered the question. "That's Baer, he's our best," he said, then stopped to frown. "What are you still doing here? Weren't you supposed to be…"

Baer slid his hands into his pockets. "She told me to meet her at Gatson's," he said. "I've got time."

"Time to call Christine?" the other man asked.

Baer raised his attention to the wall clock. "Again?"

The man smiled once more, an amused, yet cocky smirk. "Again," he said. "Always again... Imelda left a message too and Rosemarie."

On hearing that name, Baer's smile was instant. "I called Rosie," he said. "We set something up."

"Sunderland will be pissed."

"Sunderland is always pissed," Baer said and switched on the dazzling smile she'd first seen downstairs. "You haven't introduced our guest, Conrad... Allow me..." Moving away, Baer went around the couch and extended a hand to her cousin. "Holly, I assume."

"Yes, Mr. Baer," Holly said, accepting his hand and laughing when he bowed to kiss her knuckles.

"Just Baer."

"And are you?" Holly purred. Though Baer's back was to her, the angle still allowed Freya to drink in her cousin and Baer fixating on each other. Oh, and there was the nausea. Holly's eyes glittered with excitement. "A bear?"

"If that's what you need me to be, sweetheart."

Holly laughed again. "I'll have to think about what I need from you, Baer."

Conrad interrupted the couple's mooning. "Now that we've found your cousin, we can go through our introductory meeting," he said. "Find out what you ladies need and if Baer is in your price range..."

Holly laughed, but it was Baer who spoke. "Conrad, you've lost that gentle touch... You've been spending too much time with Ilsa."

"And I've got the scars to prove it, buddy."

"Haven't we all?"

There was a lightness to the way the men spoke to each other. It wasn't as measured as Baer had been with Holly or as seductive either. These men were friends. Familiar, maybe even close... maybe they trusted each other... they could've worked together a long time.

Conrad would know the answers to all her wonderings about Baer. She'd bet he knew Baer's background, his marital status, his family and friendships... Attraction was one thing, but as she adjusted to this bizarre set up, the more truth she grasped.

Baer was an employee. His job was to make women feel the way he'd made her feel. It was his job to soothe and seduce, to kiss and coddle. It was a sales pitch. The pathetic thing was how well, and how quickly, it worked. She'd fallen for it so fast, it was embarrassing. Was she so starved of affection?

One thing she'd never been with men was easy. From her father's protection to her grandfather's, contact with men had never been straightforward. Relationships were never simple. That was part of the reason she'd given up hope of ever finding a happy one.

In saying that, getting a date had never been a problem.

Finding a man she could trust, that had proved impossible. No, that wasn't fair, there were men she trusted, just none who bewitched her hormones and her heart.

"If you ladies aren't in a rush," Baer said, skimming a hand onto Holly's shoulder as he turned to look at her. "I have twenty minutes if you want to get a drink downstairs."

"No drinks for you," Conrad said. "These ladies have an appointment, we're going to the office. You have to sign something out of the garage."

"I've got time," Baer said.

Though she could feel his eyes on her, she didn't meet them, unwilling to be drawn in again.

Conrad stepped back and opened the door. "Please, ladies," he said. "Come with me before this man does my job for me. He already does the work of ten guys around here."

"Don't ever say I don't pull my weight," Baer said.

"Never do," Conrad said. "Ladies?"

Holly seemed loathed to step out of Baer's grip. No judgment, not so long ago, she'd felt the same way. Crossing the room, she made a point of averting her attention from the man who'd been kissing her just minutes before.

Conrad was in the hallway, Holly followed in his wake. As Freya was about to step out, Baer's voice rose behind her.

"Little Skit," he said. Turn around, say nothing, be calm. Good advice. She still had to breathe a second before looking at him. "It was a pleasure."

Nodding once, she kept her expression passive. "Likewise."

Her heart pounded so hard that her tongue throbbed. Holding on to her composure, she went to join Conrad and Holly in the hallway.

"If you'll follow me to my office," Conrad said, walking away with the women falling into step behind him.

Holly linked their arms to pull her closer. "Wow. I want that one," she whispered on a giggle, a renewed spring in her step.

Good for Holly knowing what she wanted. Freya, on the other hand, had no clue. Already Squires had given her more than she'd bargained for.

# FOUR

SETTLING THEMSELVES in Conrad's office didn't take long. Yet the setup felt wrong. The masculine man seemed out of place in a room designed more like a boudoir than a business. At that moment, seated on a chaise longue next to her cousin, perpendicular to the one Conrad had to himself, their purpose was ambiguous.

"I hope you don't mind..." he began. "Holly and I spoke some about your situation while on the hunt for you."

While she was being seduced away from good sense. "My situation?"

"Our situation," Holly said, joining their hands.

Since when was her cousin so tactile? Could be the environment brought it out in her.

"With engagements leading to weddings, we tend to assume you'll need contact for up to a year. Sometimes that goes longer. Vacations, meals, dates, it's all fine. We just need to ensure that you get the right match."

"I don't want sex," Freya said, recognizing her own voice only after it left her lips.

Conrad's smile quirked. "That's acceptable. We're paid for it, not in it."

Another stupid thing to say, what a talent she was discovering. "No, I meant, I would like to be matched with a man who doesn't… offer sexual services."

Bobbing his head, Conrad was completely at ease on his chaise longue. "We do have operators who only provide company and companionship. Operators who don't go all the way… However, they don't tend to be available for this kind of long-term work. I can check, but those operators tend to work on a date-to-date basis, what you'll need is someone willing to make regular appointments. Sometimes at short notice… Although the more notice you can give us, the better."

"We will always give as much as possible," Holly said. "The vacation is the most important thing. Other things, one-off things, we can always say a boyfriend has a work commitment or something if schedules don't match."

Conrad was smiling and nodding again. "You're flexible, that's good." Straightening, he reached for two folders and handed them one each. "We ask you to fill out these questionnaires and contracts."

Flicking through the pages, the volume shocked her. There had to be more than twenty, maybe as many as thirty sheets.

"This is a lot."

"I know, we're thorough," he said and produced two booklets from the table behind his chaise. "You should take solace we're as thorough in every area."

He gave them the booklets.

"What's this?"

"Our user manual." Holly laughed. It wasn't funny, not to her, this was a whole new world. "I know, it sounds funny. But it explains everything that's in the forms and it has a glossary, which should help you when making your selections." He grabbed two full sized folders. "We'll fill out your forms today and I'll talk you through a couple of potential matches. We don't just make one. You can list two or three from these folders. We'll double-check they meet your requirements. After that, we'll process everything and match you with a maximum of five candidates. We'll set up a date with each of them. They can be double dates if you're both more comfortable with that. Those initial five dates are on us, you meet five men and pick which one you want to see this process through with. After that, we'll have a meeting, the five of us, and hammer everything out."

"Sounds perfect," Holly said. "How do you decide on the five?"

"As I said, if anyone stands out, you can list them. As long as they meet your requirements, time, scheduling, pricing, services offered, we'll put them on the list of five. Five is the maximum we offer complimentary."

"But we can keep going?"

"If you want, at your own expense, of course," he said. "We want to find you the perfect fit."

"What about Baer?" Holly asked. "Is he available?"

Conrad's smile was warm but apologetic. "Scheduling is always a problem with Baer. He has more regulars than anyone else on our books." Holly's shoulders sagged as Conrad's strengthened. "Fortunately, I know he's desperate for the money. So I can't see him not working out the time off with his regulars."

Holly squealed, prompting Conrad's laugh. The room felt positively giddy. How was this her life right now?

"Oh goodie," her cousin said. "This is going to be so much fun."

"It is fun," their host replied. "Let's get started."

Five dates with five different men. Sounded like a punishment. Maybe it was. Punishment for acting the way she had with a stranger. Brazen wasn't her middle name. Then again, neither was simpering nor shy.

No man in the past had aroused her enough to be brazen. Turned out all she needed was a man on the clock.

The pendulum of emotion had gotten a workout that afternoon. This wasn't going to get any less extreme the deeper she waded in.

# FIVE

THE CAR WAS supposed to arrive at ten o'clock. Every other car Squires sent that week had been on time. She didn't wait around for the call from her doorman that night. Instead she went down in the elevator a minute before.

This was the third of her five dates; time was running short. Choosing to be picked up late meant they could drink fast and duck out quickly. Might be a nightmare to be stuck entertaining one man for too long. What if he was a sleazy creep? No, she needed an exit strategy, just in case.

Just as Narmer, her doorman, opened the grand glass door, a limo pulled up to the curb.

"Been a busy week, Miss Dere," Narmer said. "Third night in a row. Whoever he is, he's eager."

A positive of the same black limo showing up every day was no one knew who was inside. So, like Narmer, they assumed it belonged to one person. Good, the last thing she needed was her grandfather to learn she'd been slutting it up. Not that she had but, you know, people talked.

The Squires driver would only declare which tenant they were there to pick up. As far as Narmer was concerned, she was just dating a new man. That wasn't inaccurate, nor was it entirely true.

"And why shouldn't he be, Narmer?" she asked, sharing a smile with the man which became a laugh on his lips.

"No reason at all, Miss Dere… We would like to meet this eager gentleman though, Angel."

Leaning closer, she straightened the pearls over her cleavage, keeping her eyes on his. "Simply saving you the trouble of lying to Truman."

"God bless you, Angel."

"How's Justine doing?"

"Just fine," he said, taking her hand when she offered it. "Thanks to you."

"Not to me at all," she said. "That kid's made of steel… Can I come by?"

"Any time," he said. "Any time at all."

They shared another smile. "Let me know when you're off next week and I'll come cook for you."

Shaking his head, he laughed again. "You are heaven-sent," he said. "Whoever this guy is, he doesn't deserve you."

Taking a backward step, she curtseyed. "I will be sure to tell him that."

"Do, Angel. You deserve to be worshiped."

Compliments always made her a little uncomfortable, but she smiled through it. "You are too kind, sir… Don't wait up."

She didn't expect to be out late, but if she truly was seeing a man with this regularity, the relationship would be progressing.

The driver got out the front and met her at the back just as she got there.

"Good evening, Kessler."

Since the first night, when she'd asked his name, he got a weird sort of smirk on his face whenever she addressed him.

"Good evening, Miss Dere."

He opened the rear door and she stepped forward without getting inside. From the other side of the door, she laid her focus on him.

"Can I ask you something, Kessler?" With a single nod, he granted her permission. "Do you drink scotch?"

"Do I…? Yes, ma'am… though not when I'm driving."

Pleased, she grinned. "Of course not…" Sliding her hand along the top of the door, she edged just a little closer before pausing again. "And my name is Freya… please don't call me ma'am again."

"Whatever you say," he said, that smirk still on his face.

Dipping down, she got into the car expecting to see her date for the evening: Donoghue. Except the man waiting wasn't a stranger, it was Baer, who she hadn't seen all week.

Startled, she almost didn't know what to do. He wasn't off-kilter, of course not, he'd known they were going to see each other. Removing an earbud, he pressed some buttons on his phone.

"I, uh…" she started. "I can step out if you need to take a call."

He shook his head and raised the phone. "I was listening to music."

She gasped and grabbed the strap of her clutch from her wrist to toss it onto the seat in front of them. "Can I…"

Surprise became a frown, but he handed over the earbud when she opened both hands to him.

"Thank you," she said, sliding it in under her hair.

"What do you want to listen to?"

"What were you listening to?" she asked, shaking her head. "I really don't care. I never get to listen to good music."

Unless she was in Crimson, but that wasn't the same thing as enjoying it privately.

Still wearing a confused frown, he touched the screen and music burst in her ear. When she registered what it was, her smile grew wider.

"'Hound Dog,'" she said. "You like Elvis?" He nodded. "Are you a hound dog, Baer?"

One side of his mouth twitched. "Ain't nothing but."

She balled her hands on her thighs and slid down to lie her head against the backrest as the car got moving.

"We should go dancing." When her head rolled toward him, mortification slipped in again. What was she doing? Snapping to attention, she sat up, handing the earbud back to him. "Thank you. I… apologize."

"No need," he said, wrapping the wire around the phone and tucking it into the door well. "The place we have reservations at doesn't have dancing. But we have connections at some of the—"

"No," she said. "No, drinks are fine… Are we dropping you off somewhere, Hound Dog?"

Her joke fell flat. In the moment, it felt right. She needed to learn to ignore her instincts around this guy.

If Baer had been using the car that night, they might drop him off before picking up her date.

"No," he said.

"I expected a man named Donoghue to pick me up tonight."

"Yeah, we're on our way over there now," he said. "He's across town."

"But if Donoghue's my date and you're…" Recalling Holly's matches gave her a clue. "You're Holly's date." He nodded. "Right… good."

Her wide smile wasn't genuine though she tried hard to sell it.

Focusing on the privacy screen between them and the driver, they drove in silence for a minute before he muttered, "Donoghue."

"Excuse me?"

"Nothing, I…" His concentration didn't waver from up ahead. "If you were going to ditch me for anyone, did it have to be Donoghue?"

His wince of disgust arched her brows.

"I didn't ditch you," she said. "I didn't request anyone; Squires provided my matches. Donoghue was one of them."

"I'd love to see what answer got you landed with him. You didn't think to request me?"

"Holly requested you," she said, brushing invisible lint from her knee. "Perhaps if you didn't go around seducing every woman who crossed your path, you wouldn't be so in demand."

It wasn't right that she was still smarting over the way he'd left her to kiss Holly's hand. He'd kissed her. Actually kissed her. A full, proper, very adult kiss. All Holly got was a polite introduction. Still enough to melt her cousin.

She could never be confident with a man so adept with the opposite sex, not in this scenario. She'd always wonder if he was touting for business when they were out together.

"I'd have dropped the rate," he murmured. Her attention drifted toward him. Not that she'd intended it to, but, of their own accord, her eyes tractored to his. Gazes locked, he raised his hand to her face, scooping his fingers around her cheek. "Little Skit…" He breathed the pet name, his thumb tracing her lower lip. "If you'd made the request..."

Awareness pounded in all the wrong places. He thought money was the problem? That couldn't be further from the truth. If Donoghue's rate was less than Baer's that was just coincidence, she hadn't requested anyone cheaper. Her requirements had been simple, in contrast to Holly's more complex demands. Apparently, Baer fitted with those, or at least, the system hadn't come up against hard limits that would deny Holly her request.

Staring into him, she selfishly wished for hard limits.

His heavy gaze seemed to be moving closer to her mouth—his phone buzzed in his pocket between them. Except, hadn't he just put his phone in the door well?

Leaning away, Baer drove a hand into his pocket and pulled it out with an urgency that startled her. "Yeah," he said into the handset, his voice deep and clear. A moment passed before he spoke again. "Who is this?" The serious expression on his face became grave. "Laird's Hospital? What the hell is the little..." Breathing out, he dropped his chin and moved his index finger on the middle of his forehead in a light scratch. "Is he conscious?" Another pause. "Yeah, 'cause he knows I'll kick his ass... Are you sure he was alone?" With a palm, he covered his eyes. "Did he say that...?" Raising his head suddenly, he now wore annoyance. "You need to ask him. You need to check that he was alone..." Raising his arm, he read the heavy watch on his wrist. "I don't know how long it will take to get to Laird's..."

Bouncing onto the opposite seat, she pushed her purse aside and pressed a button to lower the privacy screen.

"Three minutes," she said as the thing slid down. "If we make this light..." Turning from the front,

Kessler was startled to see her peeking through the space between the cabins. "We need to go to Laird's hospital, right now."

"Frey—"

"Please, Kessler. As fast as you can. I'll cover any tickets," she said, resting a hand on his shoulder.

When he picked up speed, she switched to sit the right way and retrieved her phone from her purse. Without looking at Baer, she dialed.

After two rings the line answered. "Squires."

This was the emergency number for client use only.

"Hello," she said, bracing as the car swung out on a turn. "My name is Freya Dere. My cousin and I are supposed to have an appointment with your service this evening—"

"Yes, Miss Dere," the male on the other end of the line said. "I apologize if the car is late—"

"No, that's not it at all. Everything is perfect. Something has come up at my end and I'll have to reschedule."

"Of course," the male said. "Do you have a day in mind for—"

"No," she said. "If you call my cousin, she will deal with that. I apologize for the short notice. If you could let Donoghue and Baer know that—"

"Of course. I hope you resolve your issues."

"I will," she said. "Thank you."

Hanging up the phone, she sent a quick message to Holly to let her know they wouldn't be going out that night. Just as she pressed send, another phone chirped. Baer grabbed the phone from the door well.

He read the message and then tucked the phone away. Their eyes met. Whoever his call had been about, it was important enough to worry and anger him. Despite knowing nothing about his personal life, the serious look on his face bore a whisper of gratitude, though the intensity on it was something else. Something powerful shivered through her.

The car pulled to an abrupt halt. They broke their stare when Baer fled, slamming the door at his back.

Flipping around, Freya touched Kessler again. "Anyone asks, you didn't pick me up tonight," she said. "Baer got the message to cancel before I got in." Opening her purse, she pulled out a couple of hundred-dollar bills and passed them to him. "Please." Kessler didn't say anything, he seemed sort of dumbfounded as he raised his hand to take the cash. "Thank you… You can take off."

Baer might not want the world to know his personal issues, but she had to make sure everything was covered. Leaving the car, home wasn't in the cards yet. This was her stomping ground.

# SIX

ENTERING THE FAMILIAR doors of the ER, conspicuous in black pearls and a dress with a plunging neckline, it wasn't the first time she'd been called in to roll up her sleeves. Passing the waiting area, she smiled at anyone familiar and got a wave or two, though most seemed perplexed.

At the front desk, Baer was arguing with Rufio, the clerk.

"I need to see ID," Rufio said. "I'm sorry, sir—"

"I got the goddamn call five minutes ago," Baer said, strain fraying his tone. "He's about yay height…" He held out a hand at his side. "Light brown hair, dark eyes—"

"You gave me his name, sir," Rufio said. "But security won't allow me to direct anyone to a patient without confirmation they're next of kin."

Widening her smile, she set her forearms on the desk, holding her clutch in both hands, and pressed her elbows down to boost her height a little.

"Hey, Rufi," she said, stretching her smile. "You're not supposed to work nights… you prefer days."

"Tell me about it," Rufio said almost rolling his eyes at Baer. "Who you got in tonight? I didn't get any flags."

"I'm here with my friend," she said, side nodding to Baer.

"He's a ChilConn kid?" Rufio asked, standing to reach across the desk. "Are you sure? He didn't say anything."

Pulling a pink sheet from the bottom of the filing tray, he put a pen on top and slid it across the desk for her signature and initials.

"Is Dennis in?"

"Not tonight," Rufio said. "You want me to call him?"

"No!" she said, casting her eyes off the form just long enough to see Rufio smile. "I want you to do the exact opposite of calling him."

Rufio laughed. "Understood."

She passed him back the form and the pen. "I'm cooking for Narmer and Justine next week… want to join us?"

"What day?"

She shrugged. "Don't know yet… but I'll promise not to make chili if you promise to come."

"You're on," he said and picked up a file. "Exam three… You want a ride upstairs?"

"Anyone else in there?" Rufio shook his head. "Just keep it clear and we'll be fine… We're not waiting for a bed, are we?"

Rufio shook his head. "No, he's not critical."

"Is he being admitted?" she asked. "If he is, I'll take him uptown."

"Don't think so… Zard will come talk to you."

She nodded. "Anyone else in tonight?"

His smile softened. "I will check the charts."

Turning, she offered a wave. "Thank you, Rufio." Nodding past the scowling Baer, she tried not to make eye contact. "End of the hall along there."

Spinning around, he stalked away, moving faster than she could with his long legs eating up the floor. There wasn't an obvious pattern to the floorplan, but there was a door plate outside each room that declared its designation.

So it was no surprise that Baer found the room after she pointed him in the right direction. Keeping her distance, she gave him a chance to assess what was going on inside. Anyone could be in there, a wife, other kids, parents.

On coming into the hospital, she been unaware the patient was a child. Institutional knowledge could be useful. All she wanted to do was help. Hopefully Baer recognized that and didn't think she was intruding on his life.

Getting closer, with no intention of going into the room, she stayed outside the open door, out of view.

"What were you doing over there this late?" Baer's voice drifted from inside.

"I dunno," came the grumbled response.

"Pres," Baer said, softening a little. "Where's Charlie? You've gotta tell me, man. Was he out there? Is he in trouble?"

"No! No, I didn't take him. I promise... He stayed home."

With his mother? Why wouldn't the mother notice the second child missing? If that's indeed what this Pres was saying. Curiosity got the better of her. As the pair continued to discuss the veracity of what was being said, she rolled her shoulder on the wall to peek around the edge of the doorframe.

The curtain was pulled part way around the rail, but she could see the boy in the bed, brown hair and dark eyes as Baer said at the front desk. Even though he was young, probably on the brink of being a teenager, she could already see he had the same coloring and features as the man standing on the other side of the bed looking down at him.

His son. Was this Baer's son? Is this why he did what he did? To support his children? Did that mean he had a wife? Where was this boy's mother? Were the two separated or had something happened to her? If they were still together, did she have a problem with what her husband did for a living? So many questions…

Oh, God, she'd kissed him. Guilt came quick. His poor wife. What she must endure knowing her husband was out there… And Baer, he had to share himself with other women just to support his family. What debt must they have? Why were they in this position? And just like that, she'd made up a whole narrative in her head. So much for questions.

"Whoa, ho," the kid said all of a sudden, startling her. "Are you hitting that?"

Blinking and pushing upright, stunned, her eyes darted from the wide-eyed kid sitting in the bed, arm on a table set at his side, to Baer whipping around to glare at her. Soon as Baer registered who the kid was talking about, he smacked the boy on the back of the head.

"You show the lady respect."

The kid ducked forward, rubbing his head as he turned a smile on her. "You're hot… Really hot… Can't you do better than my stupid brother?"

That revelation prompted a step deeper into the room. "Your…"

"Did you lose a bet?"

"He's your brother?" she asked Baer.

The kid snorted out a laugh. "She think you were the old man?" His amusement waned to a frown. "How's your girlfriend not know you don't have kids?"

"We're just friends," she said, speaking so Baer didn't need to come up with anything. Having injected herself into the scenario, it wasn't right that he be expected to explain her presence. Edging nearer, she pointed to the chart at the end of the bed. "May I?"

"You a doctor?" the kid asked. "Wow, you're a doctor?"

"She's an imposter."

The male voice in the doorway spun her around. As always, the sight of Trey Zarden brought a smile to her lips.

"An imposter you say," she said, going over to accept his one-armed hug. "You didn't call me."

Prodding a finger into his chest, she jabbed at him, gritting her teeth in a grimace.

"'Cause all you ever want to do is poach me," Zard said. "I've told you, Angel. I want sex from you. Not money."

"How unprofessional," she joked and pointed at what he was holding. "Those the x-rays."

He held them up for her to take. "Yep." Slipping them from their folder, she carried them to the light box on the wall. "Just a distal torus," he said, moving in beside her as she waited for the lights to flicker on.

"Thank God," she said, examining the x-ray.

"Cause?"

"Fall, we think," Zard said. "Kid's been kind of tight-lipped…"

"Any internal damage?"

"No," he said. "Though, I've gotta say, I was relieved to hear you were on this…" Leaning closer, he whispered above her ear. "No insurance."

"He has insurance," Baer interjected.

She hadn't even heard him approach, but when she and Zard turned, he was standing just a couple of feet away.

"I'm sorry, sir, I…" Zard stepped away, but glanced at her. "We haven't been introduced… I'm Presley's doctor, Trey Zarden."

"Baer Claymore," he said, offering a hand, and the two men shook. "Presley's brother."

"As you can see, your brother has a fractured radius. It's nothing too serious, but it will require a cast."

"No surgery?" Baer asked. Zard shook his head. "Like I said, he has insurance; money isn't a problem."

Zard turned his narrow focus to her. "I thought he was one of yours."

"If he has no insurance, he is," she said. "Is there a problem?"

Moving back, the doctor brought both her and Baer into his circle. "It seems, uh…" Clearing his throat, she didn't blame him for being nervous if he was going to say something Baer might not like. Baer was bigger than him and, right now, looked a hell of a lot meaner. "It's possible the injury was sustained during a break-in. Insurance won't cover injuries sustained during a criminal act… even for a child."

Whipping around, Baer set his sights on the sheepish Presley. "What the hell? You were inside? Why the hell were you inside—"

"Let's all be calm," she said, opening her arms and moving around to stand in front of the bed, protecting Presley while focusing on Zard. "If Presley requires additional tests or scans, do everything he needs. I've already signed the waiver. I'm paying now no matter what happens… Have the police spoken to him?"

"On their way," Zard said.

"Who's the—"

"Chapman," Zard said, doing a terrible job of hiding the laugh blocked in his throat.

Groaning, her arms dropped as she sagged. "It had to be, didn't it? Where's Higgs?"

"Florida, I think," he said. "His mom had a heart attack."

"Good one, Mom," she muttered. "I'll... I'll deal with it."

"You know, his idea of payment from you will be a lot more depraved than mine," Zard said, his lips contorting to a smile. "Don't worry, I'm sure he's over the humiliation."

"He will never be over his perceived humiliation," she said. "His ego will never be over it."

Forgetting that it was actually her who'd been disgraced.

Zard laughed. As she considered the merits of punching him in the face, he raised a finger.

"There is one saving grace."

"What's that?"

"It was a Monument site."

Hope thrust her shoulders back and her lips circled in a hiss of interest. "Really?"

Bobbing his head, Zard smiled, pleased he'd given her an out.

"Yep," Zard said. "You going to call Truman?"

"Not a chance," she said, taking her phone from her clutch. "Duncan."

Duncan, her grandfather's bodyman, coordinated more than just Truman's schedule and security. He was discreet and could keep a secret, which was exactly what she needed. Presley had broken into a Monument site. Monument was one of her grandfather's companies, which meant they could choose not to press criminal charges.

Her grandfather wouldn't be bothered about a minor break in, not perpetrated by a child. If the cops called him about something like that, or showed up about it, he'd be more likely to dismantle their department than go after the kid.

Duncan would get a call. Everything was fielded through him. Few people wanted to talk to her grandfather directly. They'd rather go through the bodyman or her, if they knew her, which a lot of people did. It didn't always pay to be approachable.

# SEVEN

JUST THEN, someone else appeared in the doorway. Looking past Zard was enough to turn him around.

"Chapman," she said to the detective, tossing her clutch onto the trolley under the lightbox. "Been a while."

"What you doing here, Angel?" Chapman asked. "Witness tampering?"

"Yes," she said, starting toward him. "That's me, the career criminal… Can we talk?"

He shrugged and stepped out of the doorway.

Zard called after her. "Frey, he one of yours or not?"

Catching the doorframe, she spun to look at him, sparing only a glance at the still-frowning Baer. "Yes," she said. "Give him the works. The usual workup."

"Yes, mistress," he said, heading for the door.

Giving them privacy, Zard went by and disappeared down the corridor.

"I have to take a report," Chapman said.

"I know." She nodded. "I'm not saying you shouldn't talk to him… You have to do your job."

"Then what are we doing in the hallway? This social?"

Touching her face, his fingers slipped down the front of her chin. She'd be kind and let him enjoy the fleeting moment.

Linking their fingers, she drew his hand down. "Chapman," she murmured. "Presley is just a kid…" And then there was the ace. "It was a Monument site."

Groaning, he extricated his hand from hers. "You ever met a kid you won't stand in front of?"

Broadening her smile, her chin went up until her hair fell from her face. "Never yet."

And proud of it.

She didn't object when, with a hand on her hip, he put her back to the wall and braced his weight on a forearm above her head to lean in.

"Have dinner with me."

"And, what?" she asked. "You won't question the kid?"

"I'll still have to question him… but I'll be nicer about it."

Toying with a button on his shirt, she avoided looking him in the eye. "You were demoted because of us. Why would you want anything to do with me?"

"I was demoted because Truman's obsessed with you… and because screwing in police cells is against the rules."

The memory, from far too long ago, still made her smile. That he returned the sentiment wasn't a surprise.

"It was a peaceful protest."

"Way you were screaming didn't sound so peaceful," he said, curling a finger under her chin.

"Scott," she whispered, pressing her hands to his chest, skimming them up to his shoulders to keep their bodies apart. "We're professionals."

"Always forget that around you," he said. "Shouldn't I get a prize for enduring the marathon. Think about it, what else can Truman take from me? That man needs to let go."

"He's not the only one," she said. "Would this be easier with Duncan?"

"The view is better with you," he said and tried to dip lower again.

Giving him a harder push, she slid out from between him and the wall. "Scott," she said. "Please, you're not making this easier… You promised you wouldn't be like this anymore."

"Yeah, that's easy to say until I have to look at you. Shit, Frey, you know how it tears me apart? How it rips at me to know what I did to you?" Coming closer, he bobbed his chin in the direction of the room. "You got here in a hurry. Who's the guy?"

Shaking her head slowly, dread sped her blood. "The kid's brother. No one," she said. "He's no one important."

The last thing she needed was Chapman's attention in all the wrong places.

"And this kid is one of yours." He scanned her outfit. "You weren't lying around your apartment in that… Where were you?"

That question, for sure, wasn't professional. Rather than address that, she went for obtuse.

"Am I under suspicion? I don't have to break into Monument sites. Why would I steal from Monument?"

"Why would anyone steal from Monument?" Chapman asked. "Did you get a call about the break in or the kid? You're not top of the Monument phone tree."

"No, I'm not," she said. "I'm here to help Presley."

Narrowing an eye, he closed in. "Who, if the report I got was right, has insurance and no recent injuries... I'm going to ask you again, Angel, and try not to lie to me this time... Who's the guy?"

"The guy is his brother," she said, lifting her hand out of his reach when he tried to touch her again.

"Are you sleeping with him?"

Glancing at her outfit, she opened her arms. "I wasn't lying around his apartment in this either, was I?"

"What you wearing under it?"

This was why she couldn't stand to be in Scott Chapman's company for more than two or three minutes, it always got personal... too personal.

"That stopped being your business a long time ago," she said, keeping her voice low because they were still just outside Presley's room.

"And if I go in there and ask him... what will he say?"

"I imagine he'll tell you to go suck eggs."

Chapman snickered. "No one says that, Frey... You've gotta get out more."

"Coming from the man who just accused me of being out," she said, folding her arms. "You know, I don't think it's a good idea for you to be on this, if you're going to be like... this."

"Hey, if the kid did nothing wrong, he's got nothing to worry about... And his brother..."

"What about his brother?" she asked. "His brother definitely didn't do anything wrong. And for your report I should tell you, Monument won't be pressing charges against Presley."

"What about payment for damages? There's criminal damage, vandalism—"

"He's alive, that's all we care about," she said. "We'll absorb the cost."

He sneered. "Just the price of doing business." She wouldn't give him the satisfaction of responding. "You've really got to look at a guy if his brother starts fucking with you the minute you start fucking him... Kids usually love you, what did you do to this one? Or maybe the brother sent the kid out there? Truman started on him already?"

"You need to pay less attention to my love life."

His brows rose. "Love? Really... And here I thought you only used guys for sex."

"Right," she said, nodding, fired by outrage. Who did this guy think he was? "That's right. Sex. Mm hmm. I'm using him for sex... It's good sex too. Maybe the best... definitely better than it was with you." The sound of him grinding his teeth fired her up, yeah, good, let him get pissed off, his mood wouldn't shrink her infuriation. "Yes, you know what he's really good at? Doing me hard and fast all night long. All damn night. Without any of that sweet nothings bullshit. All he's interested in is sticking his cock in me as often as possible. That's it. All I am to him is a pussy to pump any time he can bend me over and make me take it." Landing her eyes on his, she didn't restrain her venom. "And, boy, do I love to take it."

Yanking her arm from his fingertips, she stepped backward.

"Frey—"

"If you turn this into an agenda against Presley, his brother, or any of their family, just because you think I might have the audacity to move on from us, you will learn the real meaning of Truman's fury... You don't think I held him back? You don't think I saved you from the real misery he wanted to rain down on you? You should be kissing my goddamn feet, not standing here threatening a child and his family because you think it will get my attention."

She tried to move past him, but he took her arm again, forcing her to swing out of his reach.

"Frey—"

"Who I spend time with is none of your business, Scott. You try to make it your business and I'll make it mine to tell the world exactly what you're capable of." This time he let her pass. She stopped in the doorway to look back over her shoulder. "Presley's not well enough for visitors. You want his statement? Call Jonas Bruce during business hours."

"Are you kidding me? You're paying for his lawyer too?"

"Goodbye, Detective Chapman."

Owing no further explanation, she went back into the room only to find Baer right there near the door.

Chapman called after her. "This guy must be damn good in the sack."

She and Baer held eye contact. Oh, God. Given his position, Baer must have heard most, if not all, of her and Chapman's exchange.

"That was, uh… personal."

He didn't flinch. "Uh huh," Baer said after a few seconds of silence.

"There will be paperwork at the front desk, you'll have to fill it in. I'd… avoid Chapman if you can."

Baer didn't say anything else, just drew his eyes off her as he turned to leave the room.

# EIGHT

INHALING THROUGH her nose, she cleared out her negative mood and smiled before focusing on Presley sitting up in bed.

"How are you doing, kid?"

"I'm not a kid," he said. "I'm twelve."

"Right." She went to his bedside. "Of course you are… I'm sorry, that's practically a man…" Pointing at the end of the bed, she slipped off her shoes. "Do you mind if I join you?"

The kid's eyes almost popped out of his head. "In bed?"

"I promise not to make any inappropriate advances," she said and gestured to the chair on the other side. "I can sit there if you'd prefer."

"No!" he said, forgetting about his arm and lunging forward. In pain, he recoiled. Her wince of sympathy came in time with helping him gently lay his arm down again. "I'm sorry, Master Claymore, can I get you something? Are you hungry?"

"I'm twelve," he muttered. "I'm always hungry." The barely restrained tears in his eyes broke her heart. "Why'd you call me master?"

"Because I don't have permission to use your first name."

"You can use my first name," he mumbled.

"Thank you," she said, grinning. "And you can use mine... I'm Freya... Freya Dere...How about when we're through here, you let me take you out for a cheeseburger?"

"Won't it be too late?"

With a shake of her head, she gestured to the end of the bed again and he nodded. Gathering her skirt, she climbed on to join him.

Legs folded, back straight, she rubbed her foot. "It's up to your brother," she said. "I know this amazing place that does the best fries you will ever taste in your whole life..." Leaning over her foot, she lowered her volume. "Saying yes would really help me out. I'm only allowed to eat junk food on special occasions."

"Says who?"

"Adulthood," she said, straightening to massage again.

The youngster's frown grew while remaining intent on her massage. "Why is this a special occasion?"

"I'm making a new friend," she said and stopped massaging to tilt her head. "Unless you don't want to be my friend."

"I... I want to be your friend," he said, his expression loosening though his eyes flicked up and down when she switched her massage to the other foot. "Your feet hurt?"

"It's the shoes," she said, sharing a private smile with herself.

Slanting to the side, he peeked off the edge of the bed. "Boy, they look..."

"Lethal?" she asked. "It's a stiletto platform. Has to be. I'm short."

He blinked. "Baer is six feet four inches tall."

Raising her brows, her smile was tight. "I noticed... Why do you think I need the high shoes?"

"Dad says me and Charlie might be tall like them one day... you think maybe?"

From what she could see, he was already tall, though he probably didn't feel it next to his brother.

"It's possible," she said. "I was told someone's height is dependent on their parents'."

That disappointed him. "Huh, Mom is short. Not as short as you, I don't think."

She laughed. "Not many people are, honey."

"Are your parents short?"

It wasn't unusual for kids to ask about her parents, or for parents to ask about her parents. Still the question always caught the breath in the back of her throat.

"My dad was tall," she said. "My mom only hit five flat."

With the innocence of a child and a wariness that suggested he feared the response, he asked, "Was?"

She licked her lips. "My parents died when I was ten."

His attention dropped to his uninjured hand resting on the bed. "Charlie and me were eight when ours had their accident."

Curiosity and sympathy inspired questions, but this was Baer's private business. She doubted he'd appreciate her prying. Not that it mattered. They weren't dating each other; she wasn't his client.

"I'm sorry," she said. "It's not easy to lose someone close to you."

Perking up, he was quick to make eye contact. "We didn't lose them. We live with Dad... he was just...

he got banged up and has problems with his leg sometimes, so he can't work like he used to. That's why Baer supports us. But, Dad, like looks after us and stuff."

No mention of their mother, but she wouldn't ask. "Must be good to have a big brother living with you."

Again, he shook his head. "Baer has his own place in the attic… he does maintenance in the building, gets us a break on rent." This kid wasn't shy about sharing. "Are you going to like get with him?"

"Get with…? Oh, no, honey. We're just friends."

Even when hurting his arm or talking about his parents, he hadn't looked so dejected as he did right then, sagging against the pillows propping him up.

"Dad says Claire messed him up good. Mom and Dad were in the hospital for so long after the accident, Baer was trying to look after us and them, it was tough. I don't remember a whole lot, just that Mom wasn't around… But after that, we didn't see Claire anymore… Dad said she was only interested in the sprint."

"Not the marathon," she murmured. In the hallway, Chapman was quick to put that same label on her. Guilty, just how like this Claire might she be? Yeah, that wasn't the time for internal crises. Changing the subject, and the mood, she squeezed his ankle, then renewed her efforts to massage her feet. "So did you think about what color you want them to wrap your cast in?"

"Color?"

"Sure," she said. "They have all sorts of colors. I love the pink, it's really vibrant." Gasping in joy, she gave him another squeeze. "I saw this one girl last week with purple daisies on hers… Purple is my favorite color. That was over at Harbor North, but I could call them, see if they'll courier some… goes really well with the pink."

"Pink?" His lip curled in disgust. "Purple?"

"Sure," she said, playing with him. Her hands left her feet when her shoulders went back. "You wouldn't get pink? I asked you out for burgers and you wouldn't even get purple flowers for me?"

"Well… yeah," he muttered, his lips loosening. "But I gotta go to school tomorrow…" Suddenly optimistic, he bounced. "You want to come to my school tomorrow? It's on West Trin. If you meet me after, I can tell them I did it for my girl."

Oh, he was so sweet. Such innocence and hope.

She smiled and reached over his legs to take his uninjured hand.

"That's a date, Handsome." She put his hand on her cheek. "But, you know, I like blue too… Maybe if you got blue, you could let me draw a daisy for you… would you let me do that instead?" Eyes glazed and wide, he blinked hard and nodded. "Thank you, Handsome."

"What's going on in here?"

Baer's approaching voice attracted her attention, which loosened Presley's hand. The older brother examined the younger. Something discerning in his eye became more intense.

He tilted his head to focus on her. "You know he can see down your dress, right?"

It hadn't even occurred to her. Glancing down, she saw that, yes, she'd been giving Presley a close-up of more than just modest cleavage. She sat up, pressing a hand to the front of her dress.

"Sorry," she said to him, then winced at Presley. "I'm sorry."

Baer laughed. "Don't apologize to him," he said and handed the kid a juice box.

"I don't want that baby thing," Presley snarked, shoving the box onto the table.

Kids on the cusp of teenage-hood acted this way all the time.

"Can I have it?" she asked, opening her hand to him. "Please?"

Surprised by the question, Presley handed it over. She smiled in thanks and opened it.

"I called home," Baer said. "You're grounded forever."

Presley gaped at his brother. "But I... Freya's taking me out for burgers." Baer landed an unimpressed eye on her. She smiled and shrugged, tonguing the straw into her mouth. "We're dating now."

That widened her smile. She sucked up some of the juice before holding the box toward Presley.

"Want to share with me, Handsome?"

The kid was happier to take the juice from her.

Baer hadn't managed to crack a smile. "You're dating," he said. "My twelve-year-old brother?"

She shrugged. "What can I say? We hit it off."

"You tell him we've kissed?"

How could he announce such a thing? She gasped and swatted for him, but he swerved back. In that move, he found his smile.

"Baer!"

"You said you weren't getting with him," Presley whined.

"Oh, honey," she said, leaning forward to take his hand again. "He's just jealous. Ignore him."

"Money shot," Baer muttered, stepping back from the bed to take his jacket off.

And, sure enough, Presley's eyes dropped a little.

Sitting up fast, she held a hand out to Baer. "Can I have that, please?"

He handed over his jacket. "Won't protect the assets." Putting her arms in the sleeves, she wrapped it around her front and leaned back to massage her foot again. "If you're dating, he's entitled to the view."

Baer went around the end of the bed to the seat by Presley's uninjured hand.

"No one is entitled to anything, even in a relationship," she said. "You should know better than to send young boys that message."

"This from the woman dating a twelve-year-old," he said, loosening his cufflinks and lifting his hips to put them in the pocket of his slacks.

"Stop being jealous, Baer," Presley said while Baer folded his cuffs over his forearms. "I manned up for her first."

She swooned a little and switched her smile from him to Baer.

Presley was glaring at his brother and didn't notice her mouth, "I love him," to the elder Claymore.

In response, he rolled his eyes.

Shifting his chair closer to the bed, Baer presented her a hand. "Gimme."

"Give you, what?"

He sat straight, gliding his fingers over the apex of her knee to skim it down the front of her calf. Ah, he'd noticed her massaging.

A foot massage? Oh, God, yes. It might be polite to refuse, but she wouldn't. Uncrossing her legs to extend one toward him, if he knew what he was doing, this would be the highlight of her week.

"Take this," he said, pulling a pillow from the top of the stack behind Presley.

One the kid wasn't tall enough to notice missing.

He guided the foot she'd given him closer and surprised her by scooping up the other one to put it on the arm of his seat. With one of her legs next to him and the other in his grip, her ass shifted closer to Presley's ankles.

"Now, kid, you watch close," Baer said. "You get this right, you'll never have to worry about your view being taken away."

"Baer," she murmured, but didn't pursue her scolding.

Instead, she put the pillow under her head and lay down. And when he squeezed the sensitive spot next to the ball of her foot, her eyes closed. Exhaling, she hadn't meant to sound quite so blissed out, but in that opening gambit, he proved his skill.

"Do you trade?" Presley asked.

Her twisted upper body didn't allow for a view of the youngster. No, when she opened her eyes, Baer was all she saw. He fixated on her with that same sleepy look in his eye as before, only this time it was hotter, steamier, far from age appropriate for their audience.

Neither of them answered.

Presley spoke again, "Freya says she has to wear the shoes that hurt her 'cause of you. Is that why you have to massage her feet?"

"I massage her feet because I want to," Baer said to his brother, forcing himself to stop looking at her.

The new angle gave her a better view of his profile. Clean-shaven tonight, unlike the stubble he wore when they met. She preferred the stubble. God, talk about presumptuous. It wasn't her place to be thinking anything close to that. So new thoughts. New thoughts…

Hmm… smooth would be nice too, she'd be able to lick his jaw, to taste his skin, slide her lips across his cheek to his upper lip. Smooth meant no stubble burn. No barriers. No clues.

Baer was a gentleman; he'd been polite and courteous. Yet there was something about him that suggested he could be a little rough around the edges… if he relaxed some.

It would be so easy to take her foot from his hands, to prop it on the opposite arm of his chair and slither forward, off the bed, into his lap…

"Freya?"

Presley's voice interrupted her inappropriate fantasy. "Yes, Handsome? Sorry, my mind was drifting."

"Drifting where, Little Skit?" Baer asked, mischief dancing in him.

When he elevated her foot, his breath touched the pad of her big toe, forcing a rush of heat through her. Clenching her abs, she tried her best not to react, but he noticed how hard she swallowed. Oh. Oh. Oh. The flare of his gaze… She had him, enticed him, intrigued him.

Licking his lips slowly, he lowered his chin, routing his exhale to her sensitive instep. A tremble shimmered from her inner thighs to the most intimate corner of her enlivened body.

"Baer," she whispered, her voice almost not there.

When he next breathed against the groove of her foot, the whisper of his lips brushed her skin. Like he'd flipped a switch, she rolled onto her back, and her foot leaped from the arm of the chair to land on his chest. Curling her toes into the thick fabric of his expensive shirt, they begged to be spoiled too.

"Have you… have you had sex?" Presley asked like he wasn't quite sure what he was witnessing.

Join the club, kid.

Her overloaded senses presented a vision, both inside and out… Oh, she wanted more.

"With Freya?" Baer asked. Guy deserved credit for getting that out, getting any words out. "No."

"Would you?" Presley asked, excited.

"Would I? Hell, yeah, I would."

Because it was his job.

A trolley rattled into the room, and she sat up fast, snatching her feet from Baer.

"Who ordered one cast?" a male voice echoed behind her, but she was too engrossed by Baer to turn around.

The quick smile he offered grew curious. "You okay?"

"I'm, uh… just going to see what Rufio dug up for me."

Sliding off the bed, she was quick about skipping around it and picking up her shoes.

"Freya?" Presley called when she was nearing the door. "We still going for burgers?"

"Of course, Handsome," she said, holding onto the doorframe, supporting her balance as she put on one shoe, then the other. "I know how long this takes… I just have to see some patients, sign some paperwork… won't take long. Baer will stay with you."

That's what she said and meant… Except in the hallway, just outside the room, she needed a moment to gather herself. Okay, she was fine, good. Back to business.

Before she'd gotten a step away, someone snatched her wrist to pull her back. Again, she landed where Chapman put her, except this time Baer was the one with his forearm on the wall above her head.

"You got spooked again, Little Skit," he said. "What happened?"

"You should get back in there."

"Kid will be fine for a minute," he said. "What's in your head?" He paused. "Thinking about that kiss again?"

"No," she said, probably too quickly, planting a firm hand on his chest. "No. God, no, I wasn't thinking about kissing you…"

Not at that exact moment anyway, though those thoughts hadn't been far from her periphery. And now that he mentioned it…

Maybe he sensed her confusion. The twitch of his eyes narrowing betrayed he couldn't quite figure her out.

"If you want to take off, you can go. You're under no obligation to be here. I'll call you a cab. I'll tell Pres—"

"No." Her hand was so small against his chest. "I don't want to go…" Peeking at him, she kept her chin low. "Unless… do you want me to go?" His next blink was long and slow. "You're under no obligation either… You're not being paid to entertain me. This is personal. I shouldn't be here… I—"

Touching her lips, he silenced her. "I don't want you to leave, Little Skit." Sliding his finger south, it kept going until his hand curved around her waist with the lightest grip. "Look at me…" Moving just the tiniest bit, her hair fell from her face. "Lift your chin…" As she complied, his arm left the wall above her head to trace the line of her jaw with the edge of his finger. "Relax," he whispered. "Right here…" The digit drifted up her jaw again. Doing as told, her jaw loosened to part her lips. She didn't think beyond his instruction, but some part of her had to know what was coming. "Good, Little Skit…" His voice was the gentlest whisper as his mouth came lower and his eyes grew heavier, eventually closing just a feather away from hers. "You are so good, baby."

Joining their mouths, his soft, slow approach stretched time, minutes must've passed before he even let their lips engage all the way. He kissed like he had all the time in the world, like there was nothing around them, like it was just them and eternity.

Brushing his tongue across her mouth's threshold, he let it just touch hers then withdrew, disappearing before she was ready. Clinging tighter, an aching squeak fled her throat. She couldn't think of anything, nothing except the whisper of his tongue dipping into her mouth again, seeking permission to be somewhere it already knew.

Begging more, her nails bit into him, desperate as her tongue pressuring his, demanding it fight back, to raise the urgency from torment to gratification. Instead, his tongue retreated, and the pressure of his mouth ebbed.

He didn't let their lips lose contact. Just the hint of his kiss was tease enough to heat her. Lost in the cocoon of his aura, she couldn't open her eyes, couldn't take a full breath.

"It's not a race, Lil'," he whispered, giving her another brief taste. "Stop trying to reach the finish… You'll always get there first with me… I swear it to you, baby."

Boneless, hot and aroused, she gripped him tighter, responding to the grace granted by his mouth.

"You didn't read the right prep sheet if you think I need tender and slow."

"No prep sheet," he said, sweeping the hair from her eyes to match their gazes. "You hear me, Frey? No prep sheet… Not between us… not ever, okay? Do you understand?"

Her head moved in an involuntary nod. Did she? No. But what did that matter? It didn't, not in the light of another truth. No one was paying either of them to be there at that minute. Whether or not he knew who she was, she wanted to be sucked in and wanted this to be doing to him what it was doing to her.

"I should get back to Pres…" Yes, his brother. She licked the remnants of their kiss from her lips. Just as her tongue slipped back into her mouth, he dipped to kiss her again. Straightening up, he ran a hand through his hair and grabbed the doorframe of Presley's room to pull himself toward it. "Oh, uh… They don't know what I do… My family, they… don't ask questions and I don't offer information. I know I don't have to ask for your discretion, but—"

"Sure," she said, surprised by his sudden composure. "No, I wouldn't ever…"

He smiled and winked. "Thanks, Little Skit."

Alone in the corridor, with whiplash, she'd need another minute. Was that kiss… something, or an attempt to ensure her silence?

From one lane to the next Baer could switch gears to floor the gas or slam the brakes. What was going on? Would she ever figure it out?

# NINE

BURGERS WITH CHILCONN kids was a regular thing. The plastic tables and neon overheads may be tacky to some, not her. Though it had never been quite like that. Baer and Presley were an enthralling experience. Kidding around and messing with each other, their familiarity mesmerized her. In the arcade at the back of the burger joint, the brothers battled on various machines, Baer got the balance of competitiveness and going easy just right.

Baer paid for the meal and refused to take a penny. He wouldn't let her pay a cent for their shared cab either. She knew better than to push, especially with a youngster around.

Despite Presley's requests to see her apartment, she doubted he truly wanted to snoop. More likely his goal was to avoid facing his father, but, unfortunately for him, that appointment was inevitable. Kissing each male on the cheek, she'd bid them goodnight.

The next afternoon, she lingered over selecting ingredients at the store. Big first impression on the horizon. She couldn't mess this up. Normally, she wasn't so concerned about making a fool of herself. Why was she so worried about it? Baer. He was why.

Loitering outside Presley's school with her paper sacks was conspicuous. There she was, a stranger, standing there as kids flooded the street. No one would notice, no one would care. Would they? If you see something, say something. If anyone reported her, could she explain her presence? Yes. So what was she stressing about? It had been a long time since she'd had first date nerves. Who was she worried about dating? The kids? Their father…? Or their older brother?

Picking out Presley was surprisingly easy. His bright cast cut through the noise and drew her eye. It didn't matter though, he spotted her just as quickly.

Grabbing the boy at his side to rush through the melee of schoolkids, Presley was with her in a flash.

"You came! I can't believe you really came!"

"I said I would, didn't I?" She set her smile on the new boy. "You must be Charlie, I'm Freya. It's a pleasure to meet you."

Presley shoved his brother. "Say hello, idiot. Freya's my girlfriend."

She'd say it was never bad to be wanted, but anyone overhearing that on the street outside a school… Yeah, maybe they should get moving.

She elevated her paper sacks. "Still okay for me to cook you dinner?"

"Uh huh! Yeah! For definite!"

"Show me the way."

The boys wasted no time heading away from school. Charlie was a little more uncertain of himself than Presley, but when inspiration struck, he'd find his exuberance.

The three of them walked back to a simple, clean, apartment building. Going inside, and up one floor of the five-floor structure, the boys burst into their apartment. In a narrow entryway, they kicked off their sneakers and dumped their bookbags, so she hung her purse on an empty hook.

Free of their school wares, the pair rushed through a door to the left.

"Dad! We brought someone home!"

Straight ahead, in a living room recliner, facing the blaring TV was a man, probably in his sixties, but still in good shape. Wearing loose jeans and a tee-shirt, he could do with a haircut. The end-table beside him was filled with clutter, magazines, soda and beer cans, a coffee mug, but nothing that looked like it had been there forever.

The man gave the doorway an absent glance, he'd been focused on something in his hand. Once she registered, he did a quick double take and sat up, tossing whatever was in his hand to the table and grabbing the remote to turn off the TV.

"Well, shit, boys, what did you do?" he asked. The gruff tone wasn't threatening, just fed up. "I'm sorry, ma'am, if they damaged your vehicle or upset you in—"

"No, not at all," she said, handing one food sack to Charlie and the lighter one to Presley who was still working on maneuvering with the cast. "Put these in the kitchen, would you, please?" The boys ran off to do as told. Landing a smile on the elder Claymore, she could tell he was still confused. "Your boys are wonderful. A real credit to you."

"A credit, huh?" he asked, raising his chin to peer at her. "You a Christian?"

Of all the questions she might have expected, that one wasn't on the list.

She laughed. "I don't know how to answer that, sir. My intentions are honorable, but I'm not here to sell the Lord to you."

"She's my girlfriend," Presley announced, bouncing over to her side.

Shock and maybe a little horror crossed the older man's face. "Your girlfriend? Boy, now I don't know what you—"

"Baer wants to have sex with her!" Charlie piped up, darting across to his father. "I say they're gonna fight over her, Dad!"

That widened his eyes. He checked both of his boys until his gaze ended on her. Still suspicious, the discerning glint was familiar, it matched Baer's.

"When you said my boys, you meant all of them," he said. "Guess I should be pleased Baer still remembers how to treat a woman right… So which of my boys you want? Woman as beautiful as you can have any of them… Will say I've been trying to offload the oldest one the longest…"

"Dad!" Presley whined. "That's my girlfriend!"

When Presley tried to put his arm around her waist, she turned to wrap both arms around his shoulders.

"You are a sweetheart, Handsome," she said and looked to the father over his head. "I came to cook dinner for Presley… would that be okay?"

"To cook? In my kitchen?"

"For you all… yes."

Some of his suspicion was back. "Baer ain't here. He drops in and out. I don't know when he'll be around… If he's giving you the runaround…"

Ha! She'd prefer if Baer didn't appear.

"No, Baer and I are friends," she said. "That's all… I was at the hospital last night when Presley was brought in. I work with a foundation that caters to children with sickness and injury…This is just something I like to do for the kids I've personally overseen. I like to check in and make sure everything is okay, check they're healing."

"Oh, like follow up care," he said. "Like a candy striper who does house calls."

She laughed. "Something like that, yes. If it's a problem, I can leave."

"No," he said, shifting in his seat. "A beautiful woman comes to my home and offers to cook dinner for me and my boys... only a fool would refuse that... The boys will help you, don't have much in there but—"

"I brought everything I need," she said and let go of Presley to cross to him. "I'm Freya... Freya Dere."

"Abel Claymore," he said, shaking her hand. "It's a pleasure to meet you."

"And you, sir," she said. "Anyone have allergies or requirements I need to know about?"

"No," he said. "We eat what's put in front of us... This is very generous."

"It's what I do, sir."

Leaving him, she went into the kitchen at the back of the space to unpack her ingredients. Once everything was laid out, the kitchen got her scrutiny. It wasn't full of mod cons but had the essentials. A sink, a stove, a fridge, and the long, wide breakfast bar was a generous working space.

A groan in the living room signaled Abel getting out of his chair. He snagged a stick from next to the table, using it for balance as he came toward her. Regardless of his infirmity, his shape was impressive. There didn't seem to be extra weight on his frame, and she smiled at the stubble on his jaw... It suited him, just like it suited his eldest son.

Taking a board from the end of the counter, she checked out blade after blade in the knife block before finding the right one.

"Yo, you two, homework," Abel called out to the boys who were taking turns hitting Presley's cast in the dining/den area by the kitchen. "What you got?"

"Nothing, Dad," Presley said, holding up his injured arm. "Teacher said she was impressed I was in."

Charlie shoved his brother. "All day I had to help him... Baer said I gotta. I don't gotta, do I, Dad?"

"I heard that conversation," Abel said, propping himself on a stool. "Sounded like you came out on top of that barter, Charlie, boy... What you extort out that conversation?"

That shut Charlie up fast.

Getting ready for cleaning and prepping, she hid a smile at Presley making faces at his brother, sharing his gloating amusement.

When he was done with that, he came moseying over to watch what she was doing.

"Wash these for me, please, Handsome," she said, handing off some of the vegetables.

After taking a second to look at them every which way, Presley went to the sink.

"Pres got arrested and Baer took him out for burgers," Charlie said. "It's not fair... How come we didn't go?"

Raising the knife a little, she stopped trimming the meat. "That's my fault," she said. "I invited Presley for burgers. I didn't think about it causing trouble at home."

"I'll take you at the weekend," Abel said. "Stop starting trouble."

"He gets to go with Freya, and he'll have to go twice 'cause what will we do with him? Baer's never here at the weekend."

"If Miss Dere is free, she can join us..." Abel said, his intent gaze expected an answer.

"I would be honored. And, please, it's Freya."

Charlie was getting closer and closer by the moment. She figured he was intrigued, or hungry. Pushing the pre-tossed salad toward him, she nodded at it. Even if he finished it, there was plenty extra to make more.

"Presley can just sit and watch us eat," Charlie said, opening the tub of salad to pick at the leaves.

She handed him a bottle of dressing. "It's better with that… If you want to try it."

"Baer makes salad," Charlie said, opening the bottle.

"Yeah, and you complain before you eat it," Abel said. "Who's cooking for your family tonight, Freya?"

"I live alone."

"No husband? No kids?" Abel asked and she shook her head. "Where did you meet Baer?"

Ah, excellent, a question she didn't want to answer. "I, uh… ran into him," she said, smiling at the memory of her panic on leaving that gallery. "I was distressed about something. He took me for coffee to calm me down."

"And she kissed him," Charlie said, then froze to look at her and his father. "That's what Presley said."

"It's not a lie." Though technically, Baer had been the one to kiss her. "But we are just friends."

Presley had been a while and the faucet was still going. She went to help him finish up. There may be water everywhere, but he hadn't done an awful job. After drying up, the boys finished the dressed salad, then set the table at her request.

Everyone helped with prep, no one complained. She saw more of Baer in Abel when the elder Claymore showed patience in teaching the boys how to cut the vegetables. Once everything was prepped, she got to cooking. Abel sent the twins to get washed up and changed.

Once she and Abel were alone, somehow, they got onto the subject of Abel's wife and what the family had endured. How? No idea. She hadn't brought it up, but Abel's openness relieved some of her guilt about intruding into Baer's life. The family had been through a lot.

Abel's willingness to share suggested he hadn't talked about it for a while or that he needed to talk about it. After their car accident, Abel lost function in his leg and his wife, Sandy, fell into a coma. Taking her time with the meal, she let him talk, let him tell her about his spinal injury and how he'd almost lost his leg completely.

Even after five years, he was battling through physio and improving all the time. The pain and stiffness didn't go away. Some days were better than others. Still he fought for the woman he loved and never missed a chance to be with her.

Serving the food, she left the meat resting.

"Have you been in pain today?" she asked, washing her hands.

"Yes," he said. "Stiff, like usual."

"This might sound weird." She snagged a towel to dry her hands. "But I'm qualified in sports and therapeutic massage, if you want me to…"

The unexpected offer didn't stump him for long. "Really? You wouldn't mind?"

"It would be my honor," she said. "I have oil in my purse… You don't have any allergies, do you?"

He shook his head, so she ran to the entryway to grab her purse from its hook.

Without closing the entryway door, she dug out her toiletry bag to retrieve the oil.

"We can do it after dinner," he said, pushing himself from the stool.

"I can give you some quick relief," she said, putting her purse on the floor and shaking the bottle of oil. "Not to be too forward, but can you drop your pants?"

He wasn't shy, and grinned until he laughed. "Haven't done that for a woman since my wife last asked me," he said, but unbuckled his belt and let them drop.

As he put his hands on the breakfast bar behind him for support, she dropped to her knees, pouring oil into her hands.

She worked her palms over his thigh. "Is the pain in your hip too? After dinner, I can do it properly, if you're still getting stiffness."

"It is stiff," he said. "I skipped exercise last night and this morning. I should know better..."

"With Presley getting injured you had reason to be distracted, this morning at least," she said. "Can you reach the meat from there?"

He twisted. "Uh, yeah, I think so."

"There's an extra piece on the end, will you try it for me, please? Tell me if it's seasoned okay for the boys."

"This looks like expensive steak," he said. "Do you treat all your clients this way?"

"Often as I can," she said, peeking up to see him pop the meat between his lips. "How is it? Is it good?"

"Mm," he said with his mouth full. "Mm, it's amazing. Really good... Wow, oh, geez, girl, you're incredible."

"What the fuck is going on in here?"

Baer's voice intruded without shame. Abel swore in a hiss. She hadn't hurt him, she didn't think, but she couldn't say the same about the man standing by the door, fuming.

"Son—"

"Are you fucking kidding, Abel?"

Speak. Speak, Freya. She should explain but was having difficulty blinking. Speaking was too much. In blue jeans and a grubby white tee-shirt, Baer was less buttoned up than she'd ever seen him. In the suits, he was hot and delicious, but with the glisten of sweat on his brow and the tool belt slung around his hips, she was surprised her tongue was still in her head.

Stomping across the room, obvious anger creased his brow. "Five fucking years you've refused to move on from Mom and the first woman you put the fucking moves on—"

"No," Abel said. "Don't fucking walk in here and speak to us like that!"

Moves? Oh, good God, Baer thought they were…

On her knees between father and son, she looked from one to the other, vocal cords still frozen.

"On your feet, Little Skit. Tell me what the fuck is going on."

He tried to give her his hand, but she pulled away. "Don't. I have stuff all over me."

"Oh God," he said with disgust written all over his face. "Shit, Lil'."

Thrusting to full height, not that it made much of a difference to him, she shed her shock in the face of outrage.

"Oil," she said, showing him both palms. "I have massage oil on my hands." Raising her chin in a defiant tilt, she marched to the kitchen sink. "Your dad is right, don't come in here shouting and swearing. You don't have a clue what's going on."

"Lil—"

"Don't 'Lil' me," she said, soaping her hands. "Do you really think I would come over to your family's home to seduce your father just hours after your mouth left mine?" Everything was relative and a certain number of hours ago, still, her point was valid. "I came here because Presley asked me to meet him after school. I stayed to cook because I like to cook and I don't have anyone to cook for, so I cook for people I meet through my work." Rinsing her hands, she grabbed the towel from the counter and spun around to face them. "Yes, okay, I admit it, I'm sad and pathetic. I go to people's houses and cook for their families because I have no family to cook for. There. I'm glad you're happy to hear my pitiful truth. Are you happy now?"

She went to rub the excess oil from Abel's leg with the kitchen towel, appreciating it wasn't the best thing to use, but she didn't have anything else. When done, she tossed it aside and crouched to help him pick up his pants, something his son failed to do in his indignation.

Ignoring Baer at her back, she met Abel's eye. "Thank you for your kind hospitality, sir. Please enjoy the food and apologize to the boys for me."

"Freya, don't leave," Abel said.

It wasn't fair to ignore his plea, but there was nothing to say. Instead of answering, she snatched her purse from the floor and strode away; it wasn't like he could chase after her. Father? No. Son…

She got as far as the entryway before Baer caught her.

"Lil' Skit," he said, grabbing her wrist to tug her back, almost knocking her from her feet. "I'm sorry, baby." Crowding her close to the wall, he scooped a hand under her jaw and tracked his thumb across her cheek. "Seeing you on your knees in front of any other man would drive me insane, but my father… I'm sorry, baby. I'm sorry I saw red… Since you were down there between me and that vending machine…" He groaned. "God, baby, all I've thought about is your mouth on me."

Not expecting him to confess such a thing, she relaxed enough to meet his eye. "Baer—"

"That question about you tasting a man… I've never done that with a client, been brazen like that before I got a brief. But you… Skit… in that minute, I was me and I…"

Touching his lips, she silenced him. "Don't talk about that here… someone might hear you. They asked how we met. I told them I ran into you and you took me for coffee."

Filling him in just ensured their stories were straight.

His lips curled to a smile behind her fingers before he took her wrist to free them. "Not a lie."

"No, it's not." She shook her head. "I'm sorry if you think I got too close. Maybe you're right, maybe I did. Sometimes I do overstep… I'm sorry if you thought I was stalking you."

He breathed out a laugh. "I should be so lucky," he said. "You should stay for dinner."

Exhaling, she relaxed. "I shouldn't. I stayed too long already and your dad is tired."

"All the more reason you should stay, help him get the boys to bed… I have to go out tonight."

Their eyes met, though locked on, she desperately didn't want to see the truth in his gaze.

"Client?" There was something solemn about the way he closed his mouth and nodded, just once. God, she had no right! No right at all to dislike his life choices or to judge him for them. Except it wasn't judgment, it was ridiculous jealousy. Inhaling through her nose, she breathed out as her gaze sank. "Lucky lady."

Curling a finger under her chin, he picked her attention back up. "It won't be all night. Just four hours, ten thirty to two thirty."

Touching his tee-shirt on his sternum, she drew a fingernail around one of the grimy patches. Presley said Baer worked maintenance in the building, which was how they got a break in rent. The jeans and sweat and tool-belt had to be part of his day job. It was a wonder the man ever found time to sleep.

Now she understood why he did it. Abel couldn't work. The facility his mom was in would be a small fortune in fees. Abel needed regular doctor and physical therapy visits too. All of that was on top of the boys', the family's, daily living costs.

"Two a.m. is my favorite time of the night," she said. "It's that sleepy time when those who didn't turn in early are heading home or going to bed… It's quiet… everything slows down and when you're in the arms of a man, it… feels like you're the only two people in the world."

"It won't tonight," he murmured. "Not for me."

Ducking down, on a trajectory for a kiss, she couldn't let him and turned her mouth away. "Don't Baer," she whispered. "Not when you're on your way to another woman's bed."

"It's work, baby. Just work, that's all."

"I know," she said, making a point of meeting his eye. "I know what it is, and I know why you do it." That piqued some curiosity in him; she didn't waver. "I don't judge you for it. I understand why and I would do the same thing if I were in your position… Doesn't mean I want to think about you doing things with other women that you'll never do with me."

His frown was quick, but they were interrupted by Abel.

"Good, you got her," Abel said. "Please stay for dinner, Freya… The boys will do the dishes."

Pasting on a smile, she eased Baer away to join his father. "I would be honored… now where are those boys?"

# TEN

WATCHING BAER WALK out his father's place was an experience she didn't want to repeat. He'd stayed as long as he could, eating with them, remaining intent as the twins recounted details of their school day. With boastful exuberance, each vied to outdo the other. Much as they might tease, those youngsters idolized their big brother.

Eventually the time had come for him to stand up and bid them farewell. She'd been in the kitchen, organizing the twins at the sink when he came over to lay a hand on her hip and kiss the corner of her mouth.

With his eyes on hers, blazing their usual intensity, he'd asked if she was okay. What was she supposed to say to that? Her heart and her mind had two different reactions. Regardless, she'd nodded. The man had to do his job, whatever the cost. Why should she make it more difficult for him?

So he'd walked out, and she'd stayed to help Abel get the boys to bed.

What was she doing playing house with…? She'd done it dozens of times. Hundreds. Visiting foundation kids and—oh, who was she kidding? This was completely different.

Why, a whole day later, was she still obsessing? There she was at her building's entrance, chatting with Narmer about his daughter, and still Baer was on her mind. More specifically, what he might've done for his client.

Get over it. This was a new night. If she wanted to enjoy it, the previous one had to be consigned to history.

When the Squires limo pulled up, she bid Narmer goodbye and dashed to the curb.

"Good evening, Kessler," she said to the driver waiting by the open back door.

"Evening, Freya, how are you?"

"Well," she said. "Thank you. And you?"

"Think I'm coming down with something."

His smile suggested that may have been a tease, she went with it anyway.

"Oh, I'm sorry to hear that," she said, tilting her head. "Maybe this will cheer you up."

Holding up a wooden box by its rope handle, she presented it to him.

"What is it?"

"Scotch," she said. "You've been so gracious; this is my thank you."

Leaving him to absorb the gratuity, she slid into the backseat.

It was insane to be disappointed by the waiting stranger. Attractive, smiling like a person happy to see her, the guy didn't know he couldn't compete.

"Miss Dere, I presume?" he asked, showing his palm. "I'm Donoghue."

She shook his hand. "Pleasure."

"Oh, that's all mine." He reached behind himself as the car got moving. "I brought you a gift."

Interesting. "A gift?" she asked, excited by the prospect. Apparently, performing a good deed earned one in return. If she didn't give Donaghue the chance to impress her, he wouldn't get a fair shake. And if nothing else, fair was the most common of courtesies. "Why thank you, I…"

When he turned back, the object in his hand shut her up in an instant. It was a gut punch. Not his fault, just one of those things. And it was stupid, childish. Yet there was a symmetry to that. The trauma came from her past, way deep down in her past, it was only logical her emotion should react in the same immature way.

"Do you like it?"

Did she like it? A single white rose. He could've brought a machete and it wouldn't have cut her deeper. No one who knew her would bring a rose, let alone a white one. But there it was, in his fingertips between them.

"I…"

What could she say that wouldn't offend or upset him? The alternative was…? Feigning delight was beyond her. Not that she'd ever get giddy over a flower.

Stop it, don't be rude. He hadn't done it out of malice. It was a nice gesture. Supposed to be a nice gesture.

"Are you okay?" he asked, probably sensing her hesitation.

Probably? It had been half a minute since he'd produced the thing and she was still just staring at it.

"Yes, I… I'm just allergic… that's all."

Okay, good deflection. Now he wouldn't expect her to take possession of it. God, she couldn't even think the noun.

"Oh," he said, his smile dropping.

Just at that, the car came to a stop and the door opened. Kessler didn't open it, someone else did.

Baer.

Climbing in, he sat in the opposite seat, reaching over to do some kind of handshake thing with Donoghue. She smiled. The twins would love to have a secret handshake with their big brother.

Donoghue said nothing, neither did she.

For a block, Baer glanced back and forth between them. "What's going on?"

A polite smile was her only response. It wasn't like she could tell him why the rose unsettled her with Donoghue sitting right there.

"Uh…" Donoghue shifted in his seat, clearing his throat. "Sorry, I… have you met? Freya, this is Baer, Baer—"

"Yeah, we've fucking met. What's going on?"

Anger? Why? His expression gave it away. On getting in, he'd been loose, now he was scowling at Donoghue.

"Calm," she whispered.

His gaze snapped to her. "If he made a fucking move on you—"

"Calm," she said, leaning forward to take his hand on his thigh. "Would you calm down?"

"You can't have been alone for more than five minutes. It was two blocks. I should've just walked over and—"

"Baer—"

"She's allergic to the flower," Donoghue said, raising a hand to let it flop.

After fixating on it for a few seconds, Baer looked from her to Donoghue. "No, she's not," he said, releasing her hand as he leaned across to roll down the side window. Picking up the flower, he tossed it out, then closed it up. "She's too polite to tell you the real reason it upset her."

"No, I..." she started. Roles now reversed, Donoghue was the scowler, while Baer was more relaxed. "You didn't have to be rude about it."

Baer straightened his cuffs, ignoring her assertion. "Was it on the prep sheet?" he asked. "What was under the flowers section?"

Donoghue lost his irritation in the face of sheer surprise. "I... nothing, it said nothing," he said, lowering his voice to a hiss. "What the hell you doing talking prep sheets in front of a client?"

"It's okay." She showed a palm to each of the men. "Let's start over... Have you two worked together before?"

The question amused Baer so much his smile broadened fast. "We haven't worked the same woman at the same time, if that's your question."

Threesomes? He was talking threesomes!

Her shock boosted his smile.

Donoghue's fingertips touched her knee and ascended to gather the hem of her dress. "That wasn't on her prep sheet either."

Baer's rage returned fast. "Don't do that."

"She likes forward," Donoghue said, his touch sliding higher.

"I don't," Baer growled. "Move your hand."

"Are you kidding?" Donoghue asked.

Plucking up his hand, she put it on his thigh and gave it a pat. "Maybe it would be best to just..." Pinning a glare on Baer, she couldn't for the life of her figure out what was wrong. "What is with you?"

"Wait, I thought she was a new client," Donoghue said. "You seen her off the books? You moonlighting?"

"No." She landed a broad smile on Donoghue. "We met at Squires. That's all. Just Squires."

"Clients pick us, buddy," Donoghue said, putting a heavy, almost clumsy arm around her. "Not the other way around. Get over it."

Baer's scowl didn't flinch. Even when he shifted it to the opposite side of the car, he couldn't keep it away. Donoghue said something about the bar they were going to, but she didn't hear it. All she could see was Baer's displeasure.

It would be rich if he was angry with her for being on a date with another man when he'd been sleeping with another woman last night. This was professional for him, and he was about to go on a date with her cousin. Why couldn't he see it was professional for her too? No, okay, granted, this wasn't her job, but she wasn't doing it for love. Not romantic love. Not sex. Family love. This was support for Holly. Surely Baer could understand that.

Without seeing, she stared out her window. By the time the car stopped again, silence reigned.

Holly got in, giving Freya an eyeful of what was under her cousin's scandalously short dress. Blinking, why couldn't she unsee that view too?

Shuffling past Baer, Holly dropped into the seat on his other side. "Isn't this a party?"

Sitting up, Freya gestured at the men in turn. "Holly, this is Donoghue, and you remember Baer."

"Yes... I do," Holly said, presenting Baer a hand.

And... he wasn't paying attention, not to the woman at his side. With widening eyes, she nodded to indicate he should say hello. While he was gracious in grazing Holly's knuckles with a kiss, his ease and charisma didn't match that of the first day in Squires. Holly noticed too, from the awkward air to the lukewarm engagement, how could she not?

In her purse, her phone chirped a distinctive tone.

"Uh oh," Holly said, recognizing that melody as she did.

Scrambling for her phone, Freya swiped the screen without taking it fully from her purse, diverting the call to voicemail.

"Damnit," she whispered.

That was against their rules. Justifying the diversion wouldn't be easy. Avoiding the call while hanging out with escorts sort of spoke for itself, but it wasn't a reason her grandfather would accept. No, because she wouldn't give him the chance. No way could she tell the truth. A lie? She hated lying to her grandfather. Mostly because whether he called her on it or not, he knew. Somehow, he always knew.

She couldn't leave it at that. He'd only keep calling if she didn't make contact. A text, she could text the reason for not taking his call. The made up reason that she still had to invent. Maybe it wouldn't be so easy to figure her out from text than it would be with speech. Hmm, yeah, she wouldn't hold her breath.

"Truman?" Holly asked. Casting her eyes up from the phone screen without raising her chin, she gave her cousin confirmation. "He's going to be maaad."

Duh, thank you. She didn't need her cousin drawing out the word to accentuate the obvious. "Yes, okay, thanks, Hol."

"What does he want?"

People usually phoned to tell other people what they wanted. Her relationship with her grandfather wasn't like that.

"What does he always want?" she muttered, typing one thing, then deleting it to write something else.

"For you to go home to him." Another glance over the phone, she understood Holly's sigh. "There are worse places to live."

"Says the woman who's never had to live with him."

"He's not awful. He doesn't beat you."

"No, he'd hire someone to do it for him." The joke wasn't funny. She inhaled to blow out a long breath. "You're right. He's good to me. He's a good man. He'd beat every other person on the planet before he'd raise a finger to me."

"Doesn't show his love in healthy ways though," Holly said. "He doesn't want you to be independent. If you go back, it will be just like before. He'll be all in your business... And he's more protective now... possessive... but cheating on a marriage—"

"Yeah, okay, thank you," she said, noting how both men in the car reacted to that statement.

Donoghue was the first to interject. "Hey, if a man can't satisfy his wife—"

"Oh, that wasn't a judgment on you." Holly was quick to leap in and clear up the misunderstanding. "Definitely not a judgment."

"No, it was a judgment on me," Freya said. "Thank you for airing my private business, Hol... My name is Freya Dere and I am a disgusting, sex-starved slut... Thank you, Holly. Thank you for helping me admit I have a problem."

"I didn't say that," Holly said. "You know how I feel about cheaters, but I—"

"You really think this is the place to talk about this?" she asked, giving up on texting and tossing her phone back into her purse. "I can't go back and change the past. What's done is done."

"That's what you say. Do you think Truman will ever let it go? Do you think he'll really ever give up on tearing Chapman apart? His wife—"

"Holly," Freya said, begging her cousin to shut up.

"What? I'm just saying, there would be worse things in the world than to be with Truman again. He loves you."

"So I should give up on self-respect? Give up on what I want to instead be the perfect, dutiful princess who never lives a day in her life?"

"If you're not in love with the dude divorce him," Donoghue said.

Holly's laugh spurted out. Horror whipped Freya around to blink at the guy casually sitting there, draped against the door. But his opinion wasn't the one that mattered.

Her eyes met Baer's. "I'm not... I'm not married."

All the things they'd done. The moments they'd shared. If she was married, she should've been honest. She couldn't let him believe she lied.

"You told me that when we met, Little Skit."

# ELEVEN

REACHING THEIR DESTINATION, eventually, delivered a reprieve from the heavy air of the car. Cloud, that was the name of the club. She hadn't picked it, though was thankful her usual haunt, the super-exclusive nightclub, Crimson, hadn't been floated as an option. Not because she didn't love it there, she did, it was one of her safe spaces. But Roxie, Crimson's Empress, was full-on, and the situation wasn't easy to explain in ten words or less.

More than a few people queued at Cloud's entrance. A canopy, red carpet, and security on the door... hmm, going for Crimson's audience? Good luck. She wasn't worried; Roxie wouldn't be either. Cloud was a cheap imitation not competition.

Using Baer's forearm to steady herself, she bent to straighten the strap at the back of her shoe.

"Shit," Donoghue said. "I changed my jacket before I left the office... You got the invite, Baer?"

Holly laughed. "Oh, sweetie, you don't need an invite."

"You okay?" Baer asked when she straightened again.

"I should've worn different shoes."

"If your feet hurt…"

And what memory did that immediately conjure? Her attention drifted to his, and it was right there staring back. The hospital. The foot massage… she shivered. And the power that gave him, oh, he could exploit that in so many ways. Naughty with him could be so much fun; that was a promise delivered in his gaze.

Licking her lips, she smiled at him. "You ain't nothing but a hound dog," she whispered.

Baer bowed closer, focused on her mouth. "They said you was high classed."

Her lips curved higher as she pushed to her tiptoes. "Well, that was just a lie."

"Uh…" Donoghue said from nearby. He snatched her arm to stuff her hand into the crook of his elbow. Choosing Baer wasn't meant to be an insult. In truth, she hadn't done it with conscious thought. Holding Baer's arm was just more natural. "That's my date… Yours is there."

Laying the evil eye on him, Donoghue tugged her against his side, forcing her to let go of Baer. Though reluctant, the latter had to be gracious in going to Holly.

Not that her cousin noticed the exchange, she was too busy ogling the entrance. "Uh," she said. Stepping closer to Baer, Holly waved toward the door. "Frey, you may have to…"

"Anyone I know?" she asked, hooking a finger into the cleavage of her dress to pull it further down.

When her gaze ascended, Baer's attention rose from her breasts. Their eyes met, and he crooked a brow. Not a fan of the show? Or not a fan of others enjoying it too?

"It's Milt," Holly said, grinning.

"Oh, then we're fine," Freya said, opening her clutch to peel a few bills from a stack.

Folding them twice, she tucked them into her cleavage and took Donoghue's arm again.

With all the confidence in the world, she strode on, chin high, and did what she always did when approaching a place like this, acted like she was *the* VVIP. Uncomfortable, but effective.

The security guys spotted her coming with Donoghue, Holly and Baer in their wake. One went to unhook the rope cordon. She twisted her upper body an almost imperceptible fraction closer to Milt as she passed him without missing a step.

"Milt," she said in acknowledgment.

Practiced, he plucked the money free. "Angel," he responded in kind.

The money was more of a gratuity than a bribe. Milt did a thankless job. He deserved to be acknowledged for his work. The amount of grief he must face each night would test anyone's patience.

Hustled inside, a sweeping bar area settled in a sort of funnel with staircases curving left and right, ascending to an overhanging floor. Unsettling white sheets hung everywhere, fully unfurled. Yes, they were unusual, but she liked the way muted lights danced across them, enhancing their subtle movement in an invisible breeze. Tables were set in among the drifting fabric, creating a kind of maze.

Why were they…?

Ah, "Cloud!" The material was supposed to give the illusion of being in a cloud. Yeah, it didn't really work, but points for trying.

A male host and female hostess spotted her.

Holly stepped closer. "We should've brought security," she murmured. "Everyone who's anyone will—"

"We don't need security," Freya said, tipping her chin up to meet Baer's eyes. "You won't let anyone hurt me, will you, Hound?"

His tongue moved onto his upper teeth inside his lip, but his mouth didn't open.

Holly squeezed his arm as she bowed nearer still. "There's an additional charge for security services, Frey, and not every guy offers—"

"No charge," Baer said, his eyes locked on hers.

Opening her purse, she took out a bundle of hundreds and handed them to him. "Tipping always helps."

Donoghue whistled. "You have it made, Royal."

"You have no idea," Holly said just as the hosts skidded up at their side.

"Miss Dere—"

"Please…" she said, switching her hand from Donoghue's arm to Holly's.

Her cousin let go of her date, and they angled themselves in front of Baer, the man she trusted to keep her safe. She'd seen that body, through a tee-shirt, but she'd had her hands on it and… mm, yes, it was definitely capable.

Mind drifting, she zoned out of whatever the host and hostess were saying. Donoghue replied with something about a table, then they were being ushered upstairs to a corner, apparently their best.

Champagne was already there. Donoghue went in one way of the low-backed circular booth, while Freya went in the other with Baer at her back, Holly wasn't far behind him.

"Miss Dere, if there's anything else you—"

"Does anyone drink champagne?" she asked, checking with her companions. None leaped to the defense of the bottle in the bucket or the flutes around it. "Can you take it away, please? I will have Gin and It, my friend…" Freya reached over Baer to touch Holly's wrist. "Will have a cosmopolitan." Moving her fingertips to Baer's arm, she met his eye. "What would you like? Beer? Scotch?" Turning, she glanced at Donoghue who pushed out his lower lip. "What's your best Macallan?" The host just blinked. "Whatever you have of that, or the Dalmore, whichever is the best… We'll have water for the table and whatever finger food you have… just give us a selection. Is the company aligned with a charitable cause…?"

"Uh, yes, Miss Dere…"

"If no one approaches this table for the rest of the night, except to provide refills, there will be a ten-thousand-dollar donation made to that charity in your name… Do you understand?"

Stunned, the host nodded and crowded his colleague out of the way to dash off.

Holly squealed. "And the heiress owns the night again," she said. "I love watching you do that, Angel."

"I know," she muttered, sinking back in her seat, adjusting her earring.

People usually did, few recognized it as an act rather than her genuine self. She'd never understood why she was seen as more important than others just because she had access to money. Yes, it gave her security, but it didn't make her inherently better than anyone else.

"Shit, baby, I had no idea you were worth a mint," Donoghue said. "Why do they call you Angel?"

"Because she is an angel," Holly said. "As fast as her grandfather can make money, she's giving it away."

"Not quite," Freya said.

Though not far off. Her grandfather would no doubt echo Holly's tease.

She should adjust her posture; slouching wasn't ladylike. That shame was overshadowed by another. All she really wanted to do was pick up Baer's arm and wrap it around herself to nestle in at his side and listen to the rumble of his voice in his chest. Pathetic. Just his heartbeat would soothe her. A yawn threatened her lips, she needed food and alcohol, and peace.

"Truman Dere," Donoghue murmured like he was just figuring it out. Yeah, sometimes it took people a minute. Sitting up straight so fast he jolted the table, he gasped. "You're Truman Dere's granddaughter…" This kind of reaction was normal. "I thought he didn't have kids."

"He doesn't," she said, sitting straight to push the champagne bucket and flutes to the far edge of the table. "His son was murdered almost twenty years ago… right alongside his daughter-in-law."

Sympathy bled from Holly. "Frey…"

She touched the edge of a line on the tabletop pattern. "It's okay," Freya said. "Nothing he won't get from Huddle Hunt. I'm the only Dere left… After me, it's…" Inhaling, the lights dancing on the sheet around their booth caught her attention. "Truman protects me because walking in to find nothing but blood where your family should be sticks with a person…" And she'd hung up on him. Guilt. Oh, it was heavy and sore. What was she doing? They had rules. Opening her purse to retrieve her phone, she rose to squeeze past Baer and Holly. "Excuse me."

Pushing one curtain aside led to another. Disorientated, maybe she wouldn't find her way back.

By a couple of tables in an unoccupied space, she quickly dialed her grandfather. "I'm sorry," she said as soon as the line connected. "Are you okay?"

"Am I okay?" Truman asked. "What do we say about not answering the phone?"

"I know," she said, closing her eyes, pressing a finger to her opposite ear when the music distracted her.

"I said I was sorry... I'm calling now. Tell me why you called."

"Jonas Bruce is working two sides of a case," he said. "Defense and prosecution. You do realize that's peculiar?"

Her lips contorted. "I amuse you," she said. "You called to tell me I amuse you?"

"Why else would I call my only granddaughter?" he asked. "We're not prosecuting?"

"No, we're not." Her good humor fled. "Granddaddy, I swear—"

"I don't need explanations..." No, he never did, not from her. "You had to see the leech?"

"Would you stop calling him that?" She bent over to rest a forearm on the back of the empty booth in front of her. "Chapman, his name is Scott Chapman and yes, I had to see him... I handled it. You know I can handle it."

"I would feel better if you were home."

Rolling her eyes, she didn't restrain her groan. "Granddaddy—"

"Yes, yes, I know," he said. "You despise me asking. What's this I hear about one of the Piven girls getting married?"

"Kelly. Yes. What about it? Do you want an invite?"

"Nothing would please me less."

Typical that he couldn't just say no. "Aww, and I needed a plus one too."

"If it will prevent you going with some new leech who is beneath you, I certainly will accompany you."

"And take all the focus from the bride," she said. "Either way, you'll end up paying for most of it."

"I long ago consoled myself with your life mission to squander our family's wealth," he said. She restrained a laugh. "Six generations turn in their graves when you open your purse, my little bleeding heart."

"Oh…" she said, teasing to make his point for him. "And, also, by the way, we're making a charitable donation tonight."

"To whom?"

She laughed. "I don't know. What do you care? It's charity."

"Yes, which I will have to rely on once we're turfed out by all the orphan children you no doubt plan to move onto the estate."

"Hey," she said, on another laugh. "That's an excellent idea, Granddaddy. All those bedrooms, we have space… and, hey, it would get me home, right?"

"I would rather you bring your own children home to me," he said. "Did you at least look at the profile I sent you of—"

"You can't send me profiles anymore, Granddaddy." She sighed. "It's weird. The kind of man you want me to be attracted to is not the same kind of man I want to marry."

His exhale was both pained and fed up. "You get this from your mother's side. Your father was never this difficult."

"Daddy shunned your money and lived in Southeast Asia for two years before going to college."

"Yes, and that wasn't quite enough to kill me. I see now he left you behind to finish me off," he said. "I want you secure before I'm not here to support you anymore."

His money would always be there. No matter how she tried, or how others teased, she'd never be able to spend it all, not in ten lifetimes. But he didn't mean money, he meant people.

"I know everyone you trust," she said. "I know dozens of people in the city."

"Who do you call at three in the morning when you feel alone?"

Wow, did he have to go there? The air weighed on her. No one was the correct answer, the only answer. In an emergency, she could call any number of people to come and take action. But just to hear a voice that would make her feel better? She didn't have that.

Baer.

She couldn't count him. She didn't even have his phone number. Even if she wanted to, she couldn't call him at three in the morning or three in the afternoon.

"Come to the house for dinner next weekend."

"I'm going away with the Pivens next weekend."

"With this new boy?" Only her grandfather would think it was okay to call a grown man a boy. "What do you know about him?"

"Nothing," she said. "I've never met him. We're supposed to get to know him during this vacation. That's the point."

"I don't like you going away with them alone."

"I won't be alone."

"Take Dexter."

"I am not going to take Dexter," she said. "Alan will be there."

"Oh, what use is that boy?" he chastised. "He's a wet blanket. Good for nothing but dousing a fire to save the drapes."

"Would you stop?" Should she be offended or amused? A bit of both. "That's my cousin."

"On your mother's side."

She narrowed her eyes. "And the distinction is important because…?"

"Deres protect you."

That sobered the mood. Even after all these years, the reminder could still hit with Mach-10 force.

"That's you and me, Granddaddy. We're it… and you don't have to worry about me being safe. I will be safe."

"How do you know?"

How did she know? Because Baer was going to be there… Except, maybe he wasn't. If Holly didn't choose him to go with her, Baer would stay behind in the city, and their lives would drift apart.

God, where did that come from? What happened to the lighter mood? Time to divert them back.

"Because it wouldn't be a great impression if this new boy let all of us succumb to tragedy, would it?"

Her grandfather's wit was dry. "And yet, I am unmoved," he said. "Send me the details of the resort at least forty-eight hours before you leave… Do you need the chopper?"

"I've never visited the place before," she said. "But I doubt it… I hate that thing."

"I'll make sure it's somewhere on site in case you need to leave in a hurry."

"You can't park your helicopter on someone else's lawn."

He scoffed. "You have been on this earth almost thirty years. Are you going to tell me you haven't yet learned money will buy you almost anything?"

"Almost," she said, fixating on the empty table. "Almost anything."

Silence passed for a few moments. "Freya," he said, his softening voice probing. "What's in your mind?"

"Nothing, I… there's this guy that I…"

More silence. "Freya?"

Forcing a smile, she couldn't be anything but happy. "I'll call you next week, we'll set something up."

"Hmm," he said. "No, we'll have dinner tomorrow night. Usual time."

And her driver would know the where after her grandfather decided on it.

Her mind blanked. "We don't have to—"

"I insist." And that was the end of the conversation. "When I call, you pick up."

"Yes, Grandaddy. I love you."

Hanging up the phone, she stared down at it. He did love her. He did care about her. He just didn't always understand her. She couldn't blame him for that, sometimes she didn't understand herself.

# TWELVE

STILL FIXATED ON the phone, the brush of fingertips on her hip broke her daze. Something about the feel of them, how they took their time gliding around her hip then tightened, with delicate but sure possession, closed her eyes.

That wasn't a threat.

That was Baer.

Switching her phone into her other hand, her fingers joined his, threading between them, caressing them deep. As she stood straight, she guided them up her stomach, through her cleavage, onto her opposite cheek.

Rubbing her face against his palm, she leaned on his solid body, grateful to have him in her life, even if it was only for a limited time.

"Little Skit," he murmured above her head.

"God, it's so wrong," she whispered, tasting the words more than she heard them. "It's wrong to want you like this." Insistent in her redirection, she forced him to cup her breast rather than her face. Squeezing his fingers with hers, her coerced fondling fired more guilt. "I'm sorry."

Dropping her hand, she expected his to loosen immediately. It didn't. Instead, he tucked his fingers into the fabric covering her breast to caress her skin to skin.

"You can't touch me like this," she whispered. Oh, but she wanted it, this and so much more. Her tormented clit heated and tingled as he squeezed her nipple between his strong fingers. "You shouldn't want to—"

He pinched her so hard that a quake of almost climax shot through her. On a yelp, her body bucked back against his. Her phone dropped from her slack fingers, but she didn't care, nothing except him mattered.

Proving that, eager to progress, she slid a hand up his thigh, intending to go higher until he caught her wrist and pressed her palm flat on his leg. He bent down, burying his mouth in her hair, resting his head on her shoulder, pushing his face into the side of her neck.

"Tell me to stop," he mumbled, teeth grazing her, something pained about the request. "Say I'm an asshole who has no right to put his hands on you... Tell me, Lil'... Tell me to fuck off."

"I can't," she gasped, fighting to keep her volume low. "I can't say it. I can't say it when I'm so desperate to beg you to fuck me." Grabbing her arms, he jerked her around to face him, picking her up to perch her on the back of the bench. Steadying herself, she planted her hands on his chest. "I know we can't. I know you're working, and I know..." Talk about pained. No words were harder to say than these. "I know after you go home with Hol tonight, we can't ever do this again."

"I won't." He shook her. "Complimentary dates don't include sex, and if Donoghue tries to touch you—"

"I don't want sex," she said, statement matching her paperwork. Except the documentation didn't reveal the whole, honest truth. "Not from him."

"You didn't write preferences; I'm not on your schedule."

He'd found the best and quickest way to remind her this was a terrible idea. The only way she'd ever have this man deeper between her thighs, embedded in her, was if she paid for the privilege.

"Baer…" she said, trying to push him away.

He didn't budge. "No." Blocking her way, he held her on the top of the bench. "How long is your trip?"

"Two weeks," she said. The serious line of his brow matched the movement of his jaw. "Baer, I—"

"There's no man I trust to go with you. Seeing Don's hands on you tonight—"

"Baer, what is this about?" she asked, stroking his chest in an attempt to soothe. "You were wound up in the car, and you're tense now. Something's upsetting you and I don't know what it is. Talk to me, baby."

Grabbing her hand, he squeezed her fingers, raising them to his mouth. "Why did the white rose upset you?"

"My mother loved white roses. They were her favorite. At the funeral… they were everywhere. Seeing them always takes me right back there. It's nothing, it shouldn't be a big deal."

"Goddamn," he exhaled.

"What? If you love them, I'll figure it out, I—"

"No, I… that's not it." That's not it, but he didn't tell her what it was. "I'm sorry about your mom, your parents, I… I didn't know."

"It's okay," she said, more worried about him than herself. "Why would you? I didn't know about yours. Your father told me last night. Baer, if there's anything you ne—"

"Don't pick Donoghue." He squeezed her hand tighter. Usually Baer was so together, so smooth. Seeing him frazzled wasn't fun. "Promise me you won't, Lil'."

"I promise. I'll pick whoever you recommend. It doesn't matter to me. I only came to Squires because Holly wanted a partner in crime, so to speak…"

Some of his agitation eased as he considered her. "You didn't tell me about the money… Why would a beautiful, rich, amazing woman like you ever be anywhere near Squires? Why aren't you married ten times over?"

"Fewer men notice the beautiful, amazing part compared to those who notice the rich part… My grandfather calls men who pursue me leeches. Not necessarily because they're not good enough for me, but because they see my generosity, and my access to Truman's bank balance, before they see anything else… He says I've never brought a man home he believes values me the way I should be valued. I don't know, I think it's just a cover because he doesn't want to think about me having sex… Yeah, he's biased, but most of the time, he's right. Usually, as I fall for a guy, I figure out he was only in it for the money… Makes it difficult, you know, to trust people. So… I eventually gave up trying."

"Until you met Chapman," he said. "Did you love him?"

"I don't know." She sagged against him. "Maybe I thought I did… But that is a much bigger conversation than we can shoehorn in here."

Easing him back, she slid onto her feet.

Putting a hand on the bench on either side of her, he blocked her in. "You told him we were sleeping together."

Frowning, her head tilted. "Who?"

"Chapman," he said. "At the hospital. You said all you were to me was a pussy to pump any time I could bend you over and make you take it."

"You were listening in?" she asked, socking his chest and growling at him. "I knew you were. Damnit, Baer, don't eavesdrop, it's rude."

Scooping a hand onto her face, he brushed her hair away with his thumb. "You could never be that to me, Lil' Skit."

"I know what I am to you," she said, losing the battle of pushing his hand down. "Actually, no, that's a lie, I don't know what I am to you, but I know what I'm not. I am not your client. Holly is your client."

"You know I won't sleep with her."

"I don't know that," she said. His free hand tried to sneak onto the other side of her face. "It's your job to sleep with her. You'll be paid to sleep with her. A lot probably. She picked you because that's what she wants from you: sex."

"That doesn't matter. I won't. We're allowed to refuse any job. There's no law that says we're required to take a certain client."

Even if there was, would he obey it? Not like those in his line of work didn't mind bending the rules.

"Why would you do that?" she asked, surrendering to his hands holding her face.

"Because she's your family," he said, bending to trace his mouth over the corner of hers. "And because I couldn't do it."

"I'm sure you've been with women who are less attractive than Holly," she said, not buying for a second that being intimate with Holly would be a hardship. "She's beautiful and smart… and sexy."

"That's not what I meant, I… Last night, I couldn't do it."

What? She leaned back to get a better look at him. "What?"

"I satisfied the client, I always do, I don't think she noticed that I wasn't... you know... I used my hands on her, my tongue—"

"Oh, Baer, please, I don't want to know this," she said, squirming in his hold.

He wouldn't release her. "I didn't have sex with her, Frey. And I'm not saying I won't with other women. It's my job, you're right about that. And this is... Well... I don't know what this is. But walking out on you last night... going to another woman's bed when all I wanted to do was take you upstairs to mine, it... I don't know, but we've gotta figure this out, Lil', before you ruin me."

Financially? Emotionally? Again, he wasn't specific. Either was a possibility. "You have to support your family, I would never ask you not to."

"I would never be able to make you that promise."

This was unexpected, yet, at the same time, overdue. "I don't understand. Surely there must have been other women. Women you cared about... personally, while you've been in this profession."

He shook his head. "Not like this... With the boys, and my mom, the money, it's been keeping our head above water. I haven't had time for..."

"And Claire bailed when things got tough," she said, provoking a frown. Sheepish, she shrugged. "Your family like to talk."

"Not usually this much," he said. "Anything they didn't tell you?"

Taking his hand in hers, she got space enough to lean back to retrieve her phone from the bench where it had fallen. "Let's go get a drink and I'll fill you in."

They'd been away from the table for so long that Holly and Donoghue might believe they'd been ditched. Until…

Uh, no, they got back to the table and found the two engaged in animated conversation.

That was okay. In fact, it was a relief.

Sitting at the opposite side of the booth with Baer, she got her wish of nestling under his arm. They spent the evening covering the topics his family clued her in on the previous night and then some.

Telling him about her grandfather and the foundation, getting it all out there was a relief, a joy. The noise of the bar provided cover to talk without worrying about anyone overhearing.

At the end of the night, while Baer went to pay the bill with her card and Donoghue used the restroom, she and Holly cleared up the table.

"I think you've made your choice," Holly said, putting the used napkins on a plate.

"My choice?"

"But listen…" Holly said. "Can you please not abandon me, okay? I'm happy for you and everything. I don't even mind you stealing my man. No one could mind; you two have chemistry up the yazoo. It's like watching magic in real life. But I still have two more dates, so will you please just pretend like you're not sure who you'll pick and come with me on those dates?"

"Holly, I was never going to—"

"Obviously, you two will have no trouble convincing my folks you're a thing. You better work overtime to help me with my guy, if we don't have the same… you know," Holly said and thrust her shoulders back to tease. "Don't ever tell me this wasn't fun. You didn't even want to be here and now look, you've found the goddamn love of your life."

The curtain moved and Donoghue came in with Baer just behind him.

"Ready to leave, ladies?" Donoghue asked.

Getting back to the car was a blur. The love of her life? Baer couldn't be the love of her life… could he? More thinking made the immediate problem clearer.

She needed a companion for the vacation and wedding events. Baer needed money. Whatever was going on between them might cause him financial problems if he kept avoiding going all the way with clients.

Freya hadn't wanted to hire Baer because she feared falling for him while he was working. But she wasn't just a client anymore, it wasn't just an act. There was something real between them. Given she was going away and in need of support, who else would she want with her? No man would be better for the job.

And, going away for two weeks, with another man, while Baer stayed in the city to work… other women. It would be a nightmare. Neither of them would be themselves. Was this the solution to all their problems, or an action they'd come to regret?

# THIRTEEN

ONE THING SHE couldn't do was let her grandfather see her mind plagued by thoughts that would distress him. Not for the same reasons they were distressing her, but if he found out the truth, he'd never let her leave again.

She'd worked at ChilConn all day, all the while trying to come up with a reason to cancel her dinner with Truman. The trouble was, he knew her like no one else. If she canceled, he'd see right through any excuse and send a SWAT team. Hence her in the back of her car on the way to the restaurant.

She'd just eat fast and excuse herself early, all the while ducking and weaving his probing questions and too knowing discernment. His questions were always probing; it wasn't fair the man was so adept at reading her. Hmm, did that sound like teenage petulance? In other situations, his awareness had saved her ass.

When her phone rang, a spear of hope begged it was her grandfather calling to cancel. Yes, yes, yes— nope, no such luck. It wasn't his name on the screen. Of course not. And more fool her, Truman rarely let her down.

She answered, "Roxie, is everything okay?"

"You tell me," Roxie said. "You've been avoiding us."

"Avoiding you—I have not. Why would I be avoiding you?"

"Where have you been? I miss you. What's the gossip? Are you on a tropical vacation? Planning world domination? Because if it's that last one you'll need a number two and I'm available."

Roxie Kyst. They hadn't known each other long, relatively speaking. Yet the woman was already integral in her life. If anyone would understand her internal struggle, it would be Roxie. The words, the truth, lodged in her throat. There just wasn't time. If she opened the floodgates, she may not be able to close them again. And she couldn't be more than a few blocks from her waiting grandfather. Showing up agitated would provoke him to shut down the city, hunting for the man who'd hurt her, regardless of her attempts at appeasement.

"I've been busy with… things."

"Things?" Her friend's curiosity was piqued. Talk about being good at reading people, Roxie was another one with the uncanny ability to sense unsaid meaning behind words. "More. More. More. I need more. Come to the club… or I can come to you."

"I'm having dinner with Truman tonight." The truth. Just not the full truth. "I'll come over soon."

"How soon?"

How did Roxie do it? The woman had a vast network, she should be overwhelmed with her new life and experiences. Amazingly, Roxanna Kyst had slid into her role as Zairn Lomond's better half without missing a step.

Freya had lived in this world her whole life, the world of decadence, luxury, easy living with plenty of money always backing her up. Yet it frequently overwhelmed her. Not Roxie, she was a pro, not ostentatious, she cared about people. Calling just to check in proved that. Did Roxie call all her friends to make sure they were okay? How did the woman find the time?

"I'll answer that after I get through my dinner with Truman."

"You in for a grilling? What does the old man know that I don't?"

Nothing. She hoped. It would be naïve to forget Truman had a way of finding things out. He loved her, adored her, of that she had no doubt. She adored him too; they were all each other had. Family. Blood. There was nothing she wouldn't do for the man who'd raised her with love and care. When growing up, friends recounted horror stories of absent parents, of forgotten birthdays. Some friends suffered neglect, and yes, it was possible to be neglected even with all the money in the world.

Truman wasn't like that. He'd been present, involved. Which was an achievement with her at an all-girls boarding school. He called every evening. Every morning. Was there for every event, never missed a parent-teacher night.

"Freya?"

"Sorry." She'd lost herself again for a second. "I don't want to lie to him."

"Then don't lie to him." Her friend's curiosity had become concern. "Do you want me to join you? Nothing pressing going on here. I can be there tout suite."

"Thank you." In that moment, she found her smile again. "Your support means everything to me."

"You want me to come?"

"No, I'll be fine."

"Truman loves me!" Roxie declared. "He won't mind me hanging out."

"But if I bring a human shield, he'll turn on the third degree for sure."

"I can deflect."

"Oh, he'll wait until you're in the bathroom, or until I'm home for the evening. Wouldn't be the first time he's shown up on my doorstep with his eyebrow crooked."

"We can have a slumber party. Or you can spend the night here, Zairn won't mind, there are beautiful women traipsing in and out of here all the time. He so used to it, it's blasé."

She laughed. "Unless I plan to live with you forever, Truman would get to me eventually."

"What are you so worried about him finding out?"

On a sigh, her shoulders dropped. "I'll loop you in as soon as I know."

"Are you sure you don't want to come over here?"

"Not tonight," she said. "But thank you for asking. Honestly, Rox, thank you for calling."

"Okay, you know where I am. Be safe and sensible."

"You too."

Her friend scoffed. "How likely you think that is?"

The line quieted at the same moment the car stopped. No going back now.

The door opened and she took the hand of an usher who helped her out. Old school. Just as her grandfather liked it. Inside the gentle susurration matched the intimate lighting. Her grandfather could close the whole place or secret them somewhere private. But no, instead, he was sitting at the best table in the house. No less than she'd expect.

He stood to kiss her cheek and help her into her seat.

"Any trouble?" he asked.

"Trouble? Getting here? No." Why would there be trouble? They'd used that restaurant dozens of times. It was one of Truman's favorites. "Did *you* have trouble?" Her grandfather just smiled. No, of course he had no trouble, he was Truman Dere. "I spoke to Roxie in the car."

Good way to get the conversation moving without hitting anything too personal. That was the idea anyway.

"Roxie's a good girl, she knows what she wants."

"Implying…?"

Oh, why did she ask?

"You've been avoiding me."

Same crime, different accuser. She was blessed and cursed to have so many people in her life who cared.

"No," she said. "Why would I do that?"

Discernment narrowed his eyes. "The fact you're fighting me is proof enough. What's wrong, pumpkin?"

He only called her that to remind her of their relationship, her young age to his elder. And he could fill the role, whether it was protection, offense, defense, Truman Dere would do whatever was necessary to help or fight for her.

Except she didn't need that. "I'm fine," she said, broadening her smile. "I'm not shy about asking if there's anything I need."

"Yes, if you identify there's something you need. Your outlook isn't always so sharp."

Did she need something? Depended which body part she asked. And most of those parts? She wouldn't want answering within earshot of her conservative grandfather. Okay, so Truman could be liberal, could bend, for her, and her only.

"As soon as I know, you'll be my first call."

"As your guardian, it's my job to identify your needs before you're aware of them."

"I'm not a little girl anymore, Grandaddy."

"You will always be a little girl, my little girl. Do you think I would protect you any less fiercely today than I would have when you were a child?"

No. On that he'd never wavered. Even when she didn't agree with his methods, he only ever did what he thought was in her best interest.

"No, but you don't have to protect me. Everything in my life is good. Trust me, Grandaddy, if I need a parachute, I'll call." Time to move things along. "What did Jonas tell you about the case? Was there a lot of damage?"

"No. You're fierce in your protection of your foundation kids."

"I learned love from you."

"And has it served you well? Perhaps if I were more vicious, your kindness wouldn't cost me so much." She waited, and on cue, his lips curled. "I wouldn't change a thing about you."

"Nor I you."

Life may not have played out the way either of them would've chosen, but where they were wasn't so bad. And if it came to it, they'd have each other's backs. Of that she was certain.

# FOURTEEN

THE NEXT MORNING her purpose was clear. Perspective was what she needed. Where better to get it than from the most honest and supportive woman she knew?

In the Rouge building, determination fueled her ascent to Roxie's floor. In a glass walled corner office, her friend stood behind a desk. The blonde wasn't alone, but, having come this far, that was no deterrent.

Without knocking, Freya went straight inside, focused completely on her friend. She dumped her purse on the desk. The second woman in the room didn't even get a sideways glance.

"Hey, honey!" Roxie exclaimed. "What a nice surprise, and opportune too, you two need to meet. This glowing mother-to-be is Lilya Kintyre. She's staying here in New York until she delivers. A little baby! We'll have a little baby right here—not right here, 'cause she has an apartment in town. But, bet your boots, where there's a baby, my Jane will never be far behind!"

The words went right over her head. Unblinking, her concentration remained intent on Roxie.

Rounding the desk, she grabbed her friend's wrist. "We have to talk. Alone. Now."

"I'll just… wait for you upstairs, Rox."

Lilya Kintyre slipped out of the room just as the previously clear wall went white. Roxie took her hand to lead her over to the couches in the corner and sat them down.

"Is this an 'I spilled wine on Zairn's favorite couch,' kind of conversation, or more of the 'there's a dead body in my apartment we have to chop into little pieces,' variety?"

That was—"Zairn has a favorite couch?"

Random. Didn't sound like the man she knew. A little distraction may put her thoughts in order.

"His favorite is whatever couch I'm on." They both glanced down. No wine. Roxie snagged her hand. "That's not the point. Murder or mayhem?"

"Somewhere in between."

While part of her wanted to stand and pace out her hopping energy, the rest of her was just too exhausted. This was Roxie, the ride or die friend who would never let her girls down.

"Okay…" Roxie drew the word out, stroking the hand she held. "Want to give me a hint? I can guess. I'm great at guessing. We could be here a while though; I have an active imagination. Something my Casanova loves about me… He loves everything about me."

Having seen the man admire his love more than once, she bought that. If only her own picture was so rosy.

Though her heart raced, her breathing slowed. She held an inhale for a moment, then let it out as her shoulders sagged.

"I think I'm falling for a forbidden man."

After a brief beat, Roxie laughed. "Oh, honey, is that all? Who hasn't?" The amusement on her friend's face wasn't so sympathetic. Didn't she understand the torment? "This isn't a bad thing. No one is as forbidden as we first think. You were right to come here, I have experience with this. A lot of experience. Tell me about him."

"He's… This is… It's stupid. Utterly ridiculously stupid. I can't… I just can't. He's not…"

"Why do you think he's forbidden? He's older? He's younger? He can't be your boss…" Roxie's eyes wandered as she pondered. "Is he one of Truman's friends? Because that's okay—"

"This is so much worse than that. So much worse. Truman would accept that a thousand years before he would accept… Maybe I should leave the country."

"And take your forbidden man with you?" Running away with Baer… great fantasy. One that would never work in reality. "Honey…" Drawing her cradled hand deeper, Roxie gave her a squeeze. "Whatever it is we can overcome it. If you love him—"

"Love? We haven't—it's never been like this, so instant, so visceral. Being with him, I lose myself, instinct wants to… take over."

"Instinct? Or your hormones?"

Nodding, hope fought to inspire. "You think that's what it is? I'm just caught up in the physical? If I avoid him…" No words ever tasted so wrong on her tongue. Imagine that, just for a second, never seeing Baer again… "I don't know if I'm strong enough."

"Does he feel the same way? Because if he does, I doubt he'll let you go that easy."

She'd apologized to Baer for appearing stalker-like the previous day. His joke of being so lucky echoed in her ears. Would she be so lucky, if she cut ties, that he'd come after her? She couldn't kid herself that wouldn't be a dream come true. For the first time, the idea of a man pursuing her relentlessly was appealing. Talking of persistent men…

"I saw Chapman."

"Please don't tell me—"

"It's not him." The contortion of disgust on Roxie's face eased, yet it lingered, still sickened by the thought. She almost laughed. "What if I said Chapman was my forbidden man?"

"I'd rush you to the hospital. Get you checked out for disease and insanity. Why did you see Chapman? You should stay away from him. What's he got to do with your forbidden man?"

"It doesn't matter. Except to say they met, laid eyes on each other."

"You're telling me your sleazy ex knows your forbidden man better than I do? I'm insulted. You've got to give me something, honey. You came here to talk about it. About him."

No refuting that. "Chapman's a detective. And my forbidden man he…" She wasn't worried Roxie would judge her or Baer. Roxie was all accepting. It was just… Telling Roxie would make it real, and if it was real, she wouldn't be able to kid herself that this wasn't a big deal. "He may, in what he does, wander over the line."

Roxie frowned. "Over the line? What line?" Her friend gasped. "The line! You mean he's a felon? Wow, you go all out, sister." Glee wrapped itself around the blonde. "So I wasn't far wrong with the body in your apartment thing."

"No! He's not that kind of—he's a good guy. Supporting his family. It's not like—he's a good guy."

"So what's the problem? He's a good guy, and you want him, go for it. His past is his past. You can't use it as an excuse to put up walls. Believe me, I've been there, done that. It doesn't work. The heart wants what it wants."

How many times had she heard Roxie and Zairn's tale? She never tired of it. If there was one thing Roxie knew, it was love. Seconds of seeing her with Zairn proved that. Love? That was too far for her and Baer. Wasn't it? Only... Her evening with his family had given her a glimpse of a future she wouldn't be sorry to know.

"There are other... women involved."

"How involved? He's married? Are they separated? It's the way things ended with Chapman. You don't trust yourself; you're gun-shy on the whole relationship front. We've all been there. Trust yourself, honey, and it's okay to trust him. At least he's told you about the wife, that's one better than the lying creep Chapman. Maybe this time—"

"He sleeps with other women... for... His family have a lot of financial commitments, so he works with an agency that—"

"He's a hooker?" Okay, so it was nice she wasn't the only one to instantly go there. A barb of primitive offense was totally irrational. Now knowing Baer, she really hated that word. "An escort?" On a wince, Freya nodded. "Oh, honey..." Throwing open her arms, Roxie pulled her into a tight embrace. "Does he know? Who you are? About your money?"

He did know. Since their Cloud date. Did it matter? Oh, it always mattered eventually.

"Yes. We haven't talked about it." Or what it might mean for them. Not in depth. "I haven't known him for—we met and it was... I'm insane, aren't I?"

"No!" Roxie settled back, still holding her hands. "You are not. Who cares if that's what he does?" The sheer acceptance on Roxie's face was so at ease there wasn't a chance of it being false. "And, baby, bet that guy will know some tricks. I thought my guy was talented, but he's never been paid for it. Your guy gets an extra gold star."

"Rox…"

"Okay, joking aside, if you love each other, you can help his family, they will be your family too. Wait, does he enjoy it? Is that the problem? He's saying he wants to keep sleeping with other women if you get together? Because that is a red flag. A great, big red flag. He tries that shit, send him to me. If he's yours, he's yours. No one else's. That's a hard limit, you tell him."

"We're not there yet. I don't know how he feels or… It's such a treacherous path. I can't stop thinking about him, I'm obsessing, it's sad and—"

"Delightful! You're freaking yourself out. If you came here for permission to walk away from Mr. So-Good-He's-Paid-For-Sex, you won't get it. I'll always fall on the side of love… Okay, maybe not always, in the right circumstances and—let's say I'll always fall on the side of true love, now. I always fall on that side now, I didn't always. I have to add that caveat or I swear Zairn will let me have it later."

Glancing around, she didn't see Roxie's other half. "Isn't he working?"

"Yeah, but, you know, I cover my ass. And who knows what Dyce tech he has secreted away in—never mind. Here it is: if you like this guy, go for it, embrace it."

"I don't know how he feels about—"

"I don't believe for a second any guy wouldn't fall head over heels for you."

Her friend's support was appreciated, but she wasn't addressing the ridiculous part. "What kind of an idiot falls for a man in that line of work?"

"You said he had valid reasons for doing it."

"He does, that's not—it's his job to make women feel good. Like you said, people pay him for services.

He's so good he has regulars that keep coming back for more. What if I'm... I keep coming back for more too."

Though, so far, she hadn't paid him for anything.

"You think he might be playing you? It's possible." Sitting straight, Roxie grinned. "Bring him here, I'll figure him out."

And scare him away for good.

She smiled. "I don't think he's ready for that."

"How long have you been seeing him? If you've paid—"

"I've never paid to be with him. We met because... Holly took me to the agency because she needs a guy to back up her fake boyfriend story."

"Always a bold start to any relationship. I love a good caper. Tell me more."

Recounting the whole fable, it felt good to get it off her chest. Perspective was still hazy in the relief of the burden. Roxie was exactly the right person to absorb some of it for her. It felt good to vent to someone sympathetic who may end up alibiing her if the whole thing fell apart.

"So we were there in the car... then something happened with his brother, his younger brother, his twelve-year-old brother... he ended up in hospital."

Roxie's concern interrupted her flow. "Is he okay?"

"Yeah, he's fine but... Roxie, I can't fall for this guy. I can't. Truman would disown me."

"Who says Truman ever has to know about the escort thing? Your guy would give it up if you got together. He wouldn't need the money anymore. If you don't want Truman to know, don't tell him."

"You know what my grandfather is like when it comes to the men in my life. He's relentless."

"If this is your meant to be guy, it doesn't matter what Truman thinks, it doesn't matter if he disowns you either." Her friend leaned closer to side-whisper, "Though, personally I don't see that happening in a million years. Truman adores you. Even if he stamps his feet and causes drama, he'll come around in the end."

"My grandfather doesn't cause drama, not public drama. He works in the background, meddling, without me ever knowing. Until someone like Chapman comes along and reams me for his demotion."

"Don't even deny Chapman deserved it. Truman did the right thing. That guy needed to be brought down a peg or two. Is he still with his wife?"

"I didn't ask. I don't care."

"It's not like we could believe him no matter what he said." Roxie came over more discerning. "Chapman's a detective." Yes, hadn't she made that connection already? "You're worried he'll come after your forbidden man. If your ex learns what your new man does…"

"He's not in vice, I don't even know if…" The slight tilt of her friend's head killed her knee-jerk objection. She exhaled. "I don't know how he would ever find out. Seeing him at the hospital, it's clear he hasn't let us go yet."

"Because you're fabulous." With the tips of her fingers under Freya's chin, Roxie elevated it. "If you love this guy, you can't give up for maybes. Maybe Truman will cause trouble. Maybe Chapman will. Trust me when I say it's all worth it. Waking up with your guy, your true love guy, there's nothing like it, no substitute. You have to fight for it, there's no obstacle you can't overcome."

"And the paying for sex thing?"

"You never have," Roxie said. "That's what you said. So make a rule; not paying him for sex is now a rule. If you're with him on a night he could be earning, pay for his time, and think of it more like helping a friend out with his bills. It's just the same as you paying for dinner."

Not like she'd never done that, and so much more. "Besides, if I came to you for money, if anyone you cared about did, you wouldn't hesitate to help. Think of it like that. And on the nights you're paying him: no sex. Use the time to get to know him better. To know each other better. Please promise me you'll try. No guilt. No second-guessing."

"And what about this family vacation?"

Roxie shrugged, arms loose. "Take him with you. Why not? If it wasn't for the fake boyfriend thing, I would go with you."

"That may not be a bad idea."

"The press believing I left Zairn for a tempestuous affair with you would be entertaining... think of the antics."

This woman and her antics were all wrapped up in such a good heart. "Isn't the point not to give my grandfather a coronary?"

"He'd love it! Two granddaughters for the price of one." Her friend hummed. "Hmm, no, I'm probably very expensive. Zairn would know. And we do have that pesky wedding this year."

Another wedding. Would she take Baer to— stop. No.

"Let me get over one family event before dealing with another one. Is taking him on vacation a good idea?"

"An excellent idea. Think of it the same as if I was coming," Roxie said. "You're taking a friend, one you don't pay for sex. You're hanging out. Having fun. If it happens, it'll happen naturally, off the clock. What would be so wrong about that?"

See this was why she came to Roxie. The woman had a way of cutting through the crap, of skewing her perspective to just the right angle, providing the truth of the complete picture.

"What would I do without you? I'm overthinking this, but I've never—"

Zairn came striding in, the door fell back into its place behind him.

Roxie stood up. "Excuse me, who do you think you are? You don't come storming in here. What if we'd been naked?"

"I've seen you naked. Many times. All the time. Can't seem to go ten minutes without it."

"Because you spend every waking minute drooling over the hidden camera shots you take of me illegally. You think I don't know? Your obsession is not healthy. I turn a blind eye because you're so rich, otherwise I'd be out of here like a shot, boy." These two loved to joke and spar. "And Freya is here, she doesn't want you seeing her naked."

"I've seen Frey naked too."

She couldn't see her friend's face, but there must've been a reaction.

"Ha!" Roxie started. "There's no way we believe of all the millions of naked women you've slobbered on that you remember anything about Freya's fabulous figure from some peeping tom moment in your youth."

"She dated one of my best friends for years. Crazy years when we were all young and stupid." Zairn licked his lips. "No, Freya's always been the sensible one. I apologize Frey."

"I don't care about your days of debauchery," Roxie said. "And where's my apology? You just stormed in when we could've been having sex or anything."

"Hot tip for the future, Lola, if you want to have sex with other people, don't do it with your guy in the next room."

Roxie's hands found her hips. "Did you want something, or are you just here to do a panty check?"

"Always got time for one of those," Zairn said. "I thought you were having lunch with Lilya upstairs. Have you scared her off already? Sent her into labor?"

"If I sent her into labor, would I be standing here?"

"Who knows with you? I thought you were upstairs already."

"Oh, so you came in here to snoop?" Roxie crept closer to her other half. "What are you doing in my office anyway? You come in here when I'm not here?"

"All the time. It's my building, I go where I want, when I want."

"We need to talk about boundaries," Roxie said, stroking Zairn's belt when she got close enough.

"Do we?"

"There are rules with boundaries…"

"Yeah?"

"Decide your boundaries and no matter what, under all circumstances, stick to them."

The way the couple fixated on each other left no doubt as to where their words and hands wanted to go next.

She stood up. "Thanks, Roxie, I'll just—"

"No!" Roxie spun to lean against her guy. "Don't go. Stay and have lunch with me and Lilya. She knows a thing or two about forbidden men."

"Forbidden men?" Zairn asked.

"Never you mind." Roxie waved a dismissive hand over her head before smiling at her again. "You'll get along great with Lilya, Frey. I promise, she's not all baby brain."

"Thanks, but I… have plans for lunch."

"With…?"

Further complications. "No one you know. I'm sorry I intruded on your day."

"It's never an intrusion," Roxie said. "I'm always here for you. For all my girls. I do want to meet this guy."

"What guy?" Zairn asked.

Roxie tipped her head back. "Didn't I say never you mind? Make believe we're in bed." Zairn's brows went up as hers did the same. "He's not allowed to repeat what he hears in our bed."

"Okay. If there's no tragedy… or sex…" Zairn kissed the top of Roxie's head. "I'll leave you to it."

Reaching behind her, Roxie snagged his belt. "No, I have use for you." Her friend refocused. "Freya, honey, you have to embrace this. Trust me when I say it's worth it. You have to take the leap. Embrace the danger. Make it work. You'll never forgive yourself if you let this go."

Roxie did know what she was talking about. As stated, this was the woman's area of expertise. Had she come to Rouge for permission, or an out? Whatever the reason, her friend provided purpose. One she had to hold onto during her next visit. Boundaries: she'd get them straight and, as Roxie said, stick to them no matter what.

# FIFTEEN

PURPOSE, YES, REASON. Resolute, she wouldn't be shaken from her decision. Sometimes a person just had to leap. Roxie would leap, so this was her, leaping.

"I want the works," Freya said at her emergency meeting with Conrad.

The surprise of her request made him pause in his descent to his chair. With one hand on the arm, his brows rose as he sank the rest of the way. "Uh... okay... are you sure?" She nodded with as much vigor as she could muster. "Really? Because when you were in here before you said you didn't want sex at all."

Dropping her purse to the floor, she flattened her hands, splaying them in the air, indicating an array. "I want everything. Your top package."

Resolute.

Top package meant top money. What better way was there to guarantee she got what she needed?

Clearing his throat, he hid his smirk by dipping his head and scratching his forehead. Attempted to hide it anyway, he wasn't doing a very good job.

"Okay…" The Squires boss was gracious enough to clear his amusement before carrying on. "We will update your profile on the system and find new matches to—"

"No," she said. Purpose. "No need for that. I know who I want."

Clutching the arms of his chair, he rocked back. "Do you? Who would you like?"

With a single nod, she gave her unequivocal answer. "Baer."

Determination. No shame here, no siree.

Again, his surprise took the form of a brow raise and not so well disguised smile. Let him be amused, if Baer was the prize, she'd take it.

"A popular choice." Not something she liked to think about. "But, unfortunately, he doesn't offer the top package."

Damn, that was an unexpected dent.

Taken aback, she frowned. "He doesn't?"

"No," Conrad said, just letting his smile go. No more mystery here. Opening a drawer, he produced a brochure, which he passed to her. "Maybe you'd like to remind yourself of what's available at the top tier."

Given how little attention she paid when perusing the brochure the first time, his suggestion wasn't a bad one.

A mass of interwoven naked bodies greeted her when she opened it. Immediately, she closed it. That was enough of that.

"No," she said, pushing it onto the desk and putting a hand to her throat. "Just to me… I want him to… to do everything to me. Not…" She waved a finger in the direction of the brochure. "Not that." Composure, calm, just pretend he's not laughing on the inside. Purpose was funny, apparently. "It's short notice, I know, I will pay top tier rates… whatever it takes."

"Okay," he said. "Maybe we can negotiate. Hold on."

Reaching for the phone on his desk, Conrad pressed a few buttons until ringing pierced the air.

"I said not today, Con," Baer's voice came through the speakerphone.

Oh, God, more humiliation. Should she smile or weep? The point of visiting Conrad was to get a measure of how this would work before Baer was introduced into the equation. If she convinced his boss, he couldn't object, could he? Having Conrad on her side may be useful in encouraging Baer's agreement.

"Yeah, I know, but, look, I've got a client—"

"What part of not today do you not follow?" Baer asked. "Someone told you I'm around? I came in for the gym. I'm not in… not in, in. I've been in every day this week. I'm entitled to a damn minute."

Part of that week included her, but she couldn't be offended he was frayed, he wasn't the only one.

The more relevant point? He was there, in the building. Unnerving, he could be close by.

"You gonna let me finish a goddamn sentence, Baer?" Conrad snapped then took a breath. "I have a client, who doesn't care about seeing you today."

He looked to her for confirmation; she shook her head fast.

"Oh," Baer said. "Cool, what's the problem?"

Conrad's irritation faded to a smile. "She wants the full package from you."

"I don't do men."

"Yeah, I know," Conrad said and smirked as he leaned back in his seat. "She says she wants you to do it all to her. Do everything to her… Everything a man can do with a woman… one on one… And she'll pay for the privilege…" Silence. "Never heard you hesitate before, buddy... This is top dollar for a job. And I gotta tell you, I wouldn't mind doing this one myself."

He winked at her. A signal he wasn't hitting on her or being leery? The comment was a prompt for Baer. And maybe for her too. Did he think Baer cared about her or was he amused that she had such a hard-on—no pun intended—for Baer?

"Then do it yourself," Baer said. "Use your patter. She won't care who—"

"No, she's pretty adamant, man," Conrad said. "She asked for you by name."

"Recommendation?"

"No, you know this one."

Interrupting would be rude, but she was dying to butt in.

"Regular?" Baer asked, trying to figure it out. "My clients want something, they ask for it and are billed. Who would come to you instead of asking me next time we're together?"

"Hound."

The word leaped out of her. All on its own. Unintentionally.

In the following quiet, her intense cringe wished the ground would swallow her whole. Conrad stared at her—just stared—awaiting Baer's response.

"Wait there," Baer said. "Don't move. Do nothing."

The line died.

On another inhale, Conrad opened his arms. "That went well," he said. "The gym's two floors down, he'll be up in just a minute... We could do the paperwork while we wait."

Opening a different drawer, he retrieved some documents to go through them, letting her read as he explained different clauses.

Conrad was still talking when she plucked a pen from a holder on the desk intending to sign the latest page.

Until someone came rushing in.

"Do not sign that," Baer said, tossing what sounded like a bag to the floor.

Twisting around, her intention was to object to his barking. But, damn, the bright white tee-shirt, the damp hair, gray sweats… She could smell soap and deodorant and… man. That was a tempting combination, she could go over there and—

"Thought you weren't in today, buddy?" Conrad semi-mocked.

"I'm not, and neither is she. Lil'—"

"I am here," she said, finding her voice. "I have decided to do this, Hound. Don't even—"

"Don't even, what?" he asked, marching over to drop into the seat next to hers. With his elbows on his parted knees, he leaned in. "Frey—" Stopping himself, he turned to Conrad. "Want to give us some privacy?"

"Privacy?" Conrad said like he'd never heard the word before. "She's a client. Why would… I…" Quieting, he puffed out his cheeks and stood up. "Sure, okay. Privacy."

Skirting the desk, he paused by the door to look at them with curious eyes before going out and closing the door.

"Baby—"

"You have every right to refuse me service, but—"

"Service? Skit, don't talk like that," he said, scooping a hand around her face, trapping her hair between his palm and her cheek. "Where is this coming from?"

"I want you to come away with me," she said. "Next weekend, two weeks, with my family... I'll pay you forty thousand dollars."

"Frey—"

"I know it's short notice and you'll be away from your family and your other job. I'll cover all expenses and get someone to cover your building's maintenance, whatever you need."

"Freya—"

"Fifty thousand," she said. "Or sixty. Whatever it will take—"

Silencing her with a fingertip on her lips, he smiled. "Now I know how frustrated Conrad was... Little Skit, you were so sure you didn't want me with you. What changed?"

His touch slid away to let her voice out. "Back then I didn't want to hire you because I... I don't know, I didn't want to fall for it. I thought it was an act. Idiot me believed it until I realized it was practiced. This is what you do, and I was a fool, it was an act, and I believed it."

Sinking back in his chair, he breathed out. "It *was* an act... until you were on your knees in front of me at that vending machine. Shit, baby, I'd have..."

"I know." She nodded, shifting in her chair to put her knees between his and lay her hands on his thighs. "At the beginning it was, it was the persona, I get that... But... things are different between us now, Baer. Aren't they different? I don't know what this is or where it's going, but I thought, why not spend some time together and find out? I need a fake boyfriend and you need the money. I won't miss the money, it's nothing to me..." Sensing he may be coming around, she pulled herself closer, digging her fingers in deeper. "You told me not to choose Donoghue." Leaning in, she lowered her volume. "And you told me you didn't want to go all the way with that client... This will give us some breathing room. It's two weeks of getting to know each other."

"And not having to worry about either of us being with anyone else."

She smiled. "Right... And the money gives us both a buffer anyway, if we decide after two weeks, or at any time, we want out, we call it business and walk away."

"Sixty grand is too much."

Though he needed every cent. "Whatever it is, I'll pay," she said, driving her hands higher while bowing lower. "You're worth it."

The corner of his mouth reacted; he exhaled a laugh. "You know how often women say that to me?"

She laughed. "Okay, so you're not worth it... I don't think of it as money for you anyway. It's money for your family, for them to live on while you're not here... In case of emergency, that kind of thing... I'm paying them for denying them your company..."

"Oh, you don't need to convince me to take the dough, sweetheart," he said. "In an ideal world I'd support you—"

"Please don't let finances come between us. It's the twenty-first century and I can't apologize for what's in my bank account. We're still equals, and I want to give you this. Don't be threatened by it."

"I'm not, and, baby, there's nothing wrong with my ego, don't worry about it. So long as we're clear it's you I want, not your bank account. But if this is business..." His eyes flicked down to take advantage of the view his younger brother enjoyed at the hospital. "What do you want for your money, Skit?"

Good progress. "Two things," she said, straightening her arms and meeting his eye. "Fidelity."

"For the two weeks, right? Because after we're back in town—"

She nodded. "I know, I know. Yes, for the two weeks... Fidelity while I'm paying you because if you're still interested in making money, there will be events after. I'd prefer it if you didn't solicit other women while we're at dinner with my family, you know?"

He laughed and reached over to tuck her hair behind her ear. "Fair enough. And number two?"

This one was more serious than the first and may be more divisive. May? Try definitely.

Licking her lips, she curled them into her mouth and took her time letting them go. "No sex."

His eyes closed before they opened wider. "Excuse me?"

"I don't want us to have sex while I'm paying you."

"What happened to wanting everything a man can do with a woman?"

"Your boss can believe that; this truth is between us."

Personal, not business.

Tilting his head, he peered into her. "Let me get this straight, you want us to explore what this might be, but you don't want us to have sex?"

"Right."

"You, the first woman in five years I've been attracted to, as me, personally... and you want me to agree I won't make moves on you?"

"Moves are okay," she said, secretly anticipating that enticement. "You'll have to be my fake boyfriend in front of everyone at God knows what kind of events." *Fake* boyfriend? Fake while there was cash involved. Why make that distinction? "Holding my hand and kissing me is the job, we'll have to be familiar. And we'll be sharing a room... and a bed, so..."

"So... sex naturally follows."

She was quick to prod him. "No! See, this is why you have to agree. We are not allowed to have sex while I'm paying you. Not while I'm paying you."

His head tilted the other way like her reiteration flagged a loophole. "What about when you're not paying me?"

She shrugged and stooped again, this time laying the points of her elbows on his solid thighs. "That's allowed. That's non-fake boyfriend."

Still didn't make him her real boyfriend, just not, not... her confuddled mind couldn't keep up. Oh, she couldn't think straight with him.

"Okay, right, good," he said. "This is boundaries." He paused. "But you'll be paying me for two weeks straight." She nodded. "No sex for two weeks?" She nodded again. "You know how long it's been since I've gone two weeks without sex?"

"According to you, if we discount all the sex you've been paid to have, it's been five years."

Unsure she'd convinced him, her butt left the seat as she slid her hands up his body. She took her time slithering onto his lap and coiling her arms around his neck.

"I'm not paying you now."

That intrigued him. "You want to have sex here?" he asked, glancing around. "Door doesn't lock, but I'm good with that. I've been watched plenty."

If he'd been doing this for years, she didn't doubt he'd probably done just about everything.

When he tried to marry their mouths, she leaned back. "Except if Conrad catches us, he'll put it on my bill and my conditions will be shot to hell..." Pouting, she wriggled in his lap. "I'll be worth waiting for."

"Waiting 'til when?" he asked. "What day do we go away?"

Squealing in delight, she bounced her fist on his shoulder. "You'll do it?"

"I'm not going to say no to you, am I? When?"

"Saturday."

"There's a lot of time between now and Saturday."

She rested her forehead on his cheek. "I'm not having sex with you on the same day you have sex with clients."

"God, these rules just keep on coming, don't they? I don't have a client tonight. There's three tomorrow, so…"

Her mouth opened. In slow motion, she slanted away. If it wasn't for his hand splaying on her back, she'd have fallen right out of the chair.

"Three? You have three dates tomorrow?"

"Breakfast, lunch, and dinner," he said, flashing her his dimple. "That's a lie, it's like lunch, afternoon delight, and then dinner."

It boggled her mind. "How do you do that?"

"How do I do what?"

"Go from one woman to the next."

"They know what I do," he said. "They don't expect me not to see other women… it's my job. It's not love. I don't care about them… not about their feelings and—"

"No, not that." Dropping her gaze, her head bobbed side to side. "How do you… do… it?"

"You think I can't get it up three times a day?"

"In close proximity like that with women you just said you don't care about… You must be exhausted by the time you get home."

He laughed and skimmed his hand up her back to draw their mouths together. "If you're worried there won't be anything left in the tank by the time I get home to you, don't be," he said. "You'll be my priority, Little Skit."

Noble. Kissing him was incredible. Their tongues tangled, his hand found its way into her top, maybe they would do it right there... Could she be with a man who did... this? Who shared himself with...? Already she was feeling something and didn't like to think about him with other women. It was jealousy, there was no other word for it.

Their attraction was still new, and he was desperate for cash. She couldn't ask him to change his life or lifestyle for her. Not... yet? Would there come a time...?

He had his father and brothers to support and a zillion medical bills. She'd happily assume the financial responsibilities, except most men wouldn't want a woman striding in and taking over. And if she did, wouldn't it be like paying him to be in a relationship with her anyway?

And then there was the other elephant: Truman. If he found out she was even considering a relationship with a gigolo, he'd cut her off for sure. Then she'd just be another mouth for Baer to feed. Another person for him to look after, she'd never be able to ask him to stop after that. Adding her to the mix would increase his burden and Squires was how he kept the family afloat.

With a palm on his chest, she separated their mouths to seek his eyes. "Baer," she said as he ran his fingers into her hair, watching it move between them. "Do you use protection?"

His hand dropped and the ease of his expression became a frown. "Yes," he said. "Always... Why would you ask me that? I'm clean. We get regular physicals."

"No, I wasn't thinking that I... I was wondering about kids."

Opening his mouth in acceptance, he nodded. "Yeah, we sometimes have women who consider us walking sperm banks, which is why we provide all protection ourselves. We don't use what the women provide and there are no exceptions. We have non-latex condoms for women who are allergic, natural alternatives, everything... There are no little Baers out there... You want to get lunch?"

From potential kids to lunch without skipping a beat. His confidence was okay, there would be time to get into all the nitty-gritty, preferably while not in Conrad's office.

Using his chest as a lever point, she got to her feet. "I can't today. I have a date."

"Oh yeah?" Pushing up in the chair, he examined her. "A date? With who?"

Bending down, she picked up her purse to hook the strap over her shoulder. "Who else? My boyfriend."

"Boyfriend, huh?"

Detecting the tease, he relaxed a little, but she wasn't giving in.

"Yes," she said. "And don't sit there all cocky, he's tough. You should watch yourself, you know..." She wiggled her finger at him. "For what we just did there. He'd take you apart for doing that."

"You sat on me, Skit... And it wouldn't be the first time I've kissed another man's girlfriend," he said, linking his fingers on the top of his head. "Tell me about this boyfriend."

"He's cute." She straightened the strap of her purse. "He's a little beat up right now, but when he's on top form, he'll take you down."

"Will he?"

"Sure," she said, coiling her fingers around the strap. "He's a criminal."

"A criminal?" One dimple peeked. "You know what I do here isn't exactly legal?"

She mock sneered. "This is kids' stuff. He's a real criminal. Wanted for breaking and entering as a matter of fact."

"Presley," he murmured, then laughed. "You're taking my little brother out for lunch?"

"Actually, his father is taking me out."

"Meeting the family, huh?" he asked, pushing out of his chair and slinging an arm around her. "My invite must have got lost in the mail."

"You're not coming."

"Why not? It's the weekend. If Abel and Pres will be there, Charlie will too… You can have the whole set."

"The whole set." They paused for him to pick up his bag and toss the strap over his head. "I like the sound of that."

# SIXTEEN

COFFEE. Back in the apartment. That was Abel's suggestion after lunch. Excellent. Not ready for the date to be over, they all piled into Freya's car for the trip back to the apartment building and got all the way to the Claymore's front door.

Coffee. She needed coffee. And she continued to believe they were going inside for beloved java. Right up until Baer squeezed her waist from behind, easing her just a little away from the rest of his family.

"I'm going to show Frey something upstairs," Baer said.

"Oh yeah? I bet you are." Abel was no fool and although she couldn't see Baer, the elder's expression was enough. The men's shared eye contact was a conversation in itself. "No prizes for guessing what that'll be."

"What'll it be, Dad?" Charlie asked with all the innocence of a child.

Abel opened the front door and, with a hand between the youngster's shoulder blades, boosted the boy toward it. "Mind your own, get inside."

Baer's fingers snagged hers and with haste got them to the end of the corridor and up the stairs to another floor.

"You're going to hell," Freya said, laughing when Baer led her into an enclosed stairwell.

Wasn't this the top floor? Where were they going? The roof?

"Yeah," he agreed. "And, for this, it'll be worth it."

At the top, just offset from the stairway, was another door. Baer unlocked it and guided her into the main body of an apartment that seemed to be... Yeah, this was the whole thing.

The angled roof limited head height around the perimeter. This wasn't even a full floor, just an extra space plopped on top of the structure. By adding some flooring, someone made it a room... that maybe wasn't supposed to be there. The bed was low, just a foot off the floor in the middle of the space. Behind the bed, to the left and right were single dormer windows, which at least gave the room lots of light.

Going past the bed and the bathroom door, the bare floorboards beneath her feet creaked. The distressed white paint on the paneled walls probably hadn't been looked after for years. No surprise, when would the guy have time?

"It's not much to look at."

Behind the headboard, between the dormers, was a shoulder-height screen. Going around it, she was amazed to find tools and a work bench with sawdust spread across the floor. And the truly wondrous sight? A low square table, a rocking chair... a partly finished... something. Definitely hand-crafted, the warm woods of varying hues were a breathtaking sight.

"Baer," she breathed, sensing him near. Transfixed, her fingertips grazed the edge of the rocking chair. "Did you do this?"

"Ah, it's nothing."

Whipping around, she was almost offended. "Baer, it's beautiful." He seemed more interested in looking at her. Backing up, she got closer to the rocking chair. "Do you know what this tells me?"

He advanced on her. "What?"

"You have a creative eye," she said, creeping around the back of the chair. "And you're good with your hands."

"Something I plan to prove now," he said, rushing forward to scoop her up. She whooped when he threw her down on the bed and landed on his side next to her. "You're not paying me today. No one is. Day off."

"You want to have sex now?" she asked, touching the neck of his tee-shirt. "Was this your evil plan all along?"

"Mm hmm," he said, lifting enough to pull off his top.

Carved into masculine perfection, his muscles were honed and his form so defined, her fingers couldn't resist. He did the bit removing her top, his boots, her shoes, her skirt... she just stroked.

There might be no prep sheet, but he wasn't asking permission, just the way she liked it. He was taking action, and didn't seem to mind her touch getting familiar.

"Hound," she said when he hooked an arm around her waist to pull her close. "This means something to you, doesn't it?" With a slow nod, he began to descend, his mouth on course for hers. She pressed harder. "No, I mean, it's special to you. Being with me, is special."

Ever patient, he swept her hair from her cheek. "Baby, what's wrong? If this is wrong, tell me how to make it right for you."

"Don't use lines on me," she said, tracing a finger down the center of his chest. "You're so hot."

"Right back attcha, Lil'."

"You might have done this twenty minutes ago, but I didn't... I don't have any problems or hang-ups about sex, but... the last man I was with was Chapman and... well he turned out to be a lying scumbag who didn't tell me he was married, so..."

"You've seen my life, Frey. No wife. No kids... I'm responsible for the twins, but—"

"I don't think you're lying to me."

Their eyes met and he exhaled. "You just want to know that this is special?" She nodded. "What reason would I have to do this if it wasn't special?"

Huh. Good point. None. No one was paying him to be there, as far as she knew. He wasn't a sex maniac, again, as far as she knew. This wasn't a dare. The Baer she knew wouldn't do something like that.

Old insecurities flared until he kissed her again, then they just faded away. She wanted this. Wanted this man. They had this moment to be together as them. She wasn't going to squander it.

His kiss softened and he rested a gentle hand on her stomach.

"We're going to be terrible at this, aren't we?" she asked, a broad smile stretched on her face.

He frowned. "Give a guy a chance, babe. Shit, we just got started and—"

"No," she said, soothing him, caressing his face. "I meant because you like it soft and slow, and I like it hard and fast."

"Maybe we find a happy medium," he said, leaning in to kiss her again. "I can give it to you anyway you want it."

Pressing a finger into his chest, she eased him back to meet his eye. "I want you to make love to me, Baer. You. Not any persona or anything you learned off a prep sheet. If you can't be you, excuse yourself."

His smirk was almost a laugh. "Excuse myself? From our bed? From sex with you?" His palm glided over her breast to her throat to catch her jaw. "Yeah, that won't be happening." Opening her mouth, she drew in a breath. "Shush now, Skit… Let a man work."

His tongue slid into her mouth, swallowing her squeak of shock while scooping her body under his. His leisurely kiss, so gentle and tender, wrapped her in the illusion of forever. When he savored her like this, it was difficult to imagine him kissing other women. No other woman existed, she was the last one in the world and couldn't help but feel special.

Her hips moved, rising and writhing, seeking an anchor. Although she pushed up against the ridge in his jeans, he didn't respond with the usual relaxing of his hips. With gradual pressure, he relaxed in increments, pressing harder, giving her more of him until…

The thick length of him imprinted itself deep. Him. Long and thick and hard… Her eyes opened. Long and thick… Whoa, boy…

Their kiss got harder by the second… and it wasn't the only thing. When he parted their mouths to look into her, she erased her frown.

"You want to talk about it?" he asked and she shook her head. Fast. Shit. Was she scared or exhilarated? Whichever it was, her heart thudded, growing so big it squeezed her lungs. Breathing out a laugh, he brushed her hair from her brow with a fingertip. "I won't hurt you."

Puffing out some of her anxiety, her smile strained. "Now I know why you're so gentle."

Widening his smile, he touched her lips with his. "Once you're used to it, I'll be as rough as you want."

Relaxed by his smile, she ran a hand up his shoulder and into his hair. "No prep sheet."

"No," he said. "But I still want to give you what you want."

"Professional pride?"

"Personal satisfaction," he said. "I want to please you, Lil'."

"Kiss me, Hound," she whispered. "Just keep kissing me."

Despite her surprise about what he was packing, her kiss was insistent. It seemed sort of unfair to other men that one man could be as good-looking and charming as Baer and be so well-hung too.

With all he endured in his life, with his parents' medical issues and his responsibility for supporting the boys, his blessing put food on the Claymore table, literally.

Conrad had said more than once that Baer was in demand. His manner and appearance guaranteed that, and this new information revealed another category of client would be sliding into his DMs too.

Wriggling, she tried to explore more, to increase the friction between them, except his weight and insistence didn't let her be more urgent or forceful. How could the man be so patient? Probably because he got off regularly, there was no rush for him, he wasn't breaking a drought.

She was.

It had been so long and she wanted to know this man. "Baer," she breathed when he broke the kiss.

"Wait here," he said and kissed her fast before retreating.

She grabbed for his shoulders to bring him back. "Where are you going?" she asked, trying to tempt his mouth. "Stay with me."

His smile grew as he traced it across hers. "I'll be right back. Just getting a condom."

"Oh," she said, her gaze dropping.

"What?" He dipped down to catch her eye, one narrowed. "Why do you sound disappointed? You don't want to use protection?"

"No, I..." The forced smile didn't convince him. "No... go get one."

Giving in, her body went limp, her hands dropped.

He didn't move. "Do you know how insane you would be to sleep with a hooker without protection?"

A reference to the day they met? She didn't feel like teasing.

"You're not a streetwalker."

"Still, I haven't had sex without a rubber since..." He thought about it but came up short. "Huh, I can't even remember."

Stroking his upper arms, she tried to connect but couldn't help being a little selfish about enjoying his muscles. "Claire?"

He shook his head. "We used 'em. She was paranoid about pregnancy, her mom and sister both got pregnant young... She didn't want kids until after she was married." He met her eye. "You didn't with Chapman?"

She shrugged. "Sometimes... I was always more particular about it than he was, which is nuts now, if you think about it. If he'd got me pregnant, his wife would've found out about us for sure."

He kissed her. "I don't want to put you at risk," he said. "That's all. I'm still waiting on the results of my latest physical, should clear us before the vacation."

Wasn't that just hilarious? "When we won't be having sex?"

Growling, he bowed to rest his head on hers. "Please don't remind me of that, baby," he said. "Might kill my buzz."

"Come on," she goaded, coaxing him. "It will be a vacation for you too. Your cock will get a rest."

"Right when it won't want one. You think it'll be easy to share a bed and not…?"

"I don't know." She shrugged. "We're both adults, I'm sure we'll contain ourselves."

Because this was important.

"'Cept all I'll be able to think about is you lying here under me telling me bareback is okay."

Wrapping her arms around his neck, she squeezed herself closer. "Bareback is okay," she whispered. Gritting his teeth, he groaned. "As long as you're using protection with everyone else."

"Always," he said, running his tongue along the seam of her lips. "I wouldn't endanger you… and I'll get tested more often." This was an odd conversation; not one she could've predicted being a part of her life. "Next time tell me what's in your head, don't hide the truth from me."

She shook her head. "No, it wasn't… I wasn't thinking about whether or not we should use protection, I just…" Exhaling, she resigned herself to revealing the truth. "It felt professional. Stopping like that for protection, it felt practiced… Sometimes I… You're so calm and controlled…"

While, in contrast, around him, she kept losing her head.

"You think it's still an act?" he asked, sounding sort of offended. "You think I—"

Touching his lips, she silenced him. "Just don't ever forget you're with me when we're together," she said. "Promise me?"

Nodding, his half frown was still dubious. "You will learn to trust me. You will."

"I do trust you." What kind of woman got herself involved with a man whose job required him to sleep with other women and didn't trust him? If that was the case, they'd be doomed before they started. "Now where's that condom, Hound Dog? You'll never catch the pussy if you don't prepare yourself."

"On it," he said, kissing her quick and leaping off the bed.

Glancing back, he seemed to appreciate the view spread out on his sheets as he unbuckled his jeans and kicked them off in a heap. His dimple flashed in unison with a wink before he disappeared into the bathroom, tossing the door into the frame behind him.

In almost the same second, her phone buzzed. Rolling to the edge of the bed, she fished it from her purse on the floor. She sat up, reading the unknown number, and frowned as she answered.

"Hello?"

"Freya? It's Conrad."

Uh, and he was calling because…? He couldn't know what they were doing right then… could he?

"Hello," she said again. "Is there a problem?" And then she remembered with a groan. "I didn't sign the paperwork."

"No, you didn't, but this is about something else," he said. "We had to move up Holly's next date. She and Marlin are available tonight, but she said you had agreed to continue double dating with her. So I was wondering if—"

"Tonight?" she asked, tucking her heels on the frame of the bed. "Sure." Ah, an opportunity for mischief. "Long as I can have Baer."

Silence. Five seconds. Ten. "Baer… uh…"

"You know, it's a shame I didn't sign that paperwork yet because—"

"Sure! Yes. Yes, you can have Baer, just let me call him and I'll call you back."

The line died. Sharing a quiet laugh with herself, she tucked her phone under the edge of the blanket and lay down again. She'd just relaxed when the bathroom door opened.

"Rubbers are expired." Baer raised a hand to his forehead to toss the box into the trash can under the window. "But, no worries, I have some from last night." Oh, did he now? "I know work product is less than ideal, but the rubbers don't care who paid for what."

Neither did their body parts, but…

"That's not what I was thinking," she said, rising to her elbows. "I was wondering why you were carrying protection on a date with my cousin who you promised not to sleep with?"

His mouth opened, but it took a second for anything to come out. "Muscle memory."

Her head tilted just as his phone rang. Apparently, more than happy to save himself, he ducked to snag his phone from his jeans pocket. To his credit, he didn't look at it or answer. Instead, he came to join her on the bed, laying over her to reignite their kiss.

Although he tried to push harder, to urge her onto her back, she stayed on her elbows.

"Are you going to get that?" she asked, accepting his kiss, eyeing the phone.

"It will stop in a second."

"You are an incredible man," she said, opening her fingers wide on his shoulders and driving them up toward his neck.

"That what I get for ditching a phone call?"

"Baer," she whispered, ascending to trace her lips over his. "My Baer."

This time her tongue took the lead and with fingertips slinking down his torso, she twisted her wrist. She'd just touched the waistband of his underwear when he growled and broke the kiss to bring the phone to his ear.

"What?" he barked into the handset, dropping his head. "No, fuck, Con, what did I—" His attention snapped up fast. She let her smile grow slowly. "Tonight... Are you shitting me?" The arousal and surprise faded to give way to suspicion. "No, Con, I don't think this girl is eager to have me at all... Yeah." Disconnecting the phone, he threw it toward the pillow. "Drinks tonight?"

Restraining a laugh, she played it coy. "Oh, well, I don't know. That's forward of you, Mr. Claymore... I was on a date with someone else today..."

"Why you..." He pinched her waist, provoking a yelp before he tickled her, pinning her body with his.

Again, her phone rang, so she pushed and squeaked, wriggling away from him to retrieve the handset from beneath the blanket. Flipping onto her front, still under him, she slithered a little higher. Baer stopped tickling just as she answered.

"Hello?"

"Freya," Conrad said in her ear.

"Conrad, what a surprise!"

Tipping her chin toward her shoulder, she expected teasing from Baer. Rather than taunt, the very tip of his tongue touched the base of her spine to ascend at an excruciating pace, tormenting a trickle of need and arousal in its wake.

"We just talked five minutes ago," Conrad said.

"Mm hmm," she managed to say, squeezing her lips together.

"You're on for tonight. Baer was a tough sell, but he's a good guy… a really decent guy… He'd do anything to keep a client happy."

And with how his tongue snaked to the back of her neck, she could believe that. "He better be available for the other date this week."

"He will be," Conrad said, a thread of concern in his voice. "Would you be able to come in this afternoon or later this evening before your date to sign this paperwork?"

"Yes," she said, her breath catching when Baer's mouth skimmed to the side of her neck. "Oh, God, yes."

Done with the call, whether Conrad was or not, she hung up and tossed the phone aside to roll over and wrap both arms around his head, forcing his mouth to accept the moan slipping from hers. Although her legs coiled around his hips, locking them together, they had a date lined up tonight; one that couldn't end with her ultimate fantasy. Rules. Rules. Rules. They couldn't follow through. As much as she wanted to…

He felt so good. His mouth. His hands. The weight of him on top of her.

"Baer, Dad says—"

The child's voice stole their kiss as both their attentions leaped toward the door. Toward Charlie, there on the threshold, screwdriver in hand.

"Charlie…" Baer said.

He gasped and pointed the screwdriver at them. "I'm telling Presley!"

Spinning around, the youngster bolted. Baer was smiling. How could he be smiling?

She didn't find it funny at all and pushed at his shoulders. "Baer! Go after him!"

"What?" he asked. "We're two consenting adults. They know what sex is."

"Presley will be hurt." Her breaking heart prompted a harder shove. "Go be a big brother, please."

He frowned. "He didn't really think you were into him… did he?"

Blinking, it was a wonder to her sometimes. "Baer, I work with kids every day, all the time. Some of them get it. Some of them are really hurt by rejection. Please… please, go be gentle about it, don't let Charlie be the one to tell him."

After searching her eyes another few seconds, he cursed under his breath and climbed off the bed. "Goddamn," he grumbled, stomping over to swipe his jeans off the floor. "This is madness." Sticking his feet into his jeans, he pulled them up. "You were mine before you were his." Despite the urgency, she rose on her elbows to smile at him. It was sweet of him to care about her feelings and his brother's. "I kissed you first."

"This will grease the skids for you, I promise."

"Grease the skids," he muttered and pointed at the bed with his thumb and forefinger just an inch apart. "We were this fucking close before the kid walked in." Turning around, he stomped out. "Goddamn."

Flopping onto her back after the door closed, she relished just being there. Hmm… naughty thoughts. She could peel off her underwear, crawl into his bed, and wait there for him to return. But they would only have to leave the sheets, unsated, to go on their date. A date he'd be paid for. They weren't supposed to have sex when he was being paid to be with her. Whose dumb idea was that?

Forcing herself to get up and dressed, she accidentally on purpose forgot to don one item and cast a slow eye over the room. She liked it. Would she be there again? If not, at least the silk panties on his pillow would be a memento of her.

# SEVENTEEN

"PLEASURE DOING BUSINESS with you," Conrad said, leading Freya out of his office and down the stairs toward the Squires reception.

The twenty guys loitering there were a surprise that halted her and Conrad halfway down.

"It's a James Bond convention," she murmured, scanning the tuxedos laid out beneath them.

"What the hell are you all doing here?" Conrad asked, checking his watch. "You should be in cars, going to your appointments."

"Garage door is broken," one of the guys said.

Conrad descended another couple of stairs, so she stayed at his side. "And no one thought to call maintenance?"

"Baer's on it," Donoghue said, holding a candy packet high over his head, offering her one. "Royal?"

She descended to dip her fingers in. Accepting the invitation, she popped the sweet treat between her lips.

Conrad wasn't satisfied. "None of you are helping him because…?"

"Didn't want to mess with the merchandise," the first guy said, gesturing at his suit. "We get dirty, we have to shower and change… That takes time… Baer said it was okay for him to be late."

Conrad's nervous laugh came with a side-eye her way. Their leader was probably trying to judge her reaction without risking full eye contact.

Breathing out, she sank to sit on the stairs. "All dressed up and no place to go… story of my life."

She didn't mind so much; Holly was her only concern.

Creeping closer to the stairs, a man she didn't know checked her out. "You could join me, sweetheart… I can handle more than one."

"That's nice," she said to be polite.

Donoghue laughed. "This one only has eyes for Baer, trust me. And he's right… she'll wait. Won't you, Royal?"

Everyone turned to the elevator when it pinged. She couldn't see what was going on through the amassed bodies.

"Well…?" Conrad asked whoever must have come off the elevator.

"I need a shower, but you're good to go," Baer's voice carried to her. "Cars are ready."

"It'll be like the president came to town all those limos pouring out the garage at once," Donoghue joked.

Conspicuous. Sure.

"How long do you need, Baer?" Conrad asked. "I have a date of my own to get to."

"So go…" Baer said. "All of you can go. I'll lock up." The guys began to move. "I just need to call—" She stood up next to Conrad, making herself known. Baer pointed at her. "Never mind."

His dirty hands were raised like a doctor waiting for surgical gloves.

"I had papers to sign," she said.

"Cool," he said and slanted his head to the side. "Come this way."

The guys stopped, which stalled Baer.

"You're taking her to the locker room?" Donoghue asked.

That warranted all focus tracking to Conrad.

"I won't let her touch anything," Baer said.

The guys laughed.

"I don't think she'll mind starting early if she paid for the night," another voice said.

Irritation ticked Baer's jaw.

Her mood differed, she smiled and descended in a bounce, aiming for light and frivolous. "Conrad can add it to my bill," she said, crossing the room to a soundtrack of whoops and whistles.

She didn't look at Baer, just headed the way he'd indicated until he nudged her toward a specific door.

Inside the swish space, individual full-height wooden lockers, thick carpet and benches, suggested high-class country club. At the end was an open archway with racks of clothes, opposite was another arch, this time to showers.

Baer went to a locker. "You're okay with them talking like that?" he asked as she got to work unbuckling his jeans so he wouldn't have to use his grease smeared fingers.

"Yes, because it doesn't mean anything," she said. "It's teasing." Dropping his pants, she was careful about picking off his tee-shirt. Despite its dirty smudge, she was careful not to mark it further as she hooped it over his hands. "Just like I'll have to get used to being the cock-hungry bunny boiler around the people in your life, you'll have to get used to people in my life assuming you're all about the money."

"Baby—"

"Can I get you a towel?"

"There are towels in the shower room," he said. "Lil', look at me."

"No," she said, unwilling to lift her head.

"If I touch you, I'll get this grease all over you and you'll have to hit the shower with me."

Not smart because they'd be naked and wet... and touching.

What choice did she have?

She elevated her chin. "I don't want to look at you because you're going to say something to reassure me either about the cock-hungry thing or the money thing."

Baer shook his head. "I won't reassure you about the cock-hungry thing. Cock-hungry works great for me, Lil'." Okay, this was Baer. Wonderful, sweet, sexy-hot Baer, she could relax. "But the money—"

"I don't want you to reassure me." Not like this was her first time on this particular train. "If you're all about the money, then you're all about the money. And if you need me to give you money, I will... I can't make you care about me. I figured that out about guys long ago. Either this works out, or it doesn't, words don't matter, actions matter."

Was that her version of reassuring him? Did it count?

"So if I just adore you..."

Grinning, she nodded, her hair fluttering against her back. "Yes, that would be perfect. Thank you."

"Okay," he said and stepped back to nod downwards. "Want to finish the job for me?"

"You sure?" she asked. He crooked a brow in assent. "I put on this pretty dress for you, you know."

Moving in closer, she dragged her thumbnails down his hips to tuck them under the elastic of his underwear.

The slight narrowing of one of his eyes betrayed his curiosity. "It's beautiful… you're beautiful…" He inhaled. "You remember you're the one with the rules, right, Lil'? If you want to join me in the shower…"

"You have no integrity," she whispered with mock outrage.

Dropping to the floor, she pulled down his boxer-briefs as she went.

What she revealed was more than ample, it was intimidating. Kneeling in front of him, her eyes trained to his member, it grew and thickened by the second. Shit, it was a rush, exhilarating, to be capable of influencing him this way.

"If you want to play with it…"

His voice startled her into blinking up. How long had she been crouched there gawping at him? Not that he seemed to mind. If there was any man with the wares to justify being cocky, this one was top of the list.

"I will," she said, rising slowly, her lower lip just grazing his dick as she returned to full height. Not so cocky now, huh? "When you're giving it up for free."

"This is a complimentary date."

Opening her hands on his bare chest, her mouth tasted him. "Are you saying you're donating your time? The agency doesn't compensate you?"

"Well, yeah, they do, but I—"

"I don't care who's compensating you. I don't want you inside me when you're on the clock."

Bowing lower, he breathed just above her mouth. "You think I wouldn't fuck my girl for free?"

"Your girl?" she asked, aroused by the words he'd never said before.

"All mine... Take off the pretty dress, Little Skit."

Unable to stop herself, her gaze devoured him again. "We're late already," she said, loathed to put space between them.

He laughed. "Baby, you snuck out on me today. We could've been in bed all afternoon."

"To leave and have you come on a date with me... a paid date."

"You requested me."

She smirked. "Would you rather another man take me out?"

"No," he said, barely allowing the complete question to hit the air before answering it. "No fucking way. Always request me."

"Even if it means you don't get laid at the end of the night?"

Walking toward the shower, he gave her an appreciated view of his magnificent ass. "That we'll negotiate on, Little Skit. Put your butt in a seat."

She'd rather admire his for as long as allowed. Just before going into the shower room, he turned, catching her drooling, but she didn't even hide it.

Feigning innocence, she shrugged. "I'm allowed to look."

Without slowing, he sauntered on, a drawl in his deep voice when he spoke. "You're allowed to do a helluva lot more than that, Lil'."

"Hound Dog!" she called after him.

He just waved and disappeared into a stall.

This was nuts.

This relationship was nuts.

Damnit, she'd never been so happy.

# EIGHTEEN

HOLLY'S MOOD wasn't so high.

In the limo at the end of the night, it would be an understatement to say Holly wasn't pleased.

Marlin, her cousin's date, got out of the car to head home. The moment the door closed behind him, Holly dropped into the vertical seat running the length of the vehicle.

They, being her and Baer, were in the shorter, horizontal seat at the back of the car. Tucked under Baer's arm with her head on his chest and arm resting between his thighs, her eyes were heavy. For some reason, Marlin picked a bar miles outside the city for drinks. During the considerable drive back, she'd fought to stay awake. It was just so… cozy back there with her guy.

Baer messed with his phone, writing messages to his dad and playing games, which had given Marlin and Holly time to talk and bond. That was the idea, though, honestly? Wow. Listening to their attempts was excruciating.

"I'm so sick," Holly huffed.

"It's not so bad." Freya closed her eyes, snuggling closer to Baer. "You still have another date."

"One shot?" Holly asked. "You think I can hit it with one shot?" She grumbled again. "We're not all as lucky as you."

"Are you cold?" Baer asked, his mouth in her hair.

"No," she said, turning her face toward him, pulling the lapel of his jacket to her nose. "You smell good."

"You want to wear it?"

"I want to take it home."

His mouth touched her scalp. "It's a company tux, babe."

"Are you taking it back to the office tonight?"

"Unless the alternative is it ends up on your bedroom floor, yes."

Still with her eyes closed, she smiled and twisted further toward him, opening a hand on his abs. "Complimentary dates don't come with sex."

Inhaling through his nose, he slouched a little. "Oh yeah, don't know why I keep forgetting that."

Wearing her satisfied smile, she could sleep right there in the car all night if it meant spending more time with Baer.

"How come it can't work like this for me?" her cousin whined.

Shifting again, she rolled her head on Baer to look over her shoulder at Holly. "What do you mean?"

"All the guys I go out with are duds… That's four guys and none my family would believe I'm with."

"You got along with Donoghue."

Holly moaned. "Yeah, I'd definitely screw him, but do you think my father would like him?"

"That's what you're looking for? Someone the family will like? Why?"

"We have to spend two weeks with them," Holly said. "I have to put up with them and I don't want my family to think I'm dating an idiot."

"No, you don't," she said, sensing a time to play. "I didn't think of that before I signed my paperwork… maybe I should've thought less about eye candy and more about picking a guy who could hold a conversation."

Baer pinched her hip. She recoiled but gave his thigh a squeeze. He knew she was teasing. How did she know? He got her. And she loved that about him.

Holly sighed. "See, you guys are great together! I need someone I can play with and joke with and talk with."

Baer made a noise that was part laugh, part scoff, part grunt, but it was so brief, she couldn't quite figure it out.

Raising her chin, she didn't relieve him of her weight but did let him know he had her attention. "What?"

"Nothing."

"No, if you have something to add…"

"Yes," Holly said. "What is it?"

"Nothing."

Digging her elbow into him, she sat up to meet his eye. "Hound?"

"Nothing. Forget it." She poked his ribs. Coiling his fingers around her extended one, he looked from her to Holly and back. "Can I be blunt?"

"With me?" she asked. "Always. Talk."

He exhaled. "Holly's prep sheet reads like a want ad," he said and her cousin's mouth fell open. "It's okay. You're not unique. A lot of women use Squires thinking it's a dating service, that they'll find true love."

"The idiots." She scoffed out mock ridicule. "Imagine falling for a gigolo."

"Desperate women, I guess," he said. "Nut jobs."

"Pathetic," she murmured, boosting up to join their lips for a flicker before sinking back down to snuggle at his side.

"I can't believe this," Holly said. "What about Freya's? Is it a want ad?"

His finger-combing of her hair was so soothing, her eyelids sank again.

"I don't know," Baer said. "I haven't read it."

"Why not?" Holly asked. "Isn't it like the law that you have to read it?"

"It's the law that I not sell sexual favors, and we all know what's going on here."

Freya patted his stomach. "Why don't you recommend someone? Someone Holly will like."

"I could," he said. "If you're interested… but he might be less than your ideal match."

Holly snorted. "Clearly even I don't know what that is."

"Okay," he said. "Then you want Lyon, Mathieson, Berwick, or Dirk."

Holly was dubious. "Dirk sounds like he's from a seventies romance novel."

"He's got a ten-inch cock."

Holly's eyes lit. "Really?"

Her cousin's quick turnaround provoked a laugh. "Tackle aside, you should pick personality."

"Personality, yes," Baer said, the arm he had around her slid higher. "Why does that sound like I have a micro situation?"

Ha! Laughable.

She patted him again. "We're not going to pretend you're insecure about the size of your cock, Hound. Your ego needs no stroking on that front."

What he was packing could give Dirk a run for his money, she wasn't about to simper like it was otherwise.

Holly's dubious eye turned suspicious. "I thought there was no sex on complimentary dates."

Baer jumped in to support her cousin. "Yeah, Little Skit, I thought there was no sex."

"It's not my fault you're so boastful," she said to him, then addressed Holly. "Sometimes he just won't shut up about it."

Her cousin's suspicion wasn't convinced. "His penis?"

"Yes," she said. "Shocking, right? It's my penis this, my penis that... all the time. Women go ga-ga for it apparently. I keep telling him that I'm more of a tongue girl, you know? All that incessant rutting and banging and thrusting—"

"Incessant?" Baer interjected and followed it with a cough of laughter. "Oh, this is going to be fun."

Skimming her hand over his, she opened his fingers to link them. "Will you set us up?" When he didn't respond, she pushed up enough to flutter her eyelashes. "Please, baby."

"Usually I get a bonus for personal recommendations," he said, his static expression giving little away.

Boosting higher, her lips grazed the shell of his ear. "I'll come cook steak and eggs for you and Abel at breakfast."

The boys would be at school, but she could bake something for them to enjoy when they got home.

Leaning back, she was proud of her suggestion.

He didn't look impressed. "That's not even in the ballpark of what I was thinking."

Giving his thigh a sympathetic rub, her smile mirrored that mood. "You know the rules, Hound Dog." It wasn't a negotiation; she tipped her head to the side. "Would you like me to be grateful... or not?"

Grumbling something, he handed the phone he'd been messing with to her and took another from his pocket to type and swipe.

"Why does he have two phones?" Holly asked.

Shifting to give him space, Freya relaxed against the backrest. "That one's work," she said, bobbing her chin toward the one in his hand while she frowned at the game he'd been playing.

Unpausing it, she tried to complete the level.

"But that means... that's personal," Holly said. "Why are you on his personal phone?"

Uh... had she misstepped? She got no prompt from Baer, he didn't even register Holly had spoken.

Turning the phone, she flashed a view of the screen at her cousin. "It's a game."

"Yeah, but you could... you know?"

She smiled. "Call his wife?" she asked. "Yeah, I guess I could."

As though on cue, the phone in her hand rang. The word "Fam" appeared on the screen; she turned it Baer's way. He bobbed his brows at it before returning to what he was doing on his other phone.

"Answer it," he said. "I have to show Holly these profiles."

Leaving his seat, he moved over to the other side of the limo to scroll through something with Holly.

Pressing receive, Freya did as requested. "Hello? Baer's phone."

There was a moment of silence.

"Freya?" came a child's voice. "Is that Freya?"

Concern creased her brow. "Yes, honey. What's up? Are you okay?"

Baer glanced up for just a moment, though his mouth kept moving, explaining whatever Holly was looking at.

"Oh, man," the young voice whined. "I'm gonna get in so much trouble."

"For what? Honey? Are you hurt? Is everyone safe?"

"Yeah, I... Is Baer at your house?"

"We're out," she said. "Do you need him to come over?"

"Well, I... yeah... I got homework I didn't do, and I can't figure it out. Pres won't help, and if I wake Abel he'll go nuts, 'cause he said we could only go for burgers with you if we had no homework."

"You lied," she said because it seemed appropriate to chastise him, but his call to Baer for help with a screw up was adorable.

"I know," Charlie whined. "I know. I just wanted to get burgers with you."

The sincerity of that was so cute that her smile broadened. This guy was a little charmer already.

"Are you sweet talking me, cutie?" Baer looked up again. Holly was engrossed, so Freya didn't mind mouthing, "I love him."

Rolling his eyes, he went back to the profiles with Holly.

Charlie spoke again, faster this time. "No! No, I... I mean it, Freya, I do... You're so pretty and you're so nice to us and—"

"Okay," she said on a laugh. "Don't belabor it... You can have him. Give Baer time to take me home and then he'll come over and help you, okay?"

"Really?" Charlie asked, both amazed and thankful. There was a moment of silence before he followed it with, "Won't he want sex?"

These kids just said it like they saw it; she loved that about them. "Yes. I don't doubt that he will," she said. "Doesn't mean he'll get it. Leave your books on the dinner table and go back to bed. He'll wake you when he gets there."

"Wow, Freya, you're like the best girlfriend ever," Charlie said. "Not like Claire at all." She squinted. Was that a compliment to her or an insult to his brother? "Are you going to marry Baer? It would be cool if you moved in."

Although they lived in separate spaces, the family did all live in the same building. The question was so optimistic. Baer was watching her; she couldn't bring herself to smile.

"I don't know, honey. We haven't talked about that."

"I hope you do," Charlie said. "I'm sorry I said I'd tell Presley about you having sex today."

Sheesh, that was that same day? It felt like so long ago she'd been ensconced in Baer's bed, maybe because she was so eager to be back there.

"That's okay, honey."

"No, seriously, after this, I'll be like... I'll be your best friend forever, Freya... Baer won't tell dad, right?"

Tucking her hair behind her ear, she lowered her chin and volume. "I'll ask him not to... but you can't lie anymore, okay? Not to anyone."

"Not even to Pres about you and Baer doing it?"

"Baer will talk to him about that."

"He will? 'Cause I think he'll be mad."

"If he's mad at anyone, he should be mad at me," she said. "Want me to walk you home tomorrow?"

"You could talk to him then," Charlie said, then a sneer touched his voice. "But do it at home, okay? 'Cause I don't wanna be there."

"Okay, honey."

"And will you make steak for dinner?"

If she made it for Abel and Baer in the morning, Abel might not want more for dinner. She could throw something else together for him. Baer would be out on his dinner date.

"We'll see," she said. "I'll rustle up something."

"You're the best, Freya."

Getting close to this family hadn't been her plan, but she was falling for all of them. Dangerous. Her and Baer's relationship wasn't exactly defined... or secure.

"Get some rest, honey. Baer will be there soon. Goodnight."

Hanging up his phone, her gaze drifted toward Baer again. There was something curious about his intense look. Holly interrupted it with a question. Just a minute or two later, the car stopped. They said goodbye and Holly slipped off home, more optimistic than earlier. That was something.

Baer came to sit beside her when the car started moving again.

"We only have a few minutes," she said when he tried to kiss her. "You have to go home."

"Everything okay?" he asked, leaning back, keeping his hand under her chin to raise it. "Thought it was your boyfriend, scenting you or something."

Twisting toward him, she slid down in the seat, resting her head against the back. "It was my boyfriend's brother," she said, smoothing his shirt. "He needs help with the homework he didn't tell his dad about..." She peeked at him. "I said you'd go over and help him..." Cringing, she braced for a potentially negative reaction. "He doesn't want you to tell Abel."

"Hey, at least the kid's trying to do the homework. I'd have fed my teacher a line."

"I believe that," she said, smiling when he slouched to lay his head on the back of the seat by hers. "I told him I'd talk to Presley too... He thinks we're cheating on him."

"I'll talk to the kid—"

"No, it's okay. I'll do it," she said. "I should've known better than to play brothers off each other."

"Can't help yourself around me, that's all," he said, edging closer until their mouths met.

The back of a car wasn't a bad place to live. First, she'd been happy to sleep there, now she'd be happy to reside there forevermore, basking in the mouth of the man pampering her.

His fingertips crept onto her knee, higher, higher, under the hem of her dress.

She caught them under the fabric and broke the kiss. "Baer—"

"Relax, baby. I'll make you come. That's all. I can make you feel good."

She didn't doubt that but didn't want him going over to his family's apartment with... *her* all over him. Leaving him in the car would be hard enough, him pleasuring her wouldn't make it any easier.

"You know the rules... And we're only a couple of blocks from mine."

His hand left her skirt to skim over her waist. "You could invite me in."

Though the privacy screen was up, she glanced toward the front like the driver might hear them. "You know we can't do that. I told you no sex while you're being paid to be with me."

"I'll pay you," he said, an unfamiliar edge of desperation in his voice. She crooked a brow. "You know what I mean, baby. This isn't about the money, Lil'."

"It doesn't matter anyway." Righting her skirt, she sat straighter. "You have to go and help Charlie."

"You could come back to mine."

Though appreciated, she had to be wary of his enthusiasm. "Are you like this with all your reluctant dates, Mr. Claymore?"

"Clayton," he said, sitting up, abandoning his seduction.

Uh… "What?"

"I use my real first name, though I spell it differently when I'm with dates. I try not to use any last name. But, if I have to, it's Clayton."

A fake name. Of course he needed a fake name in his line of work.

"And you didn't think to tell me that? I'll need to introduce you to my family. What if I'd used the wrong name?"

"Holly's last date is Tuesday. After she picks a guy, we'll have a meeting with Conrad, get our stories straight."

"I thought we weren't using prep sheets."

"We'll have our own private prep session after, Lil' Skit," he said, running a hand up her leg.

She stroked his face to guide their mouths together. "God, this is complicated," she whispered on their kiss.

All she wanted was to be with this man. Life was never as simple as that. She'd have to introduce him to her family but mislead them about his true identity. If it worked out between them, then what? She'd confess what he did for a living? What if Baer didn't want that? His family didn't know, why would he want her family to know?

Kissing him felt so right, so good, giving this up, whether in a week or a year, wouldn't be easy.

# NINETEEN

THE FINAL DATE with Lyon went better than all the others combined. Thank you, Baer. Holly now had a plus-one for their vacation. On the Wednesday, the two of them did the paperwork at Squires, then Conrad showed them to a large private room with couches and a bar. An entertaining space all to themselves.

"Make yourselves comfortable," he said, heading out. "I'll be back in a while."

Left alone, she wasn't entirely sure what would come next.

"Should we get drunk?" Holly asked, going over to the bar.

Freya went to the couch and bent to unbuckle her shoes. "Conrad said we could spend as much time in here as we have to tonight."

Hunting through bottles, Holly flashed her a grin. "We have our men for the whole night... You know what that means."

For Holly maybe. Not for her.

Monday past, she'd held good on her promise to cook brunch for Baer and Abel. The latter regarded them with some kind of... something in his expression. Were they suddenly so peculiar?

Meeting the boys from school had been fun until she sat with Presley to tell him they couldn't be boyfriend and girlfriend anymore. She'd asked permission to see Baer socially, Presley wanted time to think about it.

Fair request.

Because they didn't see each other the night of that conversation, it had been their date on Tuesday before she could fill Baer in on the development. He'd promised to talk to his little brother and that was the last she'd heard about it.

Baer came in with Lyon not far behind.

"Holly," Baer said in greeting then came straight to her.

Dropping onto the couch with a tired exhale, he was quick to slide into a slouch.

"You look tired," she said, moving onto her knees to touch her lips to the corner of his.

Closing his eyes, a wry smile appeared. "Could do with a vacation."

"Good thing you met me then," she said, loosening his tie and undoing some of his shirt buttons. "You could've changed before you got here. Was your dinner good?"

He'd eaten with another woman. Whether or not he'd been required to eat the woman too... she wouldn't ask.

"The food was good."

That was as nice an answer as he could probably give.

"Take off your jacket," she said, pulling at his lapel. "You can go and change if you want, I'll wait."

"No, I'm good." He slid an arm around her to stop her fussing. "Come give me a proper hello."

After a longer, slower, more intimate kiss, he seemed to relax. Good. She offered some benefit.

Opening his eyes to slits, he caught a section of her hair between two fingers and tucked it behind her ear. "How are you, Lil' Skit?"

"Did you talk to Pres?"

He nodded. "He says we're good so long as we don't flaunt it in front of him."

Tucking her feet to the side, she rested an elbow on the back of the couch under the arm he lay along it. "We'll be gone for two weeks, so…" the youngster wouldn't have to see them together for that. "I do feel awful though."

"Shouldn't have fallen for me," he said, exhaling and stretching to lock his fingers behind his head.

Pushing off the back of the couch, she lifted a knee over his lap, surprising him with her straddling.

Scooping his hands onto her ass, he blinked at her.

Her answer to his unasked query was a saucy smile. "You're just so irresistible."

"This went a new, and damn good, way fast," he said, skimming a hand up her back to lose it in her hair.

Pulling her down, he kissed her.

She resisted just enough and leaned back to nuzzle his mouth. "How does it look like they're getting along?"

The other couple, he probably wasn't expecting her concern.

Still, his eyes shifted past her shoulder to check. "She's a little nervous, little awkward."

"I feel like we should give them some privacy."

"We're supposed to be getting our stories straight," he said, combing his fingers through her hair, using her locks as cover to cup and squeeze her breast. "Not getting fresh."

"We don't have to worry about our story," she said. "You're Baer Clayton, we've been seeing each other a while, not sure if we're serious."

"Yeah?" he asked. "What do I do for a living? Do I have family?" Her mouth opened, but she had nothing. "Mm, yeah, Lil' Skit, not so confident."

Crunching up, he plumped the swell of her breast above the neckline of her dress and sucked her warm flesh.

"Well, there's no time for the heavy petting stuff now you've said that," she said, swatting him away, climbing off his lap to put a foot of space between them. "Teach me."

"Are you kidding? I just talked myself out of sex?"

"We weren't going to have sex," she said. "Tell me about Baer Clayton… please."

Drawing in an almost grumpy breath, he huffed it out. "Actually, you have to tell me… We have various profiles you can pick from, or you can make one of your own…" He opened his arms, letting his hands flop onto the couch. "I am whatever you want me to be."

That was… There was only one thing she wanted him to be.

"Huh, maybe this wasn't such a good idea."

Sensing her confusion, he slid a hand to her face, directing her focus to his. "What's wrong, Little Skit? Talk to me. What do you want me to be?" He smiled and ran his thumb across her lip. "It won't upset me. I've been just about everything, and I still have time to do research if you want me to be something—"

"I want you to be you," she said. "Except, I know I can't ask that of you… I don't want you to be anything you're not… But if we tell my family what you do—"

"That I'm a hooker?"

She frowned. "I'm not ashamed of you, Baer, or what you do." Though it was a little rich of him to be curt with her about it when he hadn't told his own family what he did. "I know why you do it and I have a lot of respect for that. I can't even imagine the position you're in."

"I don't need your approval," he said, shifting to sit straight. "But having it means something to me."

Oh, uh… no fight? She'd expected conflict, yet all she read in him was acceptance.

"Conrad said he was coming back." She got closer so she could whisper. "We're in a really difficult position, Hound. No one knows about us."

"I know."

"I can't ask you to be honest about your family and your personal business because that reveals Lyon too… Even if it didn't, it's not my place to—"

"It is your place, sweetheart," he said, stroking her face again. "But I understand your point…" He exhaled. "Come over here, give me a minute to think about it."

Scooping an arm around her waist, he pulled her body against his.

She rested her head on his shoulder. "I'm looking forward to having you to myself for two weeks," she admitted, caressing his chest. Shame about, you know, the inconvenience of her family. Maybe they would keep her honest. "My Baer."

For two weeks only.

"There are beds through the back if you want to claim—"

She slapped his chest, which granted her his laugh just as Conrad entered carrying two tablets.

"Okay," the boss declared. "Let's create our relationships."

Holly and Lyon came over to sit nearby while Conrad moved a seat across to face them like they were in some kind of impromptu therapy session.

"I'm nervous," Holly said. "Is it weird that I'm nervous?"

"Perfectly normal," Lyon said.

She was nervous too, but not for herself. There was a foot of space between Lyon and Holly; they couldn't look any less like a couple. Baer was stretched out next to her, slouched on the couch with his shoulder blades against the back and his legs straight, crossed at the ankle. With his arm relaxed along the backrest behind her, he included her as an extension of his being. He looked like someone's boyfriend, her boyfriend, he couldn't be more at ease.

Holly and Lyon, who were supposed to be an established couple, were awkward and ill-at-ease. This was bad. Holly had been talking about her 'Paul' for more than a month. If they didn't pull this off…

Laying a hand on Baer's thigh, she couldn't be more grateful for him. Until Baer, the idea of this vacation was not a happy one. Now, with Baer, she was kind of looking forward to it.

Twisting around, she joined their lips and brushed her nose over his, tempting his mouth to give her more.

"Uh…" Conrad said. "Plenty of time for that after we get the formalities out of the way."

"Let the woman work," Baer said, coiling an arm around her waist to hold her tighter. "You okay, Lil'?"

"What did you do before this? Before you did this?"

"Different things," he said. "Mostly carpentry. I was a personal trainer at a couple of gyms, worked security at clubs."

Considering it for just a second, she pushed her lips to the side. "Carpentry. Let's go with that."

"Carpentry?" Holly distracted her from Baer. When she laid her head on his chest, Baer's hand moved into her hair, stroking her over and over. "You could pick any job in the whole wide world, why would you want to be with a carpenter?"

Baer's hand stopped on her crown.

"Because if we say he's a personal trainer or works security someone might ask where. They might have a connection to any place we lie about. They might go there or know someone who works there. Carpentry is perfect because it doesn't have to be done at a specific location, he can be self-employed, doing jobs as and when... perfect."

"And if someone breaks a chair?" Holly asked.

"He can fix it."

"How do you know he can—"

"If he can build a chair from scratch, he can fix a broken one."

Her cousin frowned. "How do you know he can build a chair?"

Oh, yeah, another thing she wasn't supposed to know.

"I told her," Baer said with unexpected tension.

Not a lie, he had confirmed he'd built the chair she'd seen in his bedroom. Smoothing her hand down his torso, she hoped to soothe but didn't know what aggravated him.

"So we're good," she said. "Your turn, Hol."

"Lil'," Baer said, stroking her again. "I can be whatever you want me to be. If you need me to talk stocks and shares and—"

"Hound, there are important things we can fight about later. This is not important."

He didn't say anything else but must have put some sense of anticipation on the other couple because Holly suddenly straightened. "Oh, I... I already told my family about my boyfriend."

"Paul," Baer said. "Right."

Conrad held up the tablets. "That's why I have these." He handed one to Holly and the other to her. "There is a list of suggestions for things you'll want to consider, everything from family to daily habits to likes and dislikes, political views, fill in as much as you can. It will give our guys a quick reference guide to what they need to be."

Reading over the list at the top of the tablet, she was surprised by how much they could dictate. Then again, they were paying a ridiculous amount of money. It became clear right then that they weren't just paying for sex or companionship, these men had to be actors twenty-four seven.

Turning a grin on Baer, she curled her legs under her. "Will you get me a drink, please, baby? This might take a while."

"Geez," he said, leaning in to kiss her forehead. "I'm already scared to read it."

Lyon and Conrad joined Baer at the bar.

Taking the stylus from the top of the tablet, she got to work. Holly scribbled kind of furiously; her stress level didn't match. This should be fun, not a slog. Though, admittedly, she didn't have as much at stake.

When Baer brought her drink, she hugged the tablet to her chest so he couldn't see it. He laughed and kissed her. Nothing wrong with hamming it up.

Almost forty-five minutes went by before Conrad came back over. "How are you ladies doing? Can we start talking now?"

"I... uh... sure," Holly said, still writing.

They couldn't spend the whole night on their tablets, Conrad probably had better things to do. Baer came over with a fresh drink for her.

"If you're ready," the boss said, "hand the tablets to your dates and let them read your requirements. This is the time to clarify any points they don't understand."

She and Holly made eye contact, then handed over their tablets in unison. Lyon's eyes bugged. He blew out a breath and straightened to concentrate. While she... didn't want to look at Baer. Oh, but she had to. First thing he did was frown.

He looked over the top of the tablet at her. "Really?" he asked. "Are you shitting me?"

She shrugged and hooked an arm over the backrest.

"We can talk about anything, any points of disagreement," Conrad said. "If there's something outside our guy's purview, we'll find a compromise."

"She wrote two damn words," Baer said, reaching beyond her to hand the tablet to Conrad. Sweeping her hair from her shoulder, he cupped her face. "Lil' Skit—"

"Be yourself," Conrad read from her tablet. "Huh... That's a new one."

Baer was kind of staring her down.

Diverting herself, she pointed the stylus at the tablet. "Do you like my flowers?" She'd covered the bottom of the screen with a field of purple daisies. "They're my favorites."

"Freya, I'm not sure that..." Conrad looked past her at Baer. "Are you okay with this?"

"Okay with not pretending I only drink Cristal or am a proud Republican?" Baer asked and shrugged. "It's easy to remember."

"Yeah, but what about family?"

"I'd suggest we keep that vague," she said, looking to Conrad who had to be seeking a balance between protecting his employee and satisfying a client. "His parents are living, two brothers, that's all anyone needs to know."

Conrad's frown became more discerning, then seemed almost concerned as he tipped his head to the side to look closer at Baer. "There's something going on here I don't know about, isn't there?"

"Don't worry about it," Baer said, resting a hand on her back.

What an idiot! She wasn't supposed to know anything about Baer's personal life, yet she kept opening her big blabbering mouth. And Conrad was his boss. His boss! The worst part was, she knew exactly why she was doing it, and it was so immature and ridiculous that she wanted to slap herself.

Standing up, she smoothed her skirt. "Would you excuse me for a moment?" Taking her purse off the couch, she went for the door. "Please carry on without me."

It didn't matter if she knew all the details of Holly and Lyon's relationship. Holly already told her a lot about the imaginary guy anyway. For everything else, she'd vamp… not that she was good at that. Probably better to play dumb, if necessary.

She didn't stop walking until reaching the entry foyer. Actually, even when she got there, she didn't stop, she just turned to cross ten feet, then returned, pacing back and forth

It was nuts. This was easy. Should be easy. It wasn't like she couldn't be discreet in other areas of her life. She could. She could keep a confidence. This shouldn't be difficult.

"Lil'?"

Baer's voice turned her around.

She immediately held up a hand. "Don't, okay? I know. I'm sorry."

"Sorry for what?" he asked, coming to her. "Baby, you have nothing to apologize for."

"That, in there," she said, opening a hand in the direction he'd come as he laid his hands on her shoulders. "It's like I can't help myself." And he'd joked about Presley scenting her, wasn't that exactly what she was doing to Baer? And for what reason? Pique? Pride? Ego? "I shouldn't have... I'm not supposed to—"

"Hey," he said, bending his knees to bring himself closer to her level. "Lil', if you want to go in there and tell Conrad—"

"No," she said, shaking her head. "I won't risk your career here."

He laughed. "Babe, this is not a career, not for me." Skimming his hands down her upper arms and back up, he brought their bodies closer together. "I never planned to do this forever. You know why I do it."

She couldn't call herself his girlfriend. Couldn't use the word love. But she was certain this wasn't normal procedure.

"Is this against the rules?" she asked, almost afraid to meet his eye. "Whatever this is... will it get you into trouble?"

"No one can make rules about who someone falls for," he said, cradling her cheek. "Don't worry so much."

"I do worry," she said, pulling his hand away. "If you lose this job... where does that leave you? How will you make the money you need to support your family?"

"This isn't the only agency in town."

Surprised, she blinked at him. "There are... others?"

He nodded. "But I'm popular here. I make a lot of money for the agency... Some of the guys have wives, most have girlfriends, occasionally more than one. There's no rule that says I have to be single."

"But we met here," she said. "I'm a client."

"This started before you were my client... I know you're worried about me," he said, a slow smile rising on his lips. "Are you worried enough to dump me?"

She wasn't sure she was his current, let alone being an ex. "Dump you?" she asked. "Wouldn't that be kind of awkward? Your ex hiring you?"

"Long as it was you and you relaxed your sex rules, I'd be okay with that."

Opening her hands on his obliques, she ran them around to his back, sinking against him. "Everything will be better next week."

"Next week," he said. "During our no sex vacation?"

Tipping her head back, her drowsy eyes met his. "I've dreamed about falling asleep in your arms... waking up with you every day."

Wearing a smile, he hooked her hair away from her temple. "You know where I sleep, baby."

She exhaled. "I don't actually. I know where your bed is... Not where you are. I never know whose bed you'll be in."

"You know there's only one bed I'd choose to be in," he said. "I don't say it... I haven't said it... But I do appreciate that you're... understanding."

"That I don't demand you give this up," she said. "I'd be lying if I said I hadn't thought about how much easier life would be if this wasn't a part of it."

"It won't be," he said. "Not forever." Resting her head on his chest again, she sank into their embrace. "Want to get out of here? We can get caught up about Holly and Lyon whenever."

Smiling, she stayed put. "You know you're not getting laid. You're being paid to be with me all night."

"Until six a.m.," he said. "Believe me, I'm counting the minutes."

"How is your schedule this week?"

"Nothing tomorrow," he said. "I have two clients Friday... and there are some maintenance jobs I'll need to do before we leave."

"And you have to pack," she said. "Good thing you have tomorrow off."

"Believe me, that was no accident," he said, kissing the top of her head. "Come on, I'll take you home."

Breaking their embrace, he laced their fingers together to lead them the way of the elevator.

"I want dessert," she said. Stopping to peer over his shoulder, he narrowed his eyes. She laughed. "Actual dessert, Hound... Take me out for coffee and cake."

"What do I get?"

"The pleasure of my company," she said, deliberately not mentioning that he was being paid to entertain her. Stepping in close, she pouted at him. "And I'll let you cop a feel when you kiss me goodnight."

"Sold," he said, picking up her hand to kiss her knuckles. "I'll go talk to Conrad. Wait here."

Watching him go, she breathed out. This complicated and messy and wonderful and frustrating. Whoa, boy...

# TWENTY

SIX A.M.

Woken by pounding on her front door, it took a few seconds to register what was going on. Wait, what was going on?

After cake and more than one coffee, Baer brought her home. Okay, she remembered that. The all-night diner meant no impetus to say goodnight. She'd have stayed forever if Baer hadn't declared they were leaving around three a.m.

Pounding. Right. The door.

Something may have happened to her grandfather or one of her foundation kids. She grabbed her robe and ran to the door, heart hammering.

She opened it and—was brought up short.

The man standing on her threshold, hands braced on each side of her doorframe, head drooped, was the same one she'd said goodnight to less than three hours ago.

Confusion instantly became fear. "Baer," she said, overwhelmed by panic. "Oh my God, is it the boys?

I'll authorize whatever you need. Let me get dressed and—"

She started to turn, but he grabbed her arm, holding her there.

The strain on his expression came with no words, not for ten seconds, not for twenty, until...

"I have to... I have to know what it's like."

"What what's like?" she asked, stroking his hair from his temple. "What's wrong, Hound?"

"I have no clients today," he said, showing her his watch. "And I waited until six... No one's paying me to be here."

What did that mean? "I don't know what you... How did you get in here?"

The building was supposed to be manned by security twenty-four hours a day. Only Truman and Roxie were allowed to just stride up to her apartment. Not that she had a problem with Baer visiting.

"I never left," he said. "I wanted you to get some rest. It's been less than three hours; I didn't mean to keep you out so late. But I waited until after six..."

He'd wanted to take her home from Squires, she'd pushed for the dessert. If anyone should be sorry for them being out late—none of that explained his presence. After six. Her rules. After six. No one paying him. Not being with anyone else on the same day...

"Sex," she whispered, catching up with his train of thought.

"Yes, please," he said, trying to smile through his taut tension. "Lil', if you just let me hold you..."

"I don't have protection. I haven't—"

He dug a hand into his pocket to produce a strip of condoms. Hmm, prepared, impressive.

She breathed out a laugh. "It's wrong that I find that sweet," she said and cocked a hip. "I'll let you come in here and take whatever you want from my body on one condition."

He groaned, teeth clenched. "Goddamn your conditions."

She just laid a disapproving eye on him. "Did you hear me say you could take whatever you want from my body?"

"Okay," he said. "Yes. Condition. What condition?"

Gathering his hands in hers, she walked backward, leading him into her apartment. "You keep doing it until midnight."

"Midnight?"

When he kicked the door closed behind him, she heard it lock and pushed his jacket from his shoulders.

"Yes." Friday was a workday, he had clients, meaning they couldn't do it after midnight. "I don't want a quickie. I want you all to myself all day. No money." She kept on going, the bedroom not far behind her. "Be mine today, Baer. For free. Just us."

"Just us," he said, tugging her forward so hard they collided. "Those are conditions I like."

Loosening her robe, he dropped his eyes to her body when the material fluttered open. Of all the hundreds of naked females he must've seen, she had to believe she was special, and she did. Some part of her did believe that. With complete conviction. As he slipped his fingers under the fabric on her shoulders to ease it off, she wasn't self-conscious.

Naked under his scrutiny, desperate to pause the moment forever, she didn't want to breathe. The hunger in his devouring gaze whipped her arousal into a frenzy.

"I need you, Frey," he murmured in an almost growl. "Goddamnit, I've never needed anything more in my life."

She edged forward to unbuckle his belt. "I'm right here, Hound Dog."

He'd showered and changed into his jeans and tee-shirt at Squires before they went for coffee. That he was still wearing the same outfit confirmed he really hadn't left her building since bringing her home. He'd known this would happen. Wanted this. Planned this. He'd been in the damn corridor outside her apartment thinking about it for three hours. Wow. Now that was dedication. And she talked about resolve?

"Goddamn, baby."

Need stretched his restraint. The man could get laid twenty-four seven, yet she had that effect on him. Flattering. Humbling. Arousing. This wasn't sex for the sake of sex, he could get that anywhere. Hell, he was paid for it almost every day.

"I'm right here," she said, pushing his jeans and underwear down. "And I'm all yours."

Sinking onto her knees, she took him into her mouth. Most women probably wouldn't elect to do this for him. Some might. But he was paid to take care of his clients' needs. She wasn't a client, not there in that moment.

Doing her best to pleasure him, she licked and sucked, tasting him, learning him—he bent to grab her up and tossed her onto the bed.

"Please don't make me embarrass myself," he said, shedding the rest of his clothes, so he was naked when he crawled onto the bed above her.

"What does that mean?" she asked, looping her arms around his neck when he bowed to kiss her. "Being with me is embarrassing?"

"Losing my wad within two minutes of you putting your mouth on me," he said, running his lips down her chin. "Yeah, that's embarrassing... Let me worship you a while."

"You haven't slept since yesterday, if you want to rest before…"

Raising his mouth from her throat, he glared at her. "You think I'm missing a minute of this, you're insane, Little Skit. This is all I've thought about… all I want."

Stroking his face, she ran her hands into his hair. "All you want?"

"All I want," he said and kissed her. "You've gotta know I'm falling hard for you, baby… And if life was different… if my life was different—"

Laying a straight finger on his lips, she silenced him. "We'll get there, baby. We will."

"We will… God, you're amazing," he said and kissed her again.

His tongue didn't linger in her mouth, he slid it to her chest, pampering her breasts before descending to the apex of her thighs. Appreciating the skill of his mouth and the sensations of his talented tongue, she let him tease and arouse her just enough. Until, curling her fingers in his hair, she started to close her thighs as she pulled him up.

"What's wrong?" he asked, his mouth above her stomach.

"You're not working, Hound," she said, smiling at him, caressing his face.

"I know," he said on an exhale. "I want to. Let me—"

"No." She tightened her grip on his head and flattened her feet on his back, closing her thighs around his head for a second. "I am the one woman on the planet you are not obliged to eat on demand."

"I want to," he said, growing frustrated. "Would you trust me to know what I want, please?"

"You don't want to be inside me? Because that's what I want... I want my man inside me, deep inside me."

Pushing her legs from his shoulders, he rose over her, touching his lips to hers. "Because you're determined to race to the finish. I want to enjoy this."

"You promised you'd be here until midnight," she said, stroking any part of him within reach. "We have time for that later... Get a condom... Please... I want you... I need you."

Gritting his teeth, he growled. "You're too damn good at this."

Boosting away from her, he shifted to the end of the bed and dug in his pocket for the condoms. She was too good at it? This was his job and she'd never been undone by a man so quickly. If she'd let him finish her, not only would she have felt guilty, but she probably wouldn't have had the energy to participate in what came after.

"You're going to regret this," he said as he flipped back over on top of her, rolling the condom on as he did.

"I am?" she asked. "Why would—" Her words disappeared into the sharp gasp that filled her lungs when he plunged into her. "Oh, fuck!" A sinister kind of laugh warmed her lips; she smacked his shoulder. "What happened to gentle?"

"Don't have to be gentle with you," he said. "Isn't that what you keep telling me? You're not a client I can offend, who I have to worry about switching to a different guy if I don't live up to their standards."

Panting through the pulse of painful pleasure engorging her, she might split in two and he hadn't even got all the way inside her yet.

"So because…" she hissed, sucking in another breath. "Because I'm crazy about you… I get nothing but the raw Baer experience?"

One side of his mouth curled. "Got it in one, baby," he said, pushing deeper then bowing to kiss her when she puffed out another breath. "I'm not interchangeable for you like I am for them… You get me and nothing but me."

There was nothing, and no one, else she wanted.

Her nails bit into him. "Promise me," she said, wrapping her legs around him. "Promise me, Hound."

"I promise.

"Oh, thank God! Fuck me, Baer… Make me yours…"

"All mine," he said, plunging his tongue into her mouth as he forced himself deep into her.

Lost in the most intense sexual experience of her life, the burn of need pounded. He'd be the last man to ever occupy her like this. It was nuts to think it during their first sexual encounter, and maybe she'd change her mind in the light of a new day, but this was what she wanted. He was what she wanted. Him and nothing else.

# TWENTY-ONE

"DON'T PANIC," Baer said as he strode toward her in the airport lounge.

Panic? Why would that be the first thing he said?

Uncrossing her legs, she stood up next to her carry-on bag and opened her arms when he slid his hands onto her waist. "What's wrong?"

Having not seen him since he left her apartment at midnight after their day in bed together, his comment could pertain to a whole host of things.

"Where's Holly?" he asked. "Is she here?"

Nodding, she glanced to the side. "She's in the restroom. I was waiting for you. You're late. The flight leaves in half an hour... Where's Lyon?"

"You look beautiful," he said and dipped in an attempt to kiss her. Uh, no, answers first, she bowed backwards. "You won't let me say hello to you? Lil', I've thought about nothing but you since—"

"Lyon?"

It was difficult not to be flattered by such a man admitting he was enamored. Except he'd had other dates since leaving her place. She wasn't wild on the idea of him thinking about her when with other women.

"He was in a car accident," Baer said.

Grabbing for him, she gasped. "Oh my God! Is he okay?"

"He's in the hospital. Don't panic, Conrad took care of it."

"Took care of it." She didn't follow. "What does that mean?"

"Hey, Royal!"

"Donoghue?"

She couldn't believe this was happening.

"Best Conrad could come up with at short notice," Baer muttered, easing her in to rest his mouth in her hair. "I'm just glad the bastard's not your date."

"Way things are going I'm beginning to regret having a date at all," she said, pushing him aside to set a smile on Donoghue. "Hello!"

"Nice setup," he said, scanning the first-class lounge as he sauntered over. "Not too shabby."

She accepted his kiss on her cheek. "Thank you for stepping in."

"Not a problem," he said, putting an arm around her. "I got the skinny. I'm ready for this."

"Ready?" Freya asked, unconvinced by the man's confidence.

Just then movement drew her attention. Simultaneously, she spied her cousin coming out of the restroom, and the latter noticed the people with her. Neither of the men were her expected date. Okay, don't panic.

"I got this," Donoghue said, kissing her cheek again before striding away, arms open to Holly.

Watching, waiting for her cousin's reaction, she didn't blink until Baer rubbed her cheek with the cuff of his jacket.

She swatted at him. "What are you doing?"

"You shouldn't let him kiss you."

"Hound…" With an arm around her, he guided her away from the couple outside the restroom. "This won't work, it can't work."

"It will work," Baer said. "Don't worry so much."

"How can you be calm about this?"

"I've been doing this a while," he said. "It's not always so bad when a match isn't perfect. 'Specially when that match isn't heading to the altar."

That jarred her doubts to a halt in a swift redirect.

With the other couple a distant memory, he got all of her. "What is that supposed to mean?"

His ease became a frown. "Holly's not going to marry Donoghue any more than she was going to marry Lyon."

"How do you know?" she asked, stepping away to fold her arms.

"Because women who use escorts…"

He trailed off as offended incredulity tilted her head.

"What? Women who use escorts what? Please finish that sentence, Mr. Clayton."

He didn't miss her deliberate use of his alias.

"Okay…" he said, trying to lay a hand on her shoulder. She avoided it with another backward step. "I want you to remember that I have not been in a real relationship for a long time. A very long time. So if I open my big stupid mouth and upset you—"

"Frey!"

Spinning around, she found her cousin storming across the private lounge. Leaving Baer, she hurried to meet Holly halfway.

"It's okay," Freya said. "Whatever you want to do, we'll do."

"Donoghue's hot." Holly grabbed both her hands. "Am I being swayed because I think he'd be fire in the sack?"

Huh, that was unexpected.

Processing, she sought direction. "You want to go on vacation with a boyfriend, there's a guy here willing to play the role. You don't want it to be Donoghue? We'll send them both away."

Going without Baer would be payback for her judging his unfinished sentence so quickly.

Holly breathed out and looked past her. "Why do you and Baer have to be so perfect together?"

"I just jumped down his throat; I don't know how perfect we are right now."

"Wanna trade?"

Even though Holly's smile was sheepish, no way her cousin didn't already know that answer. Baer would be brilliant in the role of besotted boyfriend, no matter who he was with. But Freya couldn't imagine much worse than lying in a bed next to Donoghue thinking about Baer in bed with Holly. And under the same roof too.

Though, after how Baer reacted to Donoghue kissing her cheek, she wasn't so sure Baer would be the consummate professional if there was another man in her bed.

Donoghue was at least smart enough to give the women a wide berth as he passed to join Baer. At least she guessed that's where he was going, she didn't check.

"What do you want to do?"

"We have no choice," Holly said. "Not really... Dad thinks we're bringing our boyfriends."

"Does Donoghue know he's supposed to be Paul?"

Drawing in air through her nose, Holly tensed. "Oh God, there's so much we have to cover."

The guys were supposed to take the notes from the meeting and spend some time memorizing the details. Donoghue hadn't had the time to do that, as far as they knew.

"You have to trust your gut," Freya said.

"Miss Dere?" Her attention was drawn to an approaching attendant. "We're boarding first class; would you like us to take your carry on aboard?"

"Yes, please," she said, keeping one of Holly's hands. "So…" All expectation landed on her cousin. "What do you want to do?"

# TWENTY-TWO

THE FLIGHT WAS uneventful. Rather than sit with their dates, the women sat together. At Holly's request, Baer used the time to prep his colleague. Her point was fair, Baer knew the kind of things a man had to know about his date and what could slide by unknown. A boyfriend didn't know every single thing about his girlfriend. It was possible to be too prepared. Some things should elude him.

After disembarking, their bags were put into the waiting limo and then they were on the road.

"This is some way to live, Royal," Donoghue said, pouring champagne into flutes first for the women, then for himself and Baer.

"It's the way Truman wants Frey to live," Holly said, gesturing around the cabin. "No way I could afford any of this." After sipping her champagne, she laughed. "Why do you think I stick so close to wonderful Freya?"

Holly raised the flute at her and Donoghue copied. Freya could only muster a polite half smile. She didn't even bother to drink any champagne and instead put it on the shelf above the fridge. Baer did the same then slouched at her side. Credit where it was due, Donoghue was doing his best to distract Holly from the hiccup of losing her intended fake boyfriend.

"I'm sorry," Baer mumbled by her ear.

Having been fixated on deciphering how convincing a couple Holly and Donoghue made, her own date managed to sneak up on her. She wasn't sorry to find him only a couple of inches away. She *was* sorry to see the apology in his gaze.

"No," she said, spreading her fingers on his thigh. "I'm stressed about this stupid trip. A family vacation is my idea of a nightmare and with everything else…"

"Squires fucking up your fake love lives—"

"Hey," she said, twisting further around, digging her nails into his thigh. "You're about the only person in the world keeping me sane right now. This isn't fake…" Not that she was ready for his agreement or rejection. Her attention descended to her caress. "That's probably against your golden rule."

"My golden rule?"

Her hand rose to his cheek. "Falling for a man paid to appear in love. I said the day we met you had to be good at faking it to do this job."

"I don't fake anything with you. I'm sorry for being insensitive."

"You don't do this job to have women fall helplessly for you. I know why you do it. I understand that."

"Everything was fine when I left you the other night," he said. "You were smiling… I thought I made you happy."

"You do make me happy… That day was probably the best of my life."

"You don't look happy today." He caught her hand to press his mouth to her palm. "Talk to me, Lil'."

"I just... I guess it made me aware of what I can't have," she said, watching him kiss her fingertips.

"You have me, babe," he said, mesmerized by her skin. "God, I don't think I could fall any harder."

The point of him coming was for them to get to know each other. They weren't supposed to be so entangled already, though she couldn't regret it. Finding a man to adore, who adored her in return, wasn't a negative. She knew better than to be pessimistic. Losing her parents young taught her the virtue of appreciating what was right in front of her. Right now, that was Baer. Those she loved could be ripped away at any moment. The idea of losing Baer was so sickening that she chased it away fast.

Linking their fingers, she brought their joined hands to her lap. "I didn't want to use Squires. I was reluctant... scared." This wasn't news, he'd been there. "It's not the kind of thing I'd ever have thought of myself. Holly's colleague put her in touch with the agency... I didn't think I was, but... It turns out I am a woman who uses escorts."

"No," he said, strengthening his hold on her hand while using the other to sweep her hair from her face. "Don't think of me like that, of us like that. If it's upsetting you, I'll call Conrad and cancel—"

"No..." Shaking her head, she sat straighter. "I don't think of us like that."

And she couldn't do it to Holly. After bringing the guys all the way there, it would be killer to send them back and leave Holly empty-handed. Pasting on a smile, she pushed aside her misgivings.

"If it's jealousy, other women don't—"

"No," she said, cutting him off again and widening her smile. "Can we just forget I was snappy today and go back to adoring each other?"

His gaze dropped to her mouth; he swallowed hard. Had she missed something? Caught up in her own swirling thoughts, she hadn't taken time to ask how he'd felt since they were together and if everything was okay in his life.

"What about you?" This wasn't only about her. "Do… Do I make you happy?"

"You…?" He scoffed. "I can't get you out of my head, Lil' Skit… You're the most incredible—yes, you make me happy. But the things I can't give you…"

All she needed was him. Dangerous? Yes, but it was the truth.

"Don't think about that," she said, pushing up to trace her mouth over his. "Think about lying in bed with me… about how happy you make me."

Because in her bed, she'd been happy with him. They'd both been happy. It was only in waking alone that she faced the reality of being with him.

He got even closer. "I do that and I'll embarrass myself here in the fancy car."

Freya pressed herself against him. "We'll wake up next to each other for the next two weeks."

And then maybe never again. She wouldn't relax her smile or give him any more cause for concern, but how would it be? For the next two weeks, they'd have each other every minute. Be spoiled with each other. Real or not, they would belong to each other for the duration of their stay. And when they got home, they'd go back to how things were. He'd return to Squires and she would wake alone.

"Baer, hey," Donaghue said. "Holly says this place is on like this massive estate. It's this big building made to look like some fancy country house or something, divided up into apartments inside."

"Yeah," Baer said, retrieving their champagne. He handed hers over and took a mouthful of his own. "I know, I looked it up."

"You did?" Freya asked, lowering her glass before tasting the champagne.

"Why do you think I asked for the name of it?"

If memory served, he'd asked while they were in bed, while she was recovering, so her memory wasn't exactly clear. Even she hadn't known the name at the time and had to text Holly to get it. At some point, her cousin got back to her. Her phone had chimed anyway, Baer was the one to check it.

"Holly says there's like fishing and hiking and stuff," Donoghue said, screwing up his face. "You know how to fish?"

"You never went fishing as a kid?"

Donoghue laughed. "Any time I went to the water, I was busy catching babes in bikinis."

"Won't be doing that this time," Baer said, tucking his arm around her.

"You won't?" Wriggling a little lower, she angled to lean against him. "Maybe I'd like to be caught."

He didn't hesitate. "Then break out the bikinis, baby."

It was hardly the weather for it but…

Sigh. They were only a few hours into the vacation, and already she was frisky. The things his proximity did to her. He should come with a health warning, a Squires disclaimer that absolved the company of responsibility for minds lost and abandon embraced. God, what was wrong with her? Smart as it seemed at the time, the no sex rule weighed heavy on her.

Did he have to be so hot? So magnetic? It wasn't fair. He was hers, but not hers. They were together, but not.

"Maybe we should have a no flirt rule too."

"Baby, guy can only restrain himself so much. You want me to keep my hands to myself, and now my words too? Cool, I can do that, so long as I get to look at you. That's enough to sustain me a lifetime."

Lifetime? Would they have one of those together? Too early to be thinking that way. She wouldn't cloud her judgment, otherwise she'd be acting on confirmation bias. If they were meant to be, they'd figure it out on the vacation. Wasn't that what it was for?

They rode a while, finishing their champagne, admiring the view. The outside view, not inside. Though she may have done a little of that too. They talked about the plane ride, and various members of the Piven family, both those joining them, and those absent.

When they slowed to turn onto a gravel driveway flanked by forest, the conversation hushed. Intrigue took over, fizzing in the air, tantalizing them with what was to come. Her fingers linked through Baer's tightening as they advanced.

This was it, no going back now. Her family weren't that bad, ordinarily. Spending so much time with them in such a concentrated environment wasn't something she'd done for years. Years, as in probably since before puberty. They spent few holidays together; she tended to stick with Truman whenever there were celebrations to be had. He had no one else, and her fondness for him outweighed what she felt for the Pivens. Maybe she shouldn't think like that, but, believe it or not, she and her grandfather did enjoy each other's company, most of the time. Once, when she was a teen, Truman had joined her for Christmas, Thanksgiving, one of the holidays, with the Pivens. Note: once. Turned out once was enough.

It wasn't like he wasn't gracious. He had invited them to the house to spend holidays. While exuberant, they weren't bad houseguests. Though it was easy to say that when in such a vast house with considerable grounds. The Pivens may have been present, but Truman didn't have to hang around with them.

Knowing little about where they were going, she had no idea if the situation was the same there. The grounds inspired optimism. There was space, if not inside, then outside. Though how often would she get away with excusing herself outside? And Baer, what about him? She couldn't abandon him. God knew what her family would say to embarrass her.

They turned onto a wide parking lot that circled the main house. And that house? Huge! Good. Fantastic. Except… damn, why hadn't she spent time researching the place as Baer had? The building might look big from the outside, but they were only renting an apartment within it, and she had no idea how many dwellings occupied the structure.

"Here we go," Holly said, a whisper of trepidation in her words.

They made eye contact and she smiled, taking on the role of comforter despite her own apprehension.

"It'll be fine, it's family. Your parents, your siblings, how bad could it be?"

It was the slink of her cousin's eyes to the man at her side that revealed the true source of her anxiety. Hadn't it seemed like such a great idea at the time? That wasn't the moment for an, "I told you so," yet the words threatened her throat. Hadn't she been the one to say this was a bad idea? Nerves be damned, she squeezed Baer's hand. However this turned out, if it didn't damage her relationship with Baer, she couldn't regret it. She couldn't regret that he'd come into her life.

"I should find out if anyone's here yet," Holly said, retrieving her cellphone from her purse.

Right, because did they know where to go? Could they check-in if the named party on the reservation wasn't present? Providing they had vacancies, she could get them checked in. Were there any special requirements relevant to the rest of their group?

A massive clearing opposite the main entrance of the building was lined by trees at the far edge, not so much a forest as a perimeter. Peeking through the branches, glimmers of light reflected on glistening water. If there was a lake, maybe there would be fishing after all. Her bikini comment was meant to be a joke, it would be far too cold to swim. Let's just hope no one took her seriously. She was about to bring the others' attention to the water when two forms appeared through those trees. Swinging their joined hands, the woman was in raptures of laughter while the male grinned at his companion.

Sweet to see such a happy couple. It actually took her a minute, and a few more yards of their advance, to recognize the female as her own cousin.

"Holly," she said, flapping a hand in her cousin's general direction. "Look…" Her other hand waved at the window, finger extended, indicating the view. "It's Kelly."

"I'm supposed to be pleased to see her and I'm so not. This is really happening."

"We're fine. We're in this together, right? We will get through this." It would be nice if the guys picked up on that being a good time to also reassure Holly. They didn't. She bounced her and Baer's joined hands on his thigh. "Right, Baer, honey?"

When he didn't respond, she turned to see him fixated on something outside, what? He was just staring over the top of her head. Was it the couple, or was something else putting concern in his gaze?

"What is it?" Holly asked, her focus bouncing from one man to the next. "Why do you both look like that?"

"Don?"

"I see it."

"See what?" she asked, a whisper of desperation curling in her gut. "Would one of you talk?"

"We have a problem."

Okay, still no clearer.

"Problem? What's the problem?"

"If that's Nickson, he knows who we are."

And that served her a dose of concern too. Concern? Maybe panic was a better word. "How does he know who you are?"

It was only then that Baer's gaze met hers. "Squires. He knows us from Squires."

# TWENTY-THREE

AND THE BOTTOM fell out of her gusto. Had she had gusto? Apparently so, and now it was gone. If this was how she felt, imagine what was going through Holly's head. It wasn't shame, but the whole point was to forgo the judgment of not having stable relationships. Their partners were hired. The plan only worked if the others in their party weren't aware of that. And if Nickson recognized them...

"Wait, what do you mean?" Holly asked, the words reeking of the same desperation that bubbled in her. "How could he know you from Squires?"

"Because he's from Squires too."

Oh, she...

"He's from Squires? Squires?" The wildness of Holly's eyes didn't scream sanity. "You're saying my sister hired herself a fake fiancé? Why? Why would she do that?"

Okay, that was the pot calling the kettle black, but it wasn't exactly the time to call Holly on specifics.

And, oddly, that hadn't occurred to her. Her first thought was their ruse being uncovered, she hadn't considered why her other cousin would've set hers up at all.

"He's not Squires now," Donoghue explained. "He was Squires. Quit last year. Think he's gone out on his own?"

Nothing made sense, she hadn't seen this coming. How could any of them have seen this coming?

"Even if he has, why would Kelly be paying him to do this?"

"It's possible for a guy like him to fall in love." Baer's words felt like they were for her. "Just because you sell sex for a while, doesn't mean you give up all emotion yourself."

He was right. Nickson once sold sex, that didn't mean he would forever or that every partner in his life paid him.

"You think they met and fell in love?" Unable to miss the parallel with her own situation, her desperation morphed into hope that maybe it could be true. If Nickson could do it with Kelly, she could do it with Baer. "If you ask him to stay quiet, will he?"

"Depends."

Oh, good, that was helpful. "Depends on what?"

"Their relationship," he said. "Think I'd lie to you if another guy asked me?"

If it was real, Kelly and Nickson would, should, share everything.

"So what do we do?"

And that was the sixty-four-million-dollar question. What did they do? They needed a plan in the thirty seconds it would take the couple to finish crossing the grass and hit the gravel. There were a few other cars parked in the parking lot but no other limos. Kelly knew her just as well as Holly, therefore knew this was her typical ride.

"Shit, shit, shit." Yep, Holly's anxiety had become full-blown panic. "This is the worst thing that could possibly happen ever. What are we supposed to do?"

"We could leave," Baer said. "You two go in, say there was an issue that kept us in the city."

"Both of you?" Holly snapped. "Wouldn't we have known that before today? Unless you're running away together, why would both of our boyfriends miraculously have emergencies crop up at the same time?"

"Maybe they're family," she suggested. "Or they're best friends and they need to be around to support each other."

"Then why wouldn't we be there too? If it was such a terrible disaster, why would we abandon the men we're supposed to love?"

Maybe instead of crapping on everyone else's suggestions, Holly could come up with some of her own. She wouldn't say that, not out loud. It would just live in her head.

"We can't sit in here forever. We're here now." A quick glance back at the window confirmed Kelly was indeed heading their way. "You wanted us to bring boyfriends, we brought boyfriends. So we go in and act natural."

"There's a good chance your folks don't know Nickson's past," Donoghue offered. "Squires doesn't come up much when you're trying to impress the parents of a girl you're really into."

More proof that men in their line of work had real lives beyond it. Donoghue could have his own family. Yes, he could be abrasive, and forward, that didn't mean he couldn't be a father. Maybe he was playing up those qualities, working off a prep sheet. Maybe in his real life he was quieter and more reserved. She had to stop making assumptions; these men were more than their job.

"You think?" Holly shook her head fast, eyes squeezed shut. When they burst open, her cousin's tone changed hue. "You're right! You're right! There is no way Kelly told Mom about this. No way!"

She didn't like Holly's exuberance, like it was so blatantly obvious anyone would be ashamed of such a line of work. Though it wasn't like she was without sin on that score. Hadn't she feared Truman finding out for basically the same reason?

"We're going in?"

"You think you guys could separate Nickson, speak to him before he tells Kelly of your connection?"

"We can," Baer said. "Won't stop him telling her the truth… if he's really into her."

And if he wasn't, maybe the guys could find out and put Holly's mind at ease.

"We can offer him money." Holly's optimism bloomed. "Freya has money. Lots of it. We can pay him to keep quiet."

"My resources are at your disposal, as always, but I don't like the suggestion."

"Why not? We could pay him more than he'd make it a month."

"I don't like the suggestion that money should triumph over love. Regardless of what he's done in the past, he can still have integrity. Squires men aren't just money whores."

Did she know that for sure for each and every one of them? No, of course not. And even people not in Squires line of work would take bundles of cash for many things, integrity or not. But she knew the man sitting next to her holding her hand, and he wouldn't lie to her, he wouldn't. Tarring all escorts with that brush, male and female, tarred her guy too, and she wouldn't have that.

It all boiled down to whether the relationship was real. Otherwise, surely, there would be some standard operating procedure, something in the Squires employee handbook that would cover this eventuality. The men wouldn't out each other if they were working, but Nickson had left Squires. If he was out on his own, maybe his silence could be bought.

She doubted it. There was just no logical reason for Kelly to go through this theater if the relationship wasn't real.

"Okay, we can't sit here all day."

Baer took the cue and got out his own side of the car. She smoothed her skirt and cleared her throat. This was it. Showtime. How well would she hold up? There was no way to know, she'd never done this before.

Her one saving grace? Baer. If she was doing this with someone she had no feelings for, she'd fail miserably. That became abundantly clear when the door opened and Baer stood there, hand outstretched for hers. Just his presence was security. That man; her man. This wasn't a farce, nor theater, not for her. Whether the Pivens found out about Squires, or Truman did, this was real in her heart, that was what counted.

She slid her hand into his and went with his motion to help her to her feet. He backed them off a few steps, giving the other couple space to get out of the car.

Her chin grazed his shirt. "Are you okay?" she murmured.

With her back to the clearing, she couldn't see how close Kelly and Nickson were, but they couldn't be far away.

"Me?" The groove between his brows deepened. "I'm used to this kind of thing."

"No, you're not." Pretending to be someone's date? Sure. Pretending to be someone's true love whilst also possibly falling for them for real…? Did anyone have experience with that? "If you're uncomfortable, at any time, you can call a family emergency and leave whenever you want. The money is yours no matter what."

His fingertip grazed her jaw. "You think I'm here for the money?"

She didn't doubt it sure helped, but it wouldn't be enough for him to betray or abandon her.

"Just know I won't hold it over you." She smiled. "Thank you for being here. I couldn't be here with anyone else, and I'm sorry my family are a little crazy."

Or a lot crazy if she included Roxie as family.

He laughed. "Makes things interesting."

"Hey! You made it!" Kelly exclaimed from behind. "Let me introduce everyone!"

Oh, little did she know. Her cousin's beaming grin was matched by the man at her side, for a few seconds. Curious, she scrutinized Nickson, and there it was, the exact moment he recognized the men in their party. It only lasted a second; he pulled the mask back on fast. Names were exchanged, handshakes and cheek kisses too, everyone played their role in the performance impeccably.

"When are your parents getting here?" she asked Kelly with a few subtle sidesteps that Holly matched, giving the men a chance to split away.

Intrigued though she was, she wasn't sad to miss out on the particulars of that conversation. Baer would relay them later anyway, in a safer, less stressful, environment. No need to eavesdrop.

Kelly did glance around, probably looking for her fiancé but Holly caught her sister's hand.

"He's hot," Holly whispered wearing a saucy grin. "You never told me he was so yummy. Doesn't look like your usual type."

Was that sister sniping? He was hot, and Kelly didn't usually date hot men? Was that the implication?

If it was, Kelly let the semi-insult roll right off. "I know, right?"

The woman's excitement was understandable. Shrugging off her discombobulation, she read Kelly's glittering eyes. That glow was love. That was more than just excitement for the moment, or the vacation, Kelly's whole future was mapped out in her eager smile.

Did she know about Nickson's previous line of work? Did it matter? Kinda, yeah. Keeping their own secret inadvertently meant keeping Nickson's too, if he had one. If Kelly knew, great! If she didn't, was it their responsibility to tell her? Judging people by their past was a slippery slope. It shouldn't matter, not if they were really in love, but how true could that love be if Nickson was keeping secrets?

She tried her question again. "When is everyone else arriving?"

"Mom and Dad are here, they're upstairs. They met my guy already and want to meet yours too. Alan had a thing at work, so he's not coming until tomorrow night." The sisters' sibling. Okay, maybe it was better to do this in stages. "How great is this? We're all hooked up and settled down at the same time!"

Hooked up? Yes. Settled down? Maybe not so much. Her heart rate hadn't slowed, but at least it wasn't climbing. She'd calm down once the introductions were over. Baer would pull it off. No doubt. He'd charm the Pivens and deflect any awkward questions. Thank God for him, she wouldn't be able to do it alone.

Except now there were more variables, more secrets. How did she feel about discussing it openly, even just amongst the six of them? What would she do if Nickson said something to her about it? Challenged her on paying for love? Maybe he'd threaten her to keep his secret. In that scenario, she'd tell Baer what happened at the first available opportunity. As to what she'd say in the specific moment...

Okay, so the key would be sticking with Baer, at all times. The guy would be sick of looking at her by the end of this vacation. So much for taking the chance to get to know each other in peace and without pressure. Neither was looking likely.

"Let's go inside," Kelly said, taking both their hands then calling back over her shoulder. "We're going inside!"

Baer better be on her heels. Had the men had enough time for their conversation? Yes or no, there was no way to delay. Opening night was upon them. Each had to be at their best and give the performance of a lifetime.

# TWENTY-FOUR

TOP OF THE STAIRS, take a left, those were her aunt's instructions. She caught the newel post after the ascent. The square hall wrapped around three sides of the stairway balustrades. All the doors were visible to each other. Their room was apparently the furthest to the left. Easy to find.

Her bags were already in there. They'd seen the bedroom before her, this was her first time venturing up there. How did the luggage arrive at its destination? No idea. Could've been a bellhop, her uncle, Baer, she'd been too busy staring at her aunt to care about what happened to her clothes.

The Monopoly game going on downstairs had started not long after dinner. As expected. Board games, cards, dominoes all would be on the schedule for the vacation. Usually, she went with the flow. This time she just couldn't relax, thank God for Baer's hand on her thigh under the table. Already she was relying on his strength, she'd have to apologize for that.

Ready to give her adrenaline a chance to wear off, she wasn't sorry to be the first out of the game. Yes, there were jokes about her being the richest in real life in the poorest in Boardgame Land. Yeah, yeah, laugh it up. She'd happily be the butt of the joke if it meant a reprieve. Her poor bones couldn't take much more of the constant tension.

The bedroom wasn't particularly big, or it could be the bed was too big for the space. Still, it sufficed, they had what they needed. A small closet, their own shower room, a dresser under the window, and a full-length mirror on the back of the door.

Her suitcase was lying on the stand between the bathroom and closet doors. Was that her first port of call? No. She threw her purse on the dresser and fished out her phone to dial fast. She needed a pressure valve to release the tension, or else she might explode.

"Freya!" Oh, just the sound of Roxie's voice was enough to bolster the strength she'd lost since leaving Baer's side. "How are you doing, honey? Ready to let me meet your guy yet? I'm waiting… Can you tell I'm eager?"

If she had a choice, right then, if a genie appeared and promised to grant her wish, she'd happily switch her and Baer's location with wherever Roxie was right now.

She closed her eyes and slumped on the end of the bed, hooking an elbow over the footboard, using it to support the weight of the phone against her ear.

"Are you at the club?"

Roxie snickered. "I'm always at the club, honey. I live at the club. You want to come over?"

"I'm on vacation." The irony of her tone hopefully conveyed how she felt about that truth. "Family vacation, with my aunt and uncle, cousins, and three men being paid to be here."

"Three?" She quickly forgave Roxie her confusion. "How many boyfriends does your aunt think you have? Are you a polygamist now? 'Cause I've gotta tell you, honey, I'm into it. Or is it your cousin? You have one? She has one? Two? Or do you share? 'Cause I'm into whatever you're into, honey."

Wouldn't be her version of living her best life. "Nope, no sharing, turns out Kelly's fiancé's Squires alumni as well."

"Wow, your family sure have a type. How did that happen?"

She exhaled. "I don't know. Not yet. I'm hoping Baer has answers. I haven't had a chance to be alone with him since we got here. I feel like I'm balancing on a knife edge just waiting for the cut."

"Baer? Is he your guy? Is that his real name or somehow related to his skills? 'Cause that would be a story I'd be thrilled to hear."

"Yes, it's his real name."

His real first name, his last name, not so much. At the time, using his fake last name prickled pins through her limbs. Maybe when this was all done, if she and Baer did get together for real, she could convince her aunt that she'd misheard, not that she was wrong, or had forgotten her own boyfriend's name.

"How long have you been there?"

"We arrived this afternoon. There were pleasantries, dinner, games with the family. The mood is high so no one's asking questions."

How long would that last?

"All very wholesome. So what's the problem?"

"We didn't know Kelly's new guy was Squires too. Not until we arrived. We were in the parking lot and… They could blow the whole thing out of the water. If he tells Kelly that mine and Holly's guys are from

Squires, my aunt and uncle could find out. It's exactly what we don't need people whispering about."

Though whispering was best-case scenario. It was a much larger confrontation she feared.

"And if they find out, so what?"

Trust Roxie to have a different perspective.

"If they find out, how long do you think it will take to get back to Truman?"

"Is that what you're worried about?" Roxie asked. "Are your aunt and Truman best buds?"

"If this works out, at some point, I have to tell Truman the truth. Honestly, right now? I'm more worried about Holly. It's different for me, being here. Even if the whole truth comes out, I still have Baer's support. She doesn't have that same support structure to rely on. And, let's face it, the Pivens aren't in my life enough for it to really matter if they judge me." Truman on the other hand... "If they find out, there may be outrage, upset, I don't know. I can't predict how it will play out. If the worst comes to the worst, Baer and I can leave."

"You're worried what effect it will have on Holly's life."

"This is her sibling. Her parents. I don't know if I can support her on my own. If I'll be enough. Will they ridicule and judge her for this forever?"

"If they ridicule and judge her, they have to ridicule and judge Kelly too." And if it turned out Kelly hadn't paid Nickson? Did his previous line of work doom him to ridicule forever? "Don't forget this was Holly's idea," Roxie said, more conciliatory than teasing. "You did try to warn her. Whatever happens, it's not your fault. People are responsible for their own actions. But back up a step, if Kelly's fiancé is Squires too, is he being paid to be there? Why would she do that? He isn't being paid to marry her, is he? To hire a guy for life

would take Truman money. Though, it's not a bad idea…
hmm…" Her friend pondered. "Wouldn't be so bad to
have a guy who'd always do what he was told."

"I haven't got to the bottom of it." Not that she
planned to do the digging, Baer should have answers.
Please say he had answers. If he didn't, she may not sleep
a wink. "Kelly wouldn't have made up a fiancé, knowing
the wedding would never happen. My aunt's already
talking about the dress and flowers. God, this is going to
be a disaster."

"So you think the relationship's real? No reason
they couldn't have met and fallen in love like anyone else.
And, hey, it's hope. If she can marry her Squires man, so
can you."

In some far-off distant future. Right now she just
needed information. Her own relationship with Baer was
taking a backseat. Her cousins' men were the more
pressing issue.

"But if Kelly knows the truth, we're keeping each
other's secrets. This isn't me and Holly covering for each
other, it's out of her control. One thing goes wrong, one
word said out of turn, and everything comes crashing
down."

"It's okay, honey. Just take a breath. You've
already said it yourself, you have Baer. He is all you need.
Just because I never met him doesn't mean I doubt his
integrity. You wouldn't have picked him if he was a bad
guy. And for the sake of this argument, we're assuming
Chapman was temporary insanity. The whole cop thing
blinded you for a second. You thought it meant good
guy, you'll never make that mistake again."

"No…" She sighed. "I won't."

"I trust your judgment. Baer does too, or he
wouldn't be there. Like you said, don't forget, nothing in
your life changes if they find out the truth. The judgment
of these people doesn't matter. If it gets too much, tell

your family I'm having a meltdown and get yourself on a plane. Walk away and appreciate your guy. He'll take your mind off things."

"And if Truman finds out…?"

"Forget about that. That's next week's problem. And don't worry, I'll split the gold with you if he disinherits you in favor of me."

Oh, Roxie. This is why so many people relied on her for support. Her optimism, her charm, Roxie's acceptance gave her hope.

Relaxing, her eyes opened again. "Thank you."

"It's what I'm here for. And if you need me and Zairn to just happen upon you…"

She laughed. "At non-five-star, fend for yourself, apartments?"

"We do non-five-star sometimes."

She scoffed, amused by her friend. "Oh, yeah, when?"

"Uh… In Chicago. My apartment isn't five-star."

"Doesn't one of the guys own that now?"

"One of them owns the building, but that's nothing to do with me."

"Except they wouldn't have known it existed if it wasn't for you. Don't you have an entire security team there? Assistants bringing you anything you need?"

"We have that everywhere."

"Yes, your whole life is five-star," she said still smiling. "Welcome to the other side." Noise brought her around to see Baer entering the bedroom. "I have to go."

"Okay, keep me apprised. If you can't be safe, be naughty."

She hung up and held the footboard to twist further around. "I'm sorry, Hound. Are you okay?"

"I didn't win."

So not what she'd been referring to. "Monopoly? No one ever does. It'll descend into a rabble before they ever get there. Everyone's tired, had a few drinks… but I meant about the other thing."

He took off his jacket to hang it in the closet and loosened a few buttons on his shirt. "He's not being paid to be here."

"It's real?"

"As real as it gets."

According to him, or was he toeing a line? Was that paranoia? Was she paranoid? It wouldn't be nice to accuse Baer's friend of lying when she hadn't any measure on the man yet.

"They just happened to meet? That's one hell of a coincidence, don't you think?"

He sat on the other side of the bed to bend over and untie his shoes. "You know a woman called Loretta?"

Her shoulders went back. "Not personally, but Holly does. They work together, Holly and Loretta."

"She was what changed first." He got up to put his shoes in the closet too. "He said he was done with Loretta and quit Squires not long later."

"Because he was interested in someone?" That someone being Kelly, obviously. "In love with her? Does she know?"

"About his past? He wouldn't say."

Which she'd assume meant no, except from what she knew of Loretta, the woman was about as opposite to Kelly as any two people could be. Would Kelly accept him moving from someone like Loretta to her?

Probably. Even if it seemed unusual, how many people would go straight to assuming he was an escort being paid to date Loretta? Not many. She'd never even spent any time considering male escorts existed until her cousin introduced her to the life.

"He told you he was dating Loretta when he met Kelly? Why would he tell you one and—"

"Conrad told me about Loretta. Apparently, Loretta was one of Nickson's regulars. Then one day, out of the blue, Nickson says he won't see her anymore."

"Nickson told Loretta that?"

"He told Conrad he was done with her. Asked him to give Loretta a line."

"To lie to her?"

"Most women don't like to be dumped." Especially by a man they're paying. "Most of them want a reason too."

"And his reason was Kelly?"

"Figure that now. He didn't tell Conrad anything about her. Just said he couldn't see Loretta anymore, and it was personal. Conrad took care of the rest."

Did that mean Nickson had been into Kelly from the start? Could just be he didn't want to be "working" someone associated to the woman he was really dating. Smart move, strategic? Another reason she doubted Kelly knew the truth of his past.

"They met at a work function." That was said at dinner. They hadn't stated it wasn't one of Kelly's, now she'd bet it was one of Holly's. "Holly and Kelly go out a lot."

They were sisters. It wasn't uncommon for them to back each other up at various events. Or help each other out with obligations and sneak out for their own party after showing face.

"So Loretta must have hired him for a social function, something at work. Kelly and Holly go to the same event…"

"Nickson and Kelly meet…" He wouldn't have told her that first night, he'd be used to socializing without revealing his true purpose. "Is he going to tell Kelly? Will he tell the others about you and Donoghue?"

Facing her, he finished unbuttoning his shirt. "I think we've got to assume he will."

If he hadn't told Kelly about the escort thing, he couldn't reveal how he knew Baer and Donoghue. He hadn't made any implication to the Pivens that he, Baer, and Donoghue knew each other, that was something. Didn't that suggest he planned to be discreet? Maybe, unless he feared being outed too, and wanted to get in there first.

"I've been sitting downstairs vibrating with anxiety," she said. "I came up here to talk to my friend, she made me see…"

"Made you see what?"

How would he feel about her clarity? "I'm not worried about us. I thought I was, and I'm worried about you, if you don't want people to know… I don't want you to be upset…"

"I won't be upset, unless it coming out impacts our future."

His work was unusual, yes. At the beginning, if she'd been asked, she would've said having an escort for a boyfriend would be a major problem. With anyone else, it would've been. With Baer… she couldn't imagine anything being a barrier big enough to change her feelings. Others might have a problem. As Roxie said, that was a problem for another day.

"I'm worried for Holly. I don't want her to be embarrassed. And I don't think I have the toolkit to be a good support for her. We have each other; I can rely on you. You're not going anywhere." She hoped. "Holly doesn't have that certainty."

"I'll do whatever you need me to do."

Because she was paying him? No, she had to get away from those snap, insecure judgments. Money be damned, he was there for her because he wanted to be.

She smiled and extended a hand to him. He accepted the invitation and came to twine his fingers with hers.

"I'm not sure I'll be able to function without you. Thank you for being here. Will you come to bed with me?"

His lips curled just a little, but it was the slant of his eyes that really revealed his amusement. "No chance you mean that like I want you to mean that, is there?"

On a laugh, she used their link to pull herself to her feet. "Would you be capable right now?" With all the stress surrounding them. "I'm not sure I would."

"If that's a challenge..."

Getting closer, she rested her body weight on him. "After what we'll go through this next two weeks, I see being together when we're back home as a huge reward we'll both deserve."

If they made it through at least.

"Every second I spend with you is a reward." His arms came around to hold her tight against him. "Don't know what for, but I'll take it. I'm selfish like that."

"I've never met a man less selfish." Sliding her hands up, out of the cage of his embrace, they got as far as his shoulders. "I'm never going to stand a chance with a man like you. You know all the moves."

"Evens the playing field. One look at you and I'm sunk, gives me a fighting chance."

"No sex is a rule not because I don't want to be intimate with you. It would be so easy to..."

"I get it. I didn't at first, but I do now. You want to know this is real. Like you said, we can get to know each other, and you can be sure I'm interested in more than your panties."

"You're not like that. I would never assume you're like that. I could never think it. You're a good man, and I shouldn't have to tell you that. Do you think I would feel this way for you if you weren't?"

"I don't know…" His tone suggested a ramp up to a tease. "You did get with that Chapman guy. Suggests your judgment's not all that sound."

She socked his shoulder. "You are not the first person to remind me of that tonight. Will I ever live it down?"

"I don't know, it was a pretty big screwup if you ask me. Married or not, you deserve better than that guy."

"I know," she murmured, her fingertips meeting his jaw. "I deserve you. At least, I pray you think I do."

He bowed to kiss the top of her head. "I'm going to take a shower."

"Oh, you torture me."

He held her hand for as long as he could before disappearing into the bathroom.

She sighed. Whoever was smiling on them, whatever force brought them together, she'd never be able to express the depth of her gratitude.

# TWENTY-FIVE

SHE HAD NO memory of him coming to bed, a testament to the stress of the previous day, and his consideration. She'd been out like a light. But as daytime beckoned, she couldn't remember ever waking with such peace and contentment. She drew in breath and her eyelids opened. The reason for her morning glow was right there at her side, lying next to her, head propped on a fist, smiling down at her.

"Good morning," he said, exuding the same satisfaction that filled her.

"Good morning, how long have you been lying there like that?"

Not that she minded, unless she was drooling. Her fingertips met her lips, just to check.

His smile grew. "You don't drool. Though you'd be no less adorable if you did."

Ah, the charmer at work. Waking up with him wasn't such a bad deal.

She wriggled closer. "I like this."

"I like this too. Could get used to this. Are we hanging with the family today?"

"Do you have other ideas?"

"Plenty. I figured you'd want to stick with PG-13, rather than…"

Hanging with the rest of the family may be the best way to ensure that. If they spent too much time alone… Yes, better to keep things family oriented.

"Have you heard from the boys today?" The Claymores were just as important as the Pivens. "How is Abel doing?"

"No hope on the R-rated, huh? You're all about the family. They'll survive. I preferred watching you sleep to checking in with them, and I didn't want to disturb you. Abel's tough, he can handle things."

Her palm found his cheek. "I don't want them to think I stole you away. I understand the four of you are a package deal. I love your family, I would never—"

"If you haven't figured it out by now, they adore you. Guarantee they're missing you more than me."

What a contrast, how she felt spending time with her family versus spending time with his. She wanted more. Normality, day to day, everything in their lives intertwined, was that too much to ask?

Would they ever wake up in his apartment? Go downstairs to have breakfast with the twins and Abel, without the weight of Squires hanging over them? She didn't hate the agency; it brought them together. She did hate thinking about him with someone else even for a second.

Beyond that, she hated to think of him struggling. The pressure that he was under was immense. All expectation weighed on his shoulders; he had a family to support. If he couldn't bring in the dough, God only knew what would happen to them. And his mom, what would happen to her? Was that something that played on his mind?

"What were you thinking for today? I don't know if there's an itinerary, or if anyone has plans. I haven't heard about anything being booked at all. That doesn't mean there's no agenda. If there's something specific you would like to do or see…"

"Plenty I'd like to see."

Easing the covers down her body, he left them at her hips to slide his flat hand back up, *under* her top this time. It caught on his wrist exposing her skin as it ascended. She caught it in her cleavage, just before his view got good.

"What time is it?"

"You just said there was nothing planned. We have nowhere to be. Right now I like it right here. I'm in no hurry. Let's just take it slow…" Still beneath the fabric, his palm skimmed over her nipple before his fingers curled in a delicious fondle. Though her grip tightened, she didn't exactly move to stop him. "You don't want to play?"

Oh, she did. He had no idea just how much she wanted to let go and give him free rein. He may think he wanted it, but he had no idea. Compared to her, no one on earth understood the meaning of desire. Being in bed with him was a fantasy come to life. With so few clothes between them, it would be easy to surrender to their attraction and let biology lead the way. The same thoughts that danced in her mind, danced in his, she read them in his eyes. They had to get out of bed, away from their cozy intimacy, or they would break the rules on the very first day.

"We can play in the shower, if you want… Hound." Oh, God, where had that come from? Bad idea? Not according to the spark of blazing desire that seemed to flame around his pupils. "Unless you think we can't control ourselves."

She wasn't sure she had faith in herself, let alone him. Was the shower really a better option? It was, of course it was. Doing it in the shower required effort, and a plan. Surely one of them would speak up for their rules before it got that far.

"If controlling myself means getting you naked…"

When he put it like that…

Throwing back the covers, he leaped out of bed, driving a rapturous laugh from her lungs when he scooped her up to toss her over his shoulder. Nothing wrong with his exuberance or his stamina. He was on a mission and wasn't leaving her behind.

Fine by her. The bathroom at least had a locking door, which should prevent potentially embarrassing interruptions. There may be a lot of couples in the building, sure, but she had no idea how her aunt and uncle felt about the younger generation getting intimate while in such close quarters. Wasn't a topic one could just casually bring up while passing the peas at dinner. She hadn't heard anyone else having fun the previous night, then again, she'd been dead to the world.

Baer set her on the vanity and went to turn on the water.

Tempting though it was… "I don't think my aunt will let us stay in here all day. Someone will come looking for us eventually."

"Yeah, I figured," he said, returning to peel off her top. "Maybe if we ignore the door and stay real quiet, they'll give up and go away."

Unlikely. And if she let him follow through with what was on both of their minds, staying quiet would require Herculean effort.

This time, she didn't hinder the nudity and planted both hands behind her to lift her hips when he slid off her shorts.

"Quiet wouldn't be a bad plan, we shouldn't be loud..." He scooped his hands beneath her jaw to tilt her head back and kiss her. "Was anyone else loud last night?"

"Didn't hear anyone." Did that mean Donoghue and Nickson were good discreet lovers, sucked in bed, or were thwarted by Kelly and Holly given their parents were in the next room? "I don't care about them."

Tilting her head the other way, he angled his kiss to push deeper, though still kept his tongue from her mouth. Why was he—no, ignore the frustration. This wasn't a bad thing, it was a good thing. Restraint. Wasn't that what she asked him to exercise? If he aroused her too much...

"No sex, remember," she panted, clinging onto her last vestiges of composure.

"You meant the full penetrative kind though."

"Did I?" she teased, helping him lose the boxers. "We have to be good."

This wasn't a moment for "What would Roxie do...?" Because her friend, right then, with a guy she was crazy for...

The money. She had to remember the money going to Squires. While Baer was being paid, the full penetrative kind was definitely off the table.

Just like her.

He picked her up, both hands gripping her ass, and slid back the glass to take her under the hot spray. Oh, it was good to be in his arms, her own looped around his neck, levering her up until she finally got to taste his tongue.

Other parts of him wanted a taste too, wanted to slip over her threshold, and she wasn't immune to the temptation. It would be so good… Why couldn't they…? Oh, her and her rules. Yes, they were good rules. Rules that wouldn't muddy the waters of the true them…

"Is this crazy?" she whispered, arching her body into his descending mouth that tantalized her throat.

"I'm taking advantage before you get smart and kick me to the curb. Gotta build those memory banks."

"Crazy…" she said, writhing against him. "To think we'd ever resist…"

Inviting him into the shower was a hell of a test right up front. Naked, her body was ready, hot, wet, desperate… very accessible to his. And this guy knew sex. Was she an idiot? If anyone could do shower sex without a designated plan, it was a guy in his line of work.

She didn't bring protection. Packing it would've been tempting fate, admitting her weakness, admitting just how much she wanted to—maybe he brought condoms. Always prepared, right? Work product. It was a professional necessity. Bringing them might look presumptuous, would he think that? Could be a work policy to bring them no matter what, Conrad didn't know her rules. The boss might've forced Baer to take them. Except Baer could've worried about giving her the wrong idea. Like that he could tempt her into abandoning her rules. Wrong idea? Uh, given where she was, and what they were doing, that should be the right idea. The very right and incredibly amazing—

"Baer!"

Her eyes opened as his mouth left its post. So much for no interruptions; that voice was close. Close like right on the other side of the bathroom door perhaps. Did they lock the door? Having a lock made no difference to interlopers if they hadn't used it. She'd been otherwise indisposed, and Baer had other things in his hands when they entered.

"Who is that?" she whispered, which was stupid because no one would hear her over the shower spray.

"Don," Baer grumbled and put her on her feet. "Goddamnit."

They could ignore it, ignore him, like Baer suggested… Except they should probably be giving Donaghue a reward, he might have saved them from what they'd almost given into.

Though it was a little unsettling that…

"Did he just walk in our room uninvited?"

What if they'd followed through in bed? They'd have been… busy.

Baer left the shower and wrapped a towel around his hips. "Yeah, but don't worry, he won't be doing it again."

They better not start a fight. Her uncle wouldn't tolerate brawling in the bedrooms. But what could he really do if these tall, broad, muscular men, decided to knock lumps out of each other? What a ridiculous thought, Baer wasn't like that. He wouldn't get physical; he wouldn't do that. Not unless Donoghue provoked him. And without knowing what their unexpected visitor wanted, how could she predict Baer's mood and actions?

She couldn't leave them out there, something might have happened. They might need her. This was her family, she should be involved if something was going on. And if Donoghue had decided to split, she definitely needed to know that… and get hold of Holly fast.

# TWENTY-SIX

LEAVING THE SHOWER on, because she didn't know if they'd be back, she got out and grabbed a towel. Wrapping it around herself, she opened the bathroom door to exit quietly.

The two men stood at the bottom of the bed. Both turned in silence when she interrupted.

"Royal," Donoghue exclaimed, wearing a broad smile. "Good morning! Looking edible today."

Comments like that, and his slow perusal of her almost naked form, were exactly the kind of missteps he didn't want to be making when Baer was frowning like violence was already on his mind.

"You look at me, asshole."

Yep, her guy wasn't thinking warm and fuzzy thoughts.

Going to Baer's side, she joined their hands. Maybe the connection would give him a little reassurance, some comfort. The reminder should serve to underscore self-control was necessary.

Her focus remained on Donoghue. "Are you okay? Did something happen? Is everything okay?"

"Nothing for you to worry your pretty head about," their guests said.

Baer didn't leave her in the dark. "Nickson's being a dick."

Her guy had said he wouldn't lie to her for the sake of a colleague, now he was proving it. Just like she said in the Squires locker room, actions over words.

The honesty clearly surprised Donoghue. "Leave the clients out the loop, man. Your job is to show her a good time, not to bother her with this shit."

"I know what my job is," Baer growled under his breath. Was that tone discretion, or a sign his restraint was slipping? "And if you haven't figured it out yet, Freya isn't just a regular client for me. There's more going on."

She squeezed his hand tight. "What are you doing?" It was her turn to lay her surprise on him and lower her voice, two for the price of one. "Don't tell him that."

"You want to take Nick aside?" Baer asked his colleague, ignoring her concern. "We bring him back with bruises, people will ask questions."

"What did he say?" she asked. "Why is he being difficult?"

"Says we're causing trouble between him and Kelly."

"How are we doing that?" she asked, though neither man was forthcoming. "What did you say to Kelly?

"Said nothing to her," Donaghue responded. "But from the ice war between them, I'd say they're fighting about something."

"Where's Holly?" She let go of Baer to open her suitcase. "I'll find her. Maybe she's spoken to her sister."

"Asking questions will only make it worse."

She stopped digging through her clothes to look over her shoulder at Donoghue. "So I should do nothing? I can't do nothing. Is Nickson going to say something?"

"What can he say? It's his secret too."

Ah, an answer.

Intrigued, she straightened. "Secret? So he hasn't told Kelly?"

"Not as far as I can tell and he goes all quiet when I ask, changes the subject, gets snappy."

Rather than be angry, or even concerned, it was sympathy that welled inside her. "Poor guy. He's found the love of his life, and now he's terrified he'll lose her."

"The love of his life should know his past," Baer said. "She can't love him if she doesn't know him."

And, damn, he was right. She still felt for the guy though. And, come to think of it, Kelly too.

"She can still love him. His work history doesn't change who he is, it doesn't change his heart." Her fingers slipped between Baer's like before, apparently, she'd gone to his side again. Stuck in that tractor beam, she didn't stop until their bodies were in contact. "He should tell her but shouldn't worry about losing her. She wouldn't leave him. No woman would do that if her feelings were real."

Donaghue snickered. "Can tell you're new to the business."

"Watch it," Baer snapped.

"Look, I get it, you wouldn't be the first Jane to fall for a guy, it happens. Even get scary sometimes. But if they don't know before and you have to tell her cold, most women can't handle it. It's an even bigger deal when you sprinkle in commitment and marriage."

"Yes, but the truth will come out eventually. If they met through Loretta, there's a chance she says something. And Holly knows now too. It can't be that unusual for you to come across clients in the real world, at events or just in the street, when you're not working."

"Most don't say anything."

"Maybe not, but they're talking about a life together, a lifetime together, you don't think there's any chance of Kelly finding out?"

"Hey, babe, I'm in the full honesty camp too," Donoghue said, holding up his hands. "Does he want to be married, maybe a couple of kids running around, up to his eyeballs in mortgage payments, when the truth lands? No. Marrying her before she knows would be nutso. I'm just saying, I get why he doesn't want to put it out there. There's a chance he loses it all."

And how would a reveal work on a family vacation? Hadn't she just been saying to Baer they shouldn't be loud? If Kelly found out the truth there, the couple didn't exactly have space and privacy for long heart-to-heart talks, or screaming arguments either.

Mm, yeah, maybe the timing wasn't exactly perfect. But did they want the family to fall in love with him, only to then have him ousted when Kelly found out the truth? What reason would Kelly give the others if she dumped him?

"They'll work it out," she said, maybe because she wanted to believe love could prevail, maybe because there was a chance she'd be facing her own exposure in the not-too-distant future. "If they truly love each other." She knew what Baer did, her family didn't. Would their attitudes change how she felt about him? She just couldn't imagine it. "I'm going to get ready and talk to Holly."

Finding out a guy was a serial killer or something, sure, that may make a difference to their chances of a future together. Doing what he had to do for his family to survive? How could any woman fault a man for that?

"Holly doesn't know shit about shit." Donaghue landed the evil eye on Baer. "I don't tell my clients everything. If I stress her out, she's not having a good time."

"I guarantee she'll know if her sister is upset. I can talk to Kelly…"

Or could she? Could she trust herself not to tell her cousin the truth? Her position was still that someone should tell her. If that wasn't Nickson, maybe she'd have to fill the role. Was that just meddling? She didn't want to be the tattletale, and everyone knew what the messenger got.

Except fear of personal reprisal went further than her cousin going in a huff about her telling the truth. She could also be blamed for blasting the whole relationship apart. And for creating drama on the holiday. Was there a way out of this that didn't involve someone getting hurt or embarrassed?

"No time now anyway. Breakfast's still on downstairs, then we're going on some hike. Getting out in the fresh air, taking it all in."

Okay, so there was a plan, that didn't involve her and Baer spending the day in seclusion. Now knowing they were keeping Kelly in the dark, seclusion sounded like a much better plan. Nickson wasn't the only one with something to hide either. They'd arrived with secrets, but none that could cause the demise of the woman's love. This new information? It could turn the woman's world upside down. How could she face her knowing that?

Would there be time after breakfast to call Roxie? She needed her friend's strength to build her confidence.

One way or the other, she couldn't go out the way she was. "I'm going to finish getting ready."

After gathering a few things from her suitcase, she went back into the bathroom. As she closed the bedroom door, the men seemed to huddle closer again.

So the conversation wasn't over. Was Nickson the only one keeping things from his, temporary or permanent, other half?

No. Don't give in to paranoia. Roxie was right, after how things ended with Chapman, she was gun-shy. It wouldn't be fair to punish Baer for another man's mistakes, but it was difficult to trust her own heart.

What she did know? Baer was honest with her, would be honest with her. Maybe the men were discussing potential ways to tell Kelly the truth, maybe they were just exchanging Squires gossip, or it could be they wanted to figure out the best way to keep their friend's secret.

Friend?

Nickson was Squires, they'd said that. They didn't say whether or not he was someone they'd protect, someone they liked, someone they spent time with outside of work. She couldn't judge Nickson, she didn't know him well enough to make an accurate assessment of his character.

He loved Kelly, or at least claimed to. She needed to spend more time in his company to figure out if she could trust him to stand by her cousin, to support and love her. But was it enough? He could love her, but as long as the secret existed between them, the guillotine was waiting to fall, wasn't it?

It hung there over those in the know, invisible to the oblivious.

"I'm sorry about this." She turned to his voice when Baer joined her. "If we weren't here, none of this would be happening."

That didn't mean it was their fault. If they were assigning blame, everyone had a little of their own. As to living with private guilt, that was something a person had to figure out for themselves.

And he had to remember, it didn't start with him, or them. "If Holly hadn't lied about her boyfriend, we would never have come to Squires." Wearing a smile, she ran her fingers into her newly dried hair. "I'm not sorry we visited Squires." Because it brought them together. "Are you sorry?"

Flipping it around, the guys wouldn't be dealing with the mess if they hadn't been dragged along. It worked both ways. Now was the time to find out if maybe some part of him wished they'd never laid eyes on each other.

"You know the answer to that," he said, moseying over to prop a hip on the vanity next to her, capable arms folded. "We can get Nickson to tell Kelly the truth, if that's what you want."

"We force it out of him, he could out you too."

"And you don't want that?" he asked. "If you and me can't get past this—"

"You and I are fine," she said, her fingers leaping to his arms. "My worry is Holly, I told you that. I don't want her embarrassed."

"You're with an escort too."

"Not that, that's not the embarrassment." Not as far as she was concerned. "She lied about the boyfriend, told stories and—I don't want her to be humiliated in front of her family, it will never leave her. Even if no one talks about it direct, you know how these things are whispered about in the background."

"Then we don't force it out of him. We'll get him to keep his mouth shut."

She groaned, her head falling between her hands. "But I want Kelly to know the truth. We're all lying to her now. That's humiliating too. How can we let her marry him? Imagine how she'll feel when she finds out? As if it wouldn't be devastating enough to learn that your partner lied to you, she will also have to find out the rest of us did too. Who will she trust then?"

Was there a resolution that would keep everyone happy? Not one she could think of. She needed to have a conversation with Holly as soon as possible.

"Well—"

"I'll leave you to it."

When she started to pass him, he put an arm out to stop her, scooping her against him. "This getting to you? Is it causing problems between us? We were good before Donoghue showed up, real good."

"We're still good." She sighed. All this talk of honesty, she had to give it. Their relationship might depend on it. "It shouldn't be so difficult. Relationships. If they start with stress and upset, what does that say about their stability? How secure can a future be when your relationship starts like that?"

"Tell me if you're stressed, baby. Our relationship isn't—"

"Not us. No," she said, grabbing for his upper arms to boost a little onto her toes. "I was talking about them, not us. Living this with them proves how important honesty and openness is in a relationship. Can we promise we will always have that? No matter what, we have to be honest with each other."

"Okay. Then you should know I have little patience for this shit."

"Squires guys not confessing their profession?"

"No, that's a guy's own business. But he shouldn't be getting in deep with a girl without telling her the truth. That's bullshit. There's never a need for it. I don't want my girl hiding things from me, no reason I should hide things from her. If that's the relationship setup, it's not forever." Oh, swoon. As if he wasn't already delicious enough. "Sure, if she's a short-term deal, no problem, keep it to yourself. But meeting the family ain't no short-term deal."

No, it wasn't, he was right about that. "I'm going to talk to Holly. She wouldn't want Kelly embarrassed either. Maybe we can figure something out. Get ready and come downstairs for breakfast, don't be too long."

"'Cause you'll miss me?"

His swaggering smile was funny, but the smugness was warranted, genuine or not.

"Yes," she said, catching the door handle on her twist to look over her shoulder. "I will."

Already, she didn't want to be without him. Unfortunately, her own relationship was taking a backseat to the trials of another.

Family. Helping others was her life's purpose, didn't people say that started at home? Maybe Holly had come up with a plan of her own. Fingers crossed they could deal with this swiftly. Someone had to figure a way out of this for all of them. Maximum results with zero collateral damage, preferably no broken hearts, was that too much to ask?

# TWENTY-SEVEN

TWO THINGS became apparent when she reached the long breakfast table. Her aunt was in overdrive cooking. The spread was more than all of them could eat in a week. And the other thing? Donoghue wasn't wrong.

Although the affianced couple sat together, they wouldn't look at each other. Their body language said "get away from me" not "let's get married and have babies." Uh oh. No wonder her aunt was amped.

Pure relief lit Holly's eyes when she noticed her arrival. Her cousin sat straight and gestured her over quickly. Donoghue was keeping her uncle entertained a couple of spots up. Both men were still eating. They'd be eating for a while if they were looking to make a dent in her aunt's efforts.

The moment Freya sat, Holly grabbed both hands and tucked them on her knees under the table, getting closer.

"Where have you been?" Holly asked in a rushed breath. "I'm dying down here on my own. Kelly knows something's up."

Well, at least she'd been right that the sisters confided in each other. They were close. Usually close. She wouldn't want their bond undone by anything. But Holly wasn't telling the full truth, she hadn't revealed Nickson's past. Kelly would know, right? That her sister was holding back? This was an unnecessary stress on all of them. Unnecessary? Maybe. Avoidable? That was another story.

Though she didn't actually know what the sisters had communicated to each other. Only way to find that out was to ask.

"Have you spoken to her? About Nickson's past?"

With their voices low and heads almost touching, no one else should be able to hear them. Her aunt and uncle weren't blind though, they'd sense something going on. Hence her aunt's cooking overdrive.

"No. They've been arguing, snapping at each other, Kelly said he was fine yesterday. Enthusiastic. Excited about meeting her family. He wanted to make a good impression, she says there's a fat chance of that while he's in this mood. Since we showed up, he's been grumpy, quiet, snapping every time she speaks to him."

"She said that? Since we showed up?"

Oh no, had Kelly linked their arrival to the discord?

"No, no, she says just since we were all talking here yesterday. She thinks someone said something to upset him and is confused why he won't tell her what it was. Apparently, they have this thing about being real with each other." Whatever that meant. If being real meant honesty, the guy didn't have a great track record. "She says he's never been like this before. And is pretty sure…"

"Sure…? She's sure what?" And why wasn't Holly finishing the thought? "What does she think it is?"

Her cousin relented, releasing a held breath. "She's noticed the guys glaring at each other. Thinks one of them said or did something out of line."

Oh, shit, what did that mean? Like Kelly thought the men knew each other from before, or that one of them had spoken out of turn since they'd arrived?

"Did you tell Donoghue?"

"Not yet. There hasn't been time. I was talking to my mom in the kitchen when he came down. Kelly followed me to the bathroom to talk, this is new information. What do we do? We have to come up with a plan. Have some idea how the hell we are going to figure this out. She doesn't know. She doesn't know what he used to do. And are we totally sure that he *used* to do it? Are we sure he quit? Are there other agencies? Maybe he went there. And even if he did quit, she still has to know, right? We can't not tell her this. How can she not know? How can she marry a guy and not know the truth we know? We can't keep this from her."

Though it was reassuring to be on the same page as her cousin, it didn't really help them out. All her concerns were still valid.

"Of course we have to tell her or give him a chance to come clean. But here? With everyone around? I don't want to lie to her. To spend the next two weeks smiling and chatting while we know this thing she doesn't know. But is it a good idea for them to have a confrontation with your mom and dad around? How will they get a chance to talk it out?"

"I don't know. I don't know. This is horrible. Not in a million years could I ever have predicted... What do we do?"

"If there's any chance of them keeping their relationship, it has to come from him." Holly was nodding, her eyes widening in hope, that she was about to dash. "Except we can't force him. We don't even know him. When would we get a chance to talk? To convince him—"

"I know," Holly whispered in an exhale. "How bad will it be if she thinks we're all whispering behind her back? That we know something she doesn't know." Except they kind of were doing exactly that. "What an asshole. She shouldn't marry him at all if he's a liar. Liars are usually cheats. Maybe we should be telling her not to marry him at all. Imagine if we didn't go to Squires, if we didn't bring our guys. We wouldn't have known, she'd never have found out. This guy could be the father of her children, her children, Frey."

"I know."

"No, she would've found out. Just in like five years, in the supermarket, or a restaurant, or something. When some random woman comes over to chat it up with him. 'Oh, how do you know each other?' Kelly would ask, and then what?"

Her cousin painted quite the picture and she wouldn't like to be in that position. It was one thing knowing a guy's past and accepting it, it was another to be blindsided by something your partner kept from you for years. The escort thing was surmountable. The lying…? Not so much.

"It's never going to come to that because we're going to figure this out. She thinks there's something going on between our guys and hers—"

"We could ask them to do it," Holly said. "Get the guys to talk Nickson into telling Kelly the truth?"

"They can try, but from what I hear, he's not too open to talk to them either."

"Someone has to handle this."

"Handle what?" Kelly's voice raised their attention. How had she snuck up on them? "What's all the whispering about?"

"No whispering," Holly said, which was a ridiculous thing to say when clearly there was. Kelly was being lied to by her fiancé, she didn't need her own family gaslighting her too. "Where is this place we're going today?"

Change of subject, good plan. Though Kelly had her mother's blood, maybe she'd take up cooking too.

"Baer!" her uncle exclaimed, prompting her to twist all the way around to see her guy joining them. "Do you know Paul has never been fishing? Tell me you're a real man, tell me you fish."

"It's been a lot of years..." In a slow stroll, Baer came around to her and bowed, waiting for her to tip her head back to join their lips. It was just a slow, casual brush of skin, but it was seductive. He was seductive. She'd been his first thought, his first target. They'd been more intimate upstairs, yet that didn't stop him seeking her out. "I missed you too."

Damn, was this guy for real? Her guy. Was it possible his work at Squires changed his whole perspective of women and relationships? Did he know the difference between what he wanted and acting only to give a woman what she wanted?

Was it genuine? Did he know the difference? It felt good, she just hoped it felt the same for him.

"Our women are determined to go to some viewpoint something today," her uncle said with a flippant shake of his head. "But we've got to get him trained, whip him into shape so he'll be able to look after my daughter."

"Dad..." Holly whined. "We're seeing each other, don't make it a big deal."

"Yeah," Kelly said, finding a smile. "You'll scare him off."

"And shatter your mother's dream of a double wedding, yes, yes, fair enough." Her uncle might know there were unsteady undercurrents between the couples, one of them anyway, but he didn't get as bogged down about stressing out. "That leaves only you, Freya. Will you make an honest woman of her, Baer?"

"Dad!" Holly moaned again just as her mother came from the kitchen with another dish. "Mom, tell him to stop scaring everyone."

Her uncle laughed. "Marriage is a life goal; it's a milestone you should all be happy to shoot for. Look forward to it, your lives can start once you have that certificate in hand."

"Life's not like that these days." Holly reached over the table to snag a coffeepot. "Women can live independently without men, without marriage."

"There's something to be said for sharing your life. Okay, independence can feel like strength, but life isn't a journey you want to take alone, share it, cherish it. And for goodness' sake, marry a man who knows how to fish."

Baer sat next to her.

She retrieved a clean plate from the center of the table. "You'll have to eat something otherwise this will all go to waste." Baer loaded a few things on a plate and set it between them as she poured coffee. "I wish the twins were here."

"Yeah…" He enjoyed a bite of bacon. "It would all be gone by now with those gannets around. I'm starting to get jealous you're always thinking about my brothers when we're together."

She squeezed his thigh beneath the table and bounced up to kiss his jaw. "No need for jealousy." She rested her head on his arm. "It's actually a little embarrassing…"

He finished his mouthful and wrapped his fingers around his coffee cup. "Embarrassing? What's embarrassing? Thinking about the twins?"

"How much I think about our life together. What it might be… What it might look like… How we might be…" She couldn't say family, that would be crossing the line. Why was she telling him something so embarrassing anyway? "Sorry."

"That's what you think about? Us?"

"Presumptuous, I know, don't say it. Forget I said anything."

"I won't forget." His fingers curled around the back of her head to get it from his arm so they could look at each other. "Our life will look however you want it to look. Whatever you want, I'll find a way to get it for you."

And he would, she believed him.

"I'm getting ahead of myself. We've found each other, that's the important thing. We can take our time with the rest."

She didn't want to come across as forward or bossy, she didn't want to seem like she was taking over. Money was no concern, and they'd have to have that conversation before they made long-term promises.

It would be so easy to get caught up in the honeymoon of their new infatuation. If they wanted this to last, they had to be smart about it. Her uncle was right in one sense, there was something to be said for sharing a life. She could see Baer in hers, forever in hers, did he feel the same about her?

# TWENTY-EIGHT

AFTER BREAKFAST, everyone was instructed to put on their hiking boots and wrap up warm. It had been a while...

Their troupe left with her uncle leading the way like an intrepid explorer. The man was admirable, he kept the mood, and the pace, high. Couldn't fault him for trying. Did he know where he was going? It didn't matter, they marched away from the house into the trees, full of purpose.

Not like she had to worry about getting lost. One man from her past would track her down in no time, if the need arose. Luckily not far inside the tree line the path split and various posts with different colored markers indicated the separate routes. Good, no one's phone worked out there.

At the head of the pack, her uncle gave a commentary on the trees and plants they passed. She'd never thought of him as a horticulturist. Not that she thought of him often. She wasn't a very good niece. Maybe he was an expert botanist, what did she know?

Which was exactly the point. Everything he was saying could be complete nonsense, that was as much as she knew about the subject. Still, confidence, he sold it well.

Baer and Donoghue were little behind, hopefully discussing exactly how to get Nickson to come clean. The supposed to be happy couple were second in the group, behind her aunt and uncle, leaving her and Holly in third position.

"What do you think they're talking about?" Holly asked. "Kel and Nickson, do you think he's telling the truth?"

Oh, she wished for Holly's optimism. Was he telling Kelly the truth? Possibly, but unlikely. This wasn't exactly the safest of settings, not just because of listening ears, but if someone decided to storm off in a huff, they could walk themselves off a cliff, or into a bear's den. Did bears have permanent dens? They would if they were hibernating. Which they should be. Okay, that was the guarantee she'd be staying on the beaten path. What else might they come across?

Hmm, maybe she should've done some wilderness research of her own.

"I don't know." Get back to it, Holly was expecting an answer. Something she was coming up short on a lot these days. "Only if he's feeling the pressure."

"I didn't see Baer or Donaghue talking to him before we left, did you?"

"No. I wasn't paying much attention, but Baer was with me upstairs. Unless he did it while I was peeing, I don't think he's had the chance. It's not exactly a quick conversation."

And while she'd been peeing, with the door slightly ajar, she'd been filling Baer in on what Holly said at the breakfast table. So he better not have been wandering off to speak to Nickson leaving her talking to herself. Couldn't be, the guy was still there lacing his boots when she came out, she didn't take that long washing her hands.

"How are things going with you two?" Holly asked. "Don't need to ask if you're attracted to each other. I'm surprised the apartment didn't go on fire. You and Baer... Last night... you did... didn't you?"

Like it was a foregone conclusion. In fairness, if it wasn't for her rules they would have. She should've expected the question from her cousin sooner.

Her lips curled. "Did you and Donoghue?"

Nothing wrong with a little deflection. Though if Baer was telling Donoghue she was something special, how long would it be until Holly found out this was more than just a screw-fest for them?

"We did... stuff."

That wasn't enlightening. "Stuff?"

Holly whimpered. "It's kind of hard to be around a guy like him and not do... stuff. Especially in bed with him."

In another circumstance, she might make a quip about Holly getting her money's worth. Too right, have a little fun. Those responses didn't fit this time. It didn't feel right to think about human beings that way. Though, being particularly attached to one, she was biased. All she saw was Baer, and she didn't think of him like that.

"No reason you shouldn't enjoy each other."

True statement. If this was what Holly needed to chase her ex from her system, Donoghue was harmless fun.

"Yeah..." Holly huffed. "Except having my parents right next door kind of puts a damper on things. We want to do stuff... More stuff. I just have to figure out a way to do it without my parents hearing us. You're lucky. You and Baer's room is away in the corner. You share a wall with your bathroom, not listening ears."

And they were choosing not to take advantage of it. That was mature, right? Sensible?

"You don't have to wait until nighttime," she suggested. "There are other times and places you can... enjoy each other."

"Yeah, except my dad's on this everyone together kick. It's like being nine all over again. And what is with the fishing thing? Is he really going to teach Donoghue how to fish? Should I feel guilty about this? I don't want my dad falling in love with the guy, thinking I really have a future with him. 'Cause that won't be happening."

Would've been nice if Holly considered that eventuality before they went to all this trouble. She restrained a sigh. Hadn't her cousin said she wanted her family to like the guy? Now she was upset that they did.

"What's the harm in your dad making a new friend? And Donoghue will learn a new skill. Something else for his resume." What did he do outside Squires? Not her business. "We can't exactly ban them from spending time together." And maybe if the men were occupied with each other, it would take a little pressure off feeling like they should constantly be taking action. "Besides, it will die down when Alan shows up later. Your dad's just looking for a buddy while his son's not around."

"Mom asked me what was going on with Kel and Nickson. Talk about awkward dodge. She said Kelly won't tell her."

"Just say it's not your place. That you don't know the details."

Which wasn't entirely a lie. Though it would be more difficult for Kelly to tell her mother anything given she knew less than her sister.

"Maybe that's why dad's sticking to Donoghue. We don't have drama."

They also didn't have a real relationship. Rather than Donoghue, they should be concerned about her uncle bonding with someone else prematurely.

"Do you think your dad likes Nickson?"

"I don't know, Nickson was too busy ignoring Kelly this morning to really talk to anyone. The guy's got some nerve. He caused this. Yet she's getting all the grief for it, and she doesn't even know why."

There was a little grief trickling out elsewhere too.

"We have to give him the benefit of the doubt. There's still a chance Kelly will marry him, you said he could be the father of her children, you realize that means he'll be the father of your nieces and nephews? They get married, and there's a good chance he'll be a part of your life long-term. Give the guy a break. Maybe he's not proud of his past. We don't know what he did for Squires. I don't know if he's experienced trauma or heartache, he didn't expect this to be landed on him. He didn't expect to see his former colleagues on a family vacation with his new in-laws."

"You're too kind. You put up with too much BS from people. You think he's traumatized by having this landed on him? You want to give him a chance? All I see is a liar. All I see is a guy who probably had no intention of ever telling my sister the truth. Do I feel sorry that his hand's been forced? No. Not if it saves my sister from getting her heart broken. I think about *her* trauma, *her* heartache."

And that was a perfectly valid position. Holly was protective of her sibling, as she should be.

Someone snagged her hand and she was tugged away from her cousin at a quickening pace. Baer. He was taking her off the path, into the trees, away from the group.

"Uh... Hound... Where are we going? What's happening?" He didn't answer, just weaved around trees, stretching the distance between them and the others. Lost in the wilderness. Wasn't this exactly what she promised herself wouldn't happen? "Where are we going? The others will look for us."

And if they got eaten by a bear, it would be on her. Damn Kinloch. It wasn't like she'd never slept in the woods before. But when with a man made of the dirt and the leaves and the glorious fresh air, she didn't have to pay attention or be concerned with anything.

Baer halted and swung her around, yanking her arm so she fell against him as he pinned her between himself and a tree trunk.

"No, they won't. Donoghue knows where we are."

He crouched to kiss her. The rough bark caught in her hair as she tipped her head back to enjoy the juxtaposition of his warm slick mouth contradicting the solid monolith behind her.

She pushed just a little. "I don't want to wake any bears."

On an exhaled laugh, one of his brows twitched. "Only one Baer."

"No," she said, giving him another light push. "I mean actual bears. There will be bears around here. They'll be sleeping. I don't want to wake them up."

He tucked some loose strands of hair away from her temple. "You're scared of bears?"

"Never used to be. Never had to be. Never been anywhere like this without..."

"Without...?" Easing back, he interlaced their fingers and drew her away from the tree. "This is supposed to be our vacation too. That's why I took you from the others. We've spent enough time on them already. Forget their drama, let's enjoy each other."

Tempting. And why should she resist? He was right. "So everything on the table. Without…?"

"Kinloch Gramercy-Peake." She stepped over a branch and onto a leaf, enjoying their new leisurely pace. Still they were going a different way to the family group, but if Donoghue knew where they were going, Baer must too. How could he have told him otherwise? "A guy I used to date. This is his idea of heaven."

Roughly. His idea of heaven would be a few more miles, try a few hundred more, from civilization, but the trees, the critters, the nature, yeah, this was all him.

"Here? This place?"

"Not here specifically, somewhere like here. Anywhere without people. Where all he has to do is survive. He is a no drama kind of guy too. Though, truthfully, I don't know if it's the nature or the peace he loves. He didn't have a lot of quiet in his life."

"Sounds like you're still close."

And he said that without an ounce of accusation or jealousy. "We write. Always have. Since we were at school."

There was comfort in the routine, the nostalgia. And plenty of times that she missed him. Not that he'd ever abandon her. His stability had always been a stalwart in her life. Always would be. Somehow she just knew.

"Write? Email?"

"No," she said on a snicker. "Letters. Old style. Pen and paper, envelopes, stationery. He has a PO box. No one can get to him where he is right now. He disappears so often that his letters usually come in stacks."

Sometimes she got them one or two at a time. Occasionally. Just depended on where he was and what he was doing. Something even he couldn't typically predict. Even at the height of his responsibility, when the burden on him was greatest, and his time was precious, she could still rely on his letters. Didn't matter that they lived in the same city, their correspondence never slowed; it was cathartic.

"What do you talk about? You don't have to tell me—"

"No, it's okay. Life. I'd always keep his confidence, as I would any friends', but these aren't love letters. Nothing like that." She drew their joined hands across her body to meet the other. "Sounds ridiculous to say he had a difficult upbringing. In context, it was, everything's relative. He was born into two dynasties."

"Shorthand for he's richer than Fort Knox." It was nice he said that with a smile. "Don't worry about me, Skit."

"Regardless of the great number of people in his life, no one gave a shit about him."

"Except you. And it pisses you off."

Damn, she thought she did a good job of keeping her voice even. "How do you know that?"

"Not like you to casually swear in conversation." No, because she'd been raised better than that. Still, some things were warranted. "You still in love with him?"

"Not in that way. We used to be together, so it sounds weird to say it, but he's more like my brother than my boyfriend these days. Since before there was romance between us, he's always been there for me. After my parents…"

"He's a good guy. That's good. We should have people, friends, looking out for us."

Was he truly not threatened? If he wasn't, it would be a relief. Too many guys got the hump, or lay down ultimatums, when they learned of her continuing relationship with Kinloch. And by guys, she meant Chapman.

Baer was secure, how refreshing. Good thing too, because Kinloch was just the tip of the iceberg when it came to friends looking out for her. She'd save the Roxie conversation for another time. No need to overload the guy.

"Sometimes I can't figure you out," she said. "Whether you're really this calm, patient guy, or if you fall back on your training."

"Upbringing or training," he said as he had the day they met. "I don't act with you. You have to trust me, Lil'."

"I do. I don't worry for myself because I think you're trying to mislead me on purpose or anything like that. I worry for you."

"Something you do for everyone. Who looks out for you?"

"Truman. My friends."

"Maybe I'd like to be on that list too." And he was. He would be. She'd welcome it. "You want me to go crazy? To tell you to quit the letters, to cut this guy out of your life or we're through?"

"No. I just wonder sometimes… Do you know you anymore? I worry because I want you to be happy too. I want to make you happy. Something makes you sad or angry, if you're confused or hurt, I want that honest emotion. You're used to stifling yourself. Being who women pay you to be…"

When she said it like that, the money that had gone from her bank account to his suddenly felt dirty. It soiled them. She didn't want him to just give her what he thought she wanted. But maybe it was second nature, could he help it?

"I'm me with you," he said. "Sure, maybe a little of acting for Squires has rubbed off over the years, or maybe it's raising two young kids, dealing with my mother's carers, my father's therapists, making the tough choices, it's taught me what's important in life. Some things are worth getting upset about. Some things are drama for the sake of drama, and that pisses me off."

Like the nonsense with Nickson and Kelly, he told her last night he had little patience for it.

"You're right about Nickson. He needs to tell Kelly the truth. Better he tells her now and gets it over with. If everything's going to fall apart, better sooner than later."

Which would ease some of Holly's concern about her dad falling in love with the new men in their lives. If Kelly said that was it, over, would Nickson walk away without a fight? What would that say about the depth of the couple's love?

Easy to put it so bluntly when she was talking about someone else.

"If he does, and she kicks him out…" Baer said, "do you want me and Donoghue to go too?"

# TWENTY-NINE

SHE HEARD HIS question, but a new urgency seized her. While she had the resolve, the gumption, she had to get the decision out.

"I'm going to tell Truman when we get home," she declared.

"How does that—"

"About us. If you want me to tell him about Squires, I will. If you don't want him to know, I won't tell him. It's your choice. Though, you should know, he always checks out the guys I'm dating. I don't know how he does it, but he finds out things even I don't know sometimes. That's not to say we should tell him, I just want you to know there's a chance he finds out either way."

"We have to get through the vacation first." Implying they may not be together at the end of it? That maybe there would be nothing to tell Truman? Shh, her stupid paranoia again. "If things go off with Kelly and Nickson—"

"You want to split with Donoghue."

"I didn't say that."

"Don't put you and Donoghue together," she said because, oddly, it bothered her. "Donaghue and Holly are their own pair, he's working and she's paying him, that's their arrangement, not ours." Okay, so she was paying, but that wasn't the point. "If it kicks off and they break up, I don't know if Kelly will stay, if anyone will stay. We'll decide together if we're staying or going."

Was it reassurance he needed or was he trying to catch her out? More like he was just being the good guy she knew he was and letting her know the option was available.

"Okay. Whatever it is, we stay out of it."

"Out of it?"

"I don't want other people in our relationship, screwing with our heads," he said. "We don't do it to other people."

She would never screw with anyone's head. But, yeah, if she needed it, that was confirmation the Roxie conversation would definitely happen another time. A way, way down the line time.

"Were you friends?"

"Who?"

"You and Nickson?" she asked. "You said he was Squires; does it follow that you…?"

"Worked women together?"

"Not sex." There would be plenty of his past activities that didn't need a graphic retelling. If he wanted to tell her, needed to, for whatever reason, she'd listen. Otherwise, those mysteries could remain mysteries. "Did you hang out? Go for a beer? Watch sports? Does he know the twins? Does Conrad?"

"Conrad? Know the twins? No. He knows they exist, hasn't met them, never will."

Who would Baer invite to their wedding? Whoa, girl, where had that popped up from? Nowhere in particular, mm hmm, just an observation really. If all his friends were Squires related, would his entire list consist of the twins and Abel?

"You keep both parts of your life separate?" she asked. "Squires in one box and your family in another?"

Wasn't that complicated? Understandable, yes, though it did make his day-to-day life more difficult, that was obvious.

"What I do could hurt the twins," he said, his voice calm and even. "And if I laid out the full story for Abel, he wouldn't understand."

"You think he'd be mad?"

"Mad? Maybe. Not at me though. Knowing the lengths I had to go to—"

"Guilt. You're worried he would feel guilty that you have to sell yourself to pay the bills."

"I don't look at it that way."

"How do you look at it? I'm not judging, I'm curious. How did it start? I can't even begin to—how did you find out Squires existed?"

"An agency," he said. "A legit employment agency. I was going in, and they were giving me work, a lot of physical stuff." Yeah, because one look at him and anyone could tell he had the strength to do just about anything. "It wasn't enough. I wasn't making enough. Bills were coming due. And my mom… I lost it one day, at the agency, not in anger, just frustration, I told her I'd do anything, anything, if it would make me the amount of money I needed. She gave me a card. Under the table, you know?"

"And the rest is history," she said on a sigh. "Were you nervous? Scared?"

"I can't say I was totally comfortable. There are times even now that I'm not totally comfortable. It's just a given, the nature of the job, something I don't expect to go away."

If he was a woman, those words would be tragic. As a man, he said them with a resignation, not sadness, just inevitability. Like why should a man ever complain or moan about frequent sex with a parade of different women?

"It honestly breaks my heart that—"

"Babe, I told you, the other women… You don't have to worry about that. They're not this. This is…" Stopping, he rounded to wrap his arms around her. "You talk about boxes? You've got one all of your own, Little Skit. Nothing gets in there. Nothing but us."

Again, he was missing the point. This wasn't jealousy, she had a box for that herself, though she wasn't so good at keeping it closed all the time. Her heart didn't break because he shared his body with other women, it broke that he could admit, know, that his job was uncomfortable and wrong, yet he did it anyway. And she couldn't tell him not to do it. She wanted to, God knew she did, but she also didn't want to be her grandfather. In this situation, Truman would storm in and take over, he'd take action, fix everything…

She couldn't deny having a little of that quality herself. The foundation gave her excellent grounding, an outlet to help people all the time. But it couldn't change this, him, them. She'd never been in this position before, never had the means to fix something for someone and withheld it from them. She could make it better. She could tell him to quit. She could take over the—and there it was again. She couldn't be Truman.

"How would you feel if it was me?" she asked, squeezing herself closer. "If I shared my body with other men—"

"God, no. Don't go there." His scowl narrowed his eyes in disgust. "Fuck, I couldn't handle that."

Was that a double standard or him getting a whiff of things from her point of view?

"It's no different than what you do."

"It's different," he said. "A lot different."

Well, she hadn't expected this reaction. "How?"

"I can protect myself for one thing," he said. "Women don't usually get violent, unless it's something they've paid for, but if they did get aggressive, I could handle myself. If you came back with a single bruise, I'd…" His lips thinned as he drew in a long nasal breath. "I'd end up in prison and that doesn't help any of us."

"You'd never hurt me."

"No, I'd kill them, Lil', there's no other way to put it. I'd kill any man who laid his hands on you."

And, whoa, suddenly her meagre point paled. "Hound, you wouldn't really—"

"The way I feel about you, Frey. Baby, I'd have us live in the gutter before I'd ever allow that to happen. Why would you even say it?"

Disgust still contorted his face.

"I want you to see why it's difficult for me. It's not jealousy. Yes, okay, I hate thinking of you even looking at other women let alone touching them, but… my heart breaks for you. If I told you that my job, whatever it was, put me in awkward and uncomfortable positions, what would you do?"

"Tell you to quit," he said, matter-of-fact. "I'd do whatever it took to keep you safe and happy."

Her fingers curled into his jacket. "That's why my heart breaks, because that's what I want to do. I want to keep you safe and happy, and I know it's not…"

That he would never quit. Never? So how would this go?

"I want to be with you for you, not for your financial stability."

"I know," she said. "I know that. But if we were together… What if we decide to live together? To have kids? Couples don't keep their finances completely separate. You couldn't still do it if you were a father."

"Is that where we're at?" His disgust ebbed to concern. "Are we making plans for the future?"

Yeah, 'cause she was so desperate to scare him off. "No, I'm not saying—"

"Baby, just relax. This is getting to know you time, that's what you said." And now it seemed like she was jumping the gun. Okay, yes, maybe premature. "You knew what I did when we got together. You don't want guys laying down ultimatums—"

"I'm not laying down an ultimatum. It's just… If you won't consider what our life might be, what we have the potential to be, what's the point of getting to know each other?"

"I never planned to work at Squires my whole life. Though men have a longer shelf life than women." True. Horrific, but true. "But I can't say I'll quit tomorrow when I know there's bills due. You've got it all, babe, and that's great, but we're opposites on this. Debt collectors call me; getting caught up on one bill means falling behind on another. My mom needs a lot of care, and that's okay, I've made peace with the purpose of my life. It's to support my family and I won't let anything get in the way of that."

He'd sacrifice his own future to secure the lives of others. It was admirable, and also a little shortsighted. He said he was okay with the money, and that he didn't feel threatened by it. Though if that were true, wouldn't he at least consider their options for the future? It wasn't an unreasonable request.

His mom could be in a better facility, somewhere with professionals who might be able to do more. She could employ specialists to assess his mom's condition and—not only could she pay the bills, but she could improve the lives of the people he loved. The twins would go to college, of course, if they wanted to continue in education. She could get them out of that apartment, into somewhere bigger, somewhere with a staff who'd make sure Abel always had everything he needed. She could take care of their pain and their poverty, and it wouldn't make a dent; some people in her life paid more for vacations and diamonds.

"You're right," she said because he was in one sense. "I did know what you did when we met. I'm not trying to change you, but this would be a whole different conversation if I was a man."

"That's what you think it is? Misogyny? Pride?"

"No." She exhaled. "Let's forget it, this is a problem for way down the road."

Maybe in time he'd get used to being with her. And the twins would find out the enormity of her means, Abel would too. Would his family demand he kick her to the curb just because she had money?

"It is, so no more money talk." His embrace had loosened, so he tightened it up again, squashing her against him. "For this vacation. That's my rule. We can talk about anything else, just not the money stuff."

And she'd given him rules that he'd followed. It wouldn't be fair to refuse his request. Especially when it was clear the only place this path led was to an argument. No drama.

He bowed to kiss her. The slow rhythm of his tongue was an apology and a reassurance. The issue wasn't going to be easily resolved, but he wanted to be with her, she could taste it in the possession of his mouth.

When he lifted his head, he met her eye, almost looking for acknowledgement they were okay, that they were over it. She smiled, which was enough. The groove in his cheek warmed and he took her hand to start walking again.

"Will you tell me about your friendship with Nickson?"

"We didn't have a friendship, nothing deep and meaningful." Those last words were almost mocking, not her, just that men like him didn't have those kinds of friendships. Maybe he would if he didn't spend all his time—no, no more thinking like that. "He was a colleague."

"So you never talk to the guys?"

"Sometimes we hang out. Once in a while there's a function or event and we're all there. We double date, that kind of thing. And Conrad throws parties at the office sometimes, we'd all get together, drink, laugh, play poker sometimes... Squires has a regular turnover. Sure, there are some guys who've been there longer than me, but a lot of the young guys drift in and out."

As they needed money, no doubt.

"So there's a good chance you won't be able to appeal to his sense of morality."

"Don't even know if he has one, babe. What I do know is he seems pretty pissed this happened."

"It's not your fault; it's not anyone's fault. And it wouldn't be a problem if he'd only told Kelly the truth. Holly asked..."

"Holly asked what?"

"If we knew for sure that he'd stopped, that he wasn't seeing other women."

"Money's appealing, so it's possible. 'Specially with a wedding to pay for."

He said that like it was no big deal the guy might be selling his body while also committing himself to a fiancée. How did that work? And just for the sake of clarity, it did matter. A lot.

Which took her head right back to her and Baer. If he thought it was no big deal, might he want to keep working when they were wedding planning? She couldn't marry a man who had other sexual relationships, paid or not.

"Could you ask Conrad?"

"Nick's not on Squires books right now. I double checked on that. But there are other gigs in town."

He'd told her that before. She hadn't known there was one male escort agency, turned out there wasn't, there were several. People really could pay for any service they wanted. Bet Roxie, a new New Yorker, knew that. Didn't stack up well as a native, did she?

"Because you know that changes everything," she said. "His past? Okay. His present…" Very not okay, more so because his fiancée was ignorant to the whole deal. "They're supposed to get married."

And that sort of hung in the air. Without her saying it aloud, she inadvertently conveyed a message. The situation wasn't supposed to be about them, and yet somehow it kept coming back to their relationship.

"I'll ask around."

"You don't think Nickson would be honest if we asked?" As soon as the words were out, their ridiculousness clanged in her skull. She'd only met the guy a day ago, and the only thing she knew about him was his proclivity for dishonesty. "You should ask around."

"Yeah."

She bumped against him to get his attention just long enough to share a smile. Nothing had changed about her attraction to him, or her feelings. Yet her concern was twitchy. It wasn't such a bad thing for relationships to hit sticky spots, but theirs was a doozy. What would Roxie do?

# THIRTY

ALAN ARRIVED AFTER dinner. The distraction was enough to inflate the mood again. Her uncle spoke at length about their walk, sparing just a few comical side glances her way. He hadn't called her out for disappearing with Baer, which she appreciated, but he hadn't missed their impromptu departure either.

As the debate raged over what they should do before bed, she could already tell this would be a night more of conversation than activity.

The chill in the air prompted her upstairs to grab a sweater from the bedroom. As she came out into the hall again, Nickson was disappearing into his own bedroom. The door stayed open and she didn't hear voices. She could go talk to him. Would that be a good idea? She shouldn't meddle. Roxie would meddle. Baer didn't want them getting too involved.

This was her cousin. A woman she'd known her whole life. Whether she had a right to say something or not, didn't she have a duty to speak up?

Aware he could come out at any time, she took slow steps, craning to hear for signs he may not be alone. The affianced couple's bedroom was opposite her and Baer's. At the top of the stairs, she lingered. Do or die. Either she went back downstairs to join the merriments, or she kept on going and got herself involved.

Screw it.

Bypassing the stairs, she went around the banister and tapped a knuckle on the ajar door without giving herself a chance to hesitate. It was one thing injecting herself, it would be another if she was caught just standing there like a snooping eavesdropper.

The door was opened by Nickson and, immediately, he frowned. She bobbed a little left and right, up and down, trying to see around his formidable form, checking for his fiancée.

"Are you alone?" Maybe not the best opener; his puzzlement intensified. "Is Kelly here?" she asked, clarifying her reasoning. "And you know why am asking."

Their locked eyes fought a battle. Of judgment? Hostility? Without saying a word, she called him out.

"No." He went back into the bedroom, leaving the door open. "She's downstairs, if you want to talk to her."

"It's not her I want to talk to." Despite the lack of invitation, she crossed the bedroom's threshold and nudged the door with an elbow. Catching it as she leaned back to balance against it, she kept it open, almost closed, with the squeeze of her elbow holding it in place. "We haven't had a chance to talk. You and me. By ourselves."

She didn't cut the most intimidating figure, no kidding herself there. In that moment, being innocuous worked, this shouldn't be adversarial, she wanted him to see sense and had no interest in strongarming him… unless it was necessary.

"I say we don't need to talk." He was rifling in a holdall open on the bed. "Though I was surprised. You? Squires gets all kinds of clients. But a woman like you…? Just what are you worth? How many billions? And looking the way you do… You have to pay for sex? Fuck, you must be into some helluva kinky shit."

The tone was light, sort of conversational, yet the mocking was more than apparent.

"My crime, if one has been committed, hurts no one. Yours, by comparison, deserves its own scrutiny, wouldn't you say?"

There was a time for etiquette and breeding to be practiced. This probably wasn't it. She was tense, it came out all on its own. Maybe she should've called Roxie, asked her friend to feed her appropriate words for the moment.

"I'm not committing a crime, babes, not anymore. Your guy on the other hand…" That hung in the air, sinking and floating, trying to find its level. A statement? Threat? Whichever, she wasn't afraid. "If you're here to offer me cash—"

"Cash? Why would I offer you cash?"

"To get rid of me? I'm not going anywhere. I'm marrying your cousin."

"Are you? My whole life, others have scrutinized my relationships, I know what it's like. I know it's none of my business—"

"None of your business, that's right." He flipped the lid of the bag over again, not finding whatever he was looking for. "Stay the hell out of it."

"You're lying to her," she said, beseeching him. "How can you possibly marry her when there's this blackhole in her knowledge?

"Don't turn this into some sanctimonious crap. Admit it, there's only one reason it bothers you."

There was, yes, the lie. Somehow, she doubted that's what he was referencing. "One reason?"

"You're scared for your reputation. That's all it is. Don't come in here all righteous, telling me to do the right thing, when you're trying to destroy a man because of his history."

Slack-jawed, she could hardly believe it. Did he really just…? The gall! Who the hell did he think he was?

"For your information…" she said, affront blasting out all on its own. "I don't care what you used to do. I spend my nights sleeping next to a man who does the same job. Would I do that if I had a problem with the profession?"

"Yeah, yeah, that's just it. You don't want the world to know you pay for it, I've met plenty of broads like you. The ones who are happy to take it every which way, so long as it's in secret. You're disgusted by it." With one long stride, he put himself at the footpost of the bed. "You think if it gets out that your cousin is marrying a guy who used to make his money dirty, the world will find out your kinky secrets."

"If my concern is so selfish, why wouldn't I tell Kelly the truth? Why wouldn't I poison her against you?"

"Because if you share my secret, I'll share yours."

So much for do or die. "My secret? That Baer works at Squires? Share it." Hell, if her and Baer were going to be together, that truth was better out than in. "I'm not afraid of that. I'm not afraid of the truth. Or people knowing it." Except maybe Truman. No, that was less fear and more apprehension. Her grandfather tended to act first and ask questions later, which, on occasion, caused harm. "Baer knows my secrets and I know his. You can't damage us."

"Would damage your precious charity though, wouldn't it? What is it they call you? 'Angel'? Wonder if that would change when people discovered you're a secret sex slut."

"Oh, be thankful Baer didn't hear you say that. The people I help don't appreciate me for any reputation. They appreciate me, and the work I do, for saving the people they love."

"You're probably right, they'd take your money anyway, wouldn't stop them judging you."

"What about you? You declare to the world who I am, what Baer does, and all those other guys at Squires... Conrad, Lyon, Dirk, Berwick... Donaghue, should I keep going? How will those guys like it if you tell the world about the agency? Talk about reputations? You'd be outing a whole community of people doing what they do to survive. You take away their ability to exist with security, how do you think they'll like that?"

"You're threatening me?"

"As you did me." She exhaled. "No one needs to threaten anyone. There's no reason we can't get along. Just tell my cousin the truth. I don't want her to leave you." Unless she wanted to. She'd support whatever Kelly decided. "I want her to know the truth, so it can't blindside her later. Can't you see how much easier things would be if you just came clean? Surely it's a weight off your shoulders."

"You don't know anything about me."

"No," she said, releasing the door from her elbow to venture a couple of steps closer. "And neither does Kelly. Because it doesn't matter how many truths you tell her, if you conceal one, there's still a part of you she doesn't know. She's not marrying the whole you, she's marrying only the pieces you give her. That isn't fair. Grant her the right to make this decision herself. How would you like it if the shoe was on the other foot? If she was hiding such a big secret from you?"

"You think I know her entire work history? We don't sit down and go over each other's resumes on date night."

"If it's not a big deal, tell her."

"With her mom and dad in the next room?"

"If that's the problem, book a restaurant, talk about it over a meal. My aunt and uncle will understand you want some alone time. We can sell that."

He scoffed. "You think it's better to tell her in a crowded room?"

Okay, fair point. Kelly was her first concern. How would her cousin react to the news? If she absorbed it and it made no difference, the couple could laugh in fun and continue their meal, which would give Kelly a chance to ask questions.

But if her cousin wasn't okay with it, if it hurt and shocked her—that was probably unfair, one way or another there would be shock. She and Kelly had known each other their whole lives, yet she couldn't anticipate how her cousin would feel about this. It wasn't something that came up in conversation. And, in fairness, she hadn't known what her own reaction would be until Holly brought it up. Sometimes she still wasn't sure. Either way...

"Please trust me when I say the lie is worse. This vacation may not be the ideal time to tell her. But do you want to spend the next two weeks bonding with her family, only to break her heart when you get home?"

"Why would I want to do that? Why would you want me to do that? It's in the past, forgotten, she doesn't need to have her heart broken. I look after her."

"And in future if you need cash?"

"You accuse every Squires guy of that?"

"You're the only Squires guy who counts right now. And the way you're talking... did you ever plan to tell her? Did you ever plan to tell her about Squires?"

"What's Squires?"

Only after she turned, did the door open, and there was Kelly scrutinizing them both.

Damn. Of every way Kelly could've found out, this had to be the worst.

"Nothing," Nickson snapped and marched toward them. She was quick to get out of the way, Kelly pushed the door closer to its frame, blocking his way out. "It's nothing, baby. Let's go back downstairs."

"No, what's Squires? Is that why you've been in a mood? Why does Freya know and I don't?"

She'd really rather not be in the room for this. This should be a private conversation. Unfortunately, there was only one exit, and the couple blockaded the route. She'd be quiet. Stay quiet. Let them talk. As soon as Kelly moved out of the way—

"What is it?" Oh, bad, bad, Kelly was looking at her. "Freya, tell me. What is Squires?"

"You keep your mouth shut," Nickson barked, shaking a finger at her. "Don't say a damn word."

"It's really not my place..."

"If he won't tell me, you have to. What is it? Did you two hook up or something?"

"No!" Not that she should be so offended by the idea. "It's nothing like that."

"Then what?" Kelly's pleading tugged at her heart. "Please, someone tell me what I'm missing."

"It's nothing. I said it's nothing." Nickson adamant in the statement. "Forget about it. Trust me. You don't need to know."

"If I go downstairs and ask Holly? Baer? Donaghue? You think I'm an idiot, I get that. I've seen the way all of you whisper behind my back."

Which was exactly what she hadn't wanted.

"Tell her." As adamant as Nickson was that Kelly should forget and move on, Freya was just as adamant that she should know the truth. "You're not going to get a better time. She knows that something—"

"Because of you," Nickson barked. "Why couldn't you just keep your nose out? You think because you're rich you can tell people what to do?"

"I think because you're marrying her, she deserves to know the truth of your past. You tell her, right now, or I will."

"Try it and I'll go straight downstairs."

"I told you that doesn't scare me," she said, edging closer. Her cousin needed support, to know she had allies, that people were looking out for her. Right now, Kelly probably felt ganged up on. "It's not a big deal, Kelly, just something that you should—"

"Shut your mouth! Don't you say another damn word!"

"What is it?" Kelly begged her fiancé. "Nothing anyone could say would change the way I feel about you. I love you. We're getting married—"

"Then what does it matter?" Nickson had quickly turned from hostile to placating. "Just trust me that it's not important. It's just a dumb, stupid mistake, from a long time ago."

A long time ago? Not that long ago, in fact they hadn't got to the bottom of just how long his work at Squires overlapped with his and Kelly's relationship. Did the time elapsed really matter? Maybe not. If he'd been sleeping with other women while sleeping with Kelly, yes, that made a difference.

"Then why wouldn't you tell me? Why would you tell my cousin—"

"I didn't tell her. She found out on her own. No one's going to talk about it again. We're going to forget it, completely forget it, and have a happy, fun vacation. That's it, over. No more Squires talk."

Forgetting that two of its current employees were nestled with her family downstairs.

He tried to put his arm around his fiancée. Pushing it away, Kelly shoved his chest, sending him back a step.

Getting close, Kelly hit his shoulder with the side of her fist. "We're supposed to be real with each other. I can't marry a man who won't tell me the truth."

"You know everything. Everything important, this is just bullshit. Your cousin's interfering because she doesn't like me."

Kelly's focus darted to her. "Is that true? You don't like him? Why? Freya, what did he do? How do you know each other? If you didn't hook up—is it Chapman?" Back to Nickson. "It's Scott Chapman, isn't it? What did you do? Do you have a record?"

"Never heard of a Chapman."

"This isn't Chapman." Though she couldn't say with a hundred percent certainty the men hadn't come across each other, she didn't decipher any recognition in Nickson. "And we've never met, Nickson and me, not before this vacation. It's—"

"I told you to shut your mouth!"

"Stop talking to her like that," Kelly bit back, leaving her fiancé to approach, probably sensing she was the weaker link. Though in this scenario, was that such a bad thing? Telling the truth wasn't a sign of weakness... was it? "Whatever it is, Freya, you know I need to know. You know what it's like when your guy's lying to you. If any of us knew the truth about Chapman—"

"I know," she said because her family would've told the truth. Except did Chapman still have to come up in every conversation regarding her love life? The sooner the world knew about her and Baer the better. She needed to move on from the Chapman debacle. "I want you to know the truth, but it's better coming from him. He has to want you to know."

He had to show her that respect at least. Choosing not to should be a major red flag from Kelly's perspective, would be from hers anyway. Though they'd all been guilty of being blinded by love in the past; a relationship meant for the altar needed a different kind of scrutiny, in her opinion.

"Nick doesn't want me to know. I don't know why—"

"Because it's irrelevant." He jumped in. "Why won't you trust me?"

Now offence became affront. "Don't turn this around on her. She's done nothing wrong."

"Oh, and I have?" When he stomped closer, Kelly got between them and planted a hand on his chest. "Ignore her, baby. She's a troublemaker."

A troublemaker? And there was Roxie in her head again. Plenty may accuse her friend of that, but if Roxie heard it laid at her door… The Crimson Empress would take matters into her own hands. Roxie wouldn't see honesty as a weakness.

Nickson gathered Kelly's hand from his chest and curled her fingers into his while kissing her knuckles. "We love each other. That's enough. Haven't we always said that's enough?"

"It is enough. But you're asking me to trust you without trusting me. You have to trust me to hear this and still love you, that I'll still want to be with you regardless of this secret." Yes, exactly. Good. "What is Squires? Just tell me what Squires is."

The door moved again, she saw it first, the other eyes in the room weren't far behind. Internally, she cringed when Baer's scowl darkened the room. Whoops, boy, now it was a party.

"This is staying out of it?"

Some of that cringe seeped onto her expression in a wince. "It got away from me."

"Mm hmm." So he was unimpressed, he didn't look mad... Not too mad. "An escort agency." His honesty opened her mouth in disbelief; his cool gaze slunk to Kelly. "Squires is an escort agency."

"An—"

"What the fuck?" Nickson hollered and turned on Baer.

Her guy wasn't concerned. "You want to start something with me, Nick, I'll put you in a box anytime."

"What fucking right do you have to talk about my life, to my fiancé? Want me to start spouting your secrets?"

"Go ahead. I've got nothing to hide."

"An escort agency?" Kelly's confusion was forgiven, there's no way the woman anticipated this. Of all the things in the world... "It's an escort agency? I don't understand. Nick, you use this... escort agency? You use an escort agency? Why would you pay to...?" Kelly backed away. "You're sleeping with other women?"

"No! Not anymore." Wow, Nickson flipped his mood quick. "And it's not like that—"

"What is it like? What is it—do you have an addiction? Is that what it is? Is that what you didn't want to tell me?" And suddenly there was hope and Kelly's voice. "Is that how Freya knows? She's helped you. Through her foundation? One of her charities? She has contacts in the medical world—"

"It's a male escort agency," Baer clarified. "He's not paying to sleep with women, they paid to sleep with him."

Kelly's expression didn't change. She wasn't sure either of them breathed, that news required a little mental alone time. The poor woman hadn't wrapped her head

292 ~ SCARLETT FINN

around the first revelation, this clarity was another gut punch. Her hand moved to Kelly's loose one to lace their fingers together, hoping to give the woman some comfort and support. Not that it would mean much. Holly should be there. Ultimately to know that the news was out, yes, and she would be a better sounding post for Kelly in her time of need.

"Honey—"

"Don't you talk to her!" Nickson rounded and shoved Baer hard. She gasped though Baer hadn't so much as rocked on the spot. Hadn't she earlier anticipated a brawl, and been thankful Baer would be around to defuse it? Please say she was right about his restraint. "Who the fuck do you think you are? Who gave you the fucking right—"

"Grow a set. You make your choices, and you live with them. You choose this woman? You give her the truth. There's no other way."

"You're as bad as that bitch!"

Before Nickson could get so far as to gesture at her, Baer's form was already growing. Oops, not the right thing to say. She quickly weaved her way over there, hoping to keep her guy calm.

"Let's accept he's having a bad day and didn't mean that," she said in a singsong voice. "We're not getting involved."

In fairness, he'd been the one to say that. A little reminder wouldn't go astray. In the end, he'd been the one to tell the truth. Go figure. So who really was more involved? He'd cut to the chase. No patience for it? Boy, was that the truth. He'd cut through the bullshit so they could get to more important things. That depended, of course, on how the rest of the conversation played out.

"An escort agency..." Kelly murmured. "A male..." Her attention flew to her fiancé. "You're a gigolo?"

"Was." When Nickson tried to take Kelly's hand again, she tugged it away. "It was a long time ago." Hmm, a little lie there. "I was stupid, it was easy money and—"

"When?" Kelly demanded. "When did you do this? When were you a gigolo?"

"You said it didn't matter. That you loved me no matter what and I should trust you to still want to be with me."

"That was before... Oh my God, you weren't going to tell me? You thought I would just... How could you keep this from me?"

"I love you. I didn't want to change what we—I love you. This doesn't change anything."

"If it wasn't for Freya, for Baer—oh my God. How could you hide this from me?"

"Skit," Baer said, attracting her focus.

He dipped his head to the side. Yeah, this was the kind of conversation the couple should have alone. There was still a chance Nickson wouldn't tell the full truth, so some part of her wanted to hang around, just in case. But that really would go against Baer's request they stay out of it. Besides, Kelly could be done with him. If she was, did it matter what stories he told? And if she wasn't, Holly would get the full rundown. She trusted one cousin to set the other straight if it was needed.

"Wait a second..." Kelly halted them before they could leave. "How did you know this? How did you know that he...?"

Her eyes tracked to Baer's, whose stuck to her cousin. "'Cause I work there too."

Judgment or disgust be damned, an odd ball of pride warmed her. Wherever the chips fell, his honesty prevailed. And he hadn't hesitated.

With an arm around her, he guided her out to the hall and closed the bedroom door. His trajectory suggested he intended to take them downstairs again. She turned to him, pushing her weight against the arm he had around her to angle him her way.

"I'm sorry," she said. "You said stay out of it and—"

"It's done now. She knows. That's what you wanted."

Was that why he'd done it?

"You didn't have to tell her the truth about you."

"Nick will tell her anyway. If he's going down, he'll take someone with him."

"Not you."

"If your family find out—"

"Find out what? That I'm with a good, honest, decent man? A man willing to do whatever it takes to save his own family, people he loves, from enduring hardship and tragedy? I'm not ashamed to be with that man. I'm not ashamed of what you do, or why you do it. Our jobs, in one sense, are the same. We help people. We do for others what they can't do for themselves."

She did it with money. He did it with his body. It just so happened that the people he helped, who couldn't help themselves, were two twelve-year-old boys and his parents. The essence was the same.

"What will we tell your aunt and uncle?"

She sighed. "That the couple want an evening to themselves."

"Won't they assume that means sex?"

"If we're lucky," she said, hoping there wouldn't be too many questions. "Better they assume that than we just—"

"Detonated their relationship?"

Not quite the way she'd have put it. Was that what he thought? She'd gone in there to blast the couple apart. Now she doubted not only her role but her motive. She'd never thought of herself as someone who created drama or coveted it. It was supposed to be quiet conversation, a request Nickson tell Kelly the truth. She hadn't intended for it to play out the way it did.

"They'll be okay. It's a shock, but she'll get over it."

"Are you sure?"

No. No one could be sure of anything in this world. If it didn't work out, would that night forever tarnish her relationship with Kelly? Would they get over it? The couple had to hash this out themselves. Until that happened, there was nothing anyone else could do.

# THIRTY-ONE

"NO, THEY'RE STILL in their bedroom," Holly said, shuffling across the bed a little more.

Baer was in the shower; Freya was sitting up in their bed. Their libidos cried out to be sated, distance was turning out to be their only hope. If she followed him in there...

Thankfully, Holly saved her from the torment by appearing in their bedroom only moments after Baer departed. Dilemma diverted, though not erased for good. Her cousin was at best a distraction. She was still hyperaware that Baer was naked just a room away, so easily accessible...

"Freya!" Holly's exclamation interrupted her daydream. "I can't believe you really outed him like that."

The smile on her cousin's face was a little impressed, and maybe a little proud too.

"I didn't. I don't know if I meant to, I don't know if it would've gone that way. Baer saved me the trouble. Anyway, she knows now. It's out there. We can't take it back."

"I can't believe it." Holly's wonder was emphasized by the width of her eyes and the disbelief in her tone. "And Baer just admitted…?"

"He didn't out Donoghue, so you're fine, your secret is safe." Which was okay because Donoghue was a temporary deal and didn't owe them anything. Not that Baer did, but he'd be hanging around in their lives… she hoped. "I haven't seen or heard from Kelly since we left the bedroom last night. Do you think she's okay? Have you heard anything?"

Like her and Baer's room, Kelly and Nickson's room shared a wall with their private bathroom. Holly's room was in closer proximity though, meaning she'd be likely to overhear any drama.

"There were some raised voices," Holly said, adjusting her shoulder on the headboard. "There was laughing too." For the first time, Holly's eyes narrowed. "If they were over, Kelly would've kicked him out. Wouldn't she? He wouldn't still be here."

"Do you know for sure he is still here?"

She didn't.

The question tickled Holly's intrigue. "You think she kicked him out in the middle of the night?"

The time didn't matter. Anyone could call a cab whenever. She didn't necessarily believe Kelly ended the relationship. There would've been more shouting and crying, wouldn't there? Once he was gone, Kelly would have visited her sister's room. Ending an engagement, no matter how short, was a big deal. A monumental thing Kelly didn't have to go through alone.

"Maybe. I don't know. Have your parents said anything?"

"They already knew something was going on. They're not blind." Holly threw up her arms. "What a vacation! It's not one we'll forget."

That was true. "What has Donoghue said about it?"

"He's a guy of few words."

"Oh, is he?" she teased. "So maybe there were fireworks in Kelly's room, you were just deafened by your own?"

"No!" Holly laughed. "He is good at keeping me occupied." Which was probably the only reason Holly hadn't burst into her sister's room in the wee hours to satisfy her curiosity. Holly wasn't known for her patience. "I can tell you he's curious about you and Baer."

"Curious how?"

The last thing Baer needed was someone poking around in their business. What right did he have—okay, yes, she, the meddler, saw the irony in that affront. Maybe Roxie was contagious.

"Something Baer said about you." Freya didn't need a flashback to identify those words. "He's really into you."

She appreciated Holly's smile with her own. "The feeling is mutual."

"Haven't I always said you two had chemistry up the yazoo?"

"Chemistry is easy. And..." She shrugged. "Actually, it's just easy to be with him. In every way. I can't remember life without him. I don't ever want to be without him."

"I'm happy for you both. Truman may not say the same..."

"He'll come around. He always gives in eventually."

Or she did. Her grandfather was usually right. Their relationship didn't take too many hits after they butted heads on an issue. Usually because either he surrendered to whatever she wanted, or she admitted he was right and everything was reset. They weren't too proud to concede to each other, however her grandfather did tend to hang on to his point of view just a little longer than she did.

"You're sure?" Holly asked. "You going to make a go of it? You and Baer? For real?" Her cousin scowled. "You won't have to pay him forever, will you? I think he's a great guy, but you know him better than me. If this is a money thing—"

"He's not like that. I'm sure of that." Probably as sure as Kelly had been that her fiancé wasn't a former gigolo. "I'm not sure how it will work out. There are things that we don't... Agree on. Important things."

"Things that could break you up?"

"I hope not. We'll figure it out." She considered him a reasonable man. She was reasonable too. If they were meant to be, they'd find a compromise. "I've really never felt like this before."

Squealing, Holly grinned and grabbed her hand. "I'm so happy for you! This is so exciting! And the escort thing won't matter after he gives it up."

It mattered to Kelly even though Nickson had quit. This was different, she'd known from the start. Their issue was Baer didn't seem to be in much of a hurry to give it up, even for her. Maybe it was a trust thing. Did he trust her not to dump him and leave him destitute? He had to know her better than that... didn't he?

"I love the man, not the job he does."

"You love him?" Holly squealed again. "This is like so incredible! And you didn't even want to go to—"

"Yeah, yeah, okay." So her cousin had been right, she did admit that. "But, tell the truth, we didn't go there looking for love. You could never have predicted this."

Holly nodded. "Okay, yeah, you've got me there. Are you going to keep it a secret?" Her cousin gasped.

"If you get married? What if you have kids? Will you tell them how you met? The true story?"

She laughed. "I imagine that's something you'll take care of for me." Her fingertips touched Holly's cheek for just a breath. "It will be Baer's choice. Whatever he wants, we'll do. But that's way, way in the future. I don't think we'll talk marriage and kids for a while."

Let the guy get used to them, her world, before she roped him in deeper. Her? She thought about the money, and how it could improve the Claymores' life, would she be allowed to take on a caring role? They could wait until the twins were adults before thinking about starting their own family. Did Baer want biological children? She could help with the twins, chores—unless Baer wanted a staff. Gosh, there was such a lot to think about. Most men were happy to embrace the fortune, it didn't feel like Baer was one of those guys.

When the bathroom door opened, he got both of their attention, though they didn't move. Hair wet, white towel slung around his hips, that perfect sculpted form… it was possible she was drooling, again, Holly too.

"Mmm…" her cousin purred. "Now I think I'm in love."

She tugged Holly's hand and laughed. "Get your own!"

Baer went to the closet to pick out his clothes.

"Baer, do you want kids?" Man, her cousin was bold. Despite another nudge, Holly didn't quiet. "You know, in the future, what do you see? Big house? Big wedding? Big brood?"

"I want whatever you pay me to want, sweetheart," he muttered, tossing a tee-shirt over his shoulder and turning to face them. "You two making plans? Whose relationship you interfering with next?"

That better be a joke. Though his affect was pretty flat. "Have we heard anything from the happy couple?"

"Not yet. They're still locked up together in the room. As far as we know. Holly's too scared to go down to breakfast."

Her cousin shoved her a little. "I am not scared."

"Donoghue's down there with your parents alone? Confident women. Never know what he might say next."

Speared by alarm, Holly's shoulders went back. "What could he say? What do you think he'll say? I never told him to say anything. He doesn't know anything. We didn't talk about it."

"You didn't tell him what happened last night?"

"I didn't know what happened," Holly said. "Not the details, only what Freya said when we snuck to the bathroom before bed."

Leaving Baer and Donoghue alone with the Piven parents. They hadn't taken that long, and what choice had she had? Holly had to know about the developments, just in case something exploded. Though at that point, she hadn't known much. She still didn't know.

"Until they come out of that room…" Even then, they may not know. "Unless they hate the sight of me and curse my name."

"You didn't do shit, Lil'. If either of them starts anything with you—"

"Aww," Holly swooned. "You two really are perfect for each other." Baer headed for the bathroom with his clothes. "You don't have to change in there on my account, Baer, honey!"

Smiling, she shook her head, just as Baer did. She was paying for fidelity. Though she preferred to believe his goods were wholly hers, even if that wouldn't always be the case.

"I should get ready too," she said, stretching her back. "It won't help ease suspicions if we hide here all day."

The bedroom door opened and there was Kelly, sneaking around it, practicing stealth… not that it was necessary after she spotted her sister. Her parents were downstairs, everyone else was in the loop.

"Oh my God!" Holly hissed and clambered off the bed to go grab her sister into a hug. "What happened? We're going crazy in here. You've been locked up in there forever. He could've killed you and chopped you into little pieces or anything."

Because he might be a crazed lunatic, coincidently a psychopath and an escort? Holly couldn't mean to imply his work history was a factor. If that was the qualifier, they were all at risk.

As soon as Holly released the hug, Kelly sidestepped to blink at her. "She knows? Can't you control your employees?"

Her…? What?

"Excuse me? My what? You might be upset, you're stressed, but watch your tongue." Throwing back the covers, she was quick to get to her feet. "Baer is my boyfriend, not my employee. And he means a lot to me, more than you understand. And he's been honest with me, since the start."

"There's no need to fall out," Holly said, playing mediator. "We have each other's backs, we're here for each other. The sisterhood, right?"

"Your boyfriend?" Kelly asked, intrigued rather than angry. "Your boyfriend is an escort?"

"So is yours."

"You're not supporting him? You have all the money in the world, and your boyfriend still has to go out and sell himself to cover bills?"

Okay, so it was less of a judgment on Baer, and more of one on her. The confusion could be forgiven, she gave money left and right whenever people needed it. Her grandfather's little bleeding heart, she never saw someone in need and failed to help. Kelly had to wonder why Baer was the exception.

Before she could answer, Baer reappeared from the bathroom.

"Oh…" Kelly said, her cheeks reddening. "I didn't know you were—"

"I've been called worse for less reward." She became his focus. "Want me to stay or go downstairs and—"

"Downstairs. We can't leave Paul there alone."

Good for her remembering to reference Holly's fake boyfriend, rather than Donoghue.

"I have questions," Kelly said. "I need to—"

"Frey can answer them."

"She can't know—"

"She knows more than I'll tell you." He came over to stroke her hair and dipped to brush his lips across hers. "Holler if you need me."

"I'll go hoarse," she said and squeezed his shoulder. "Don't go too far."

She'd want to fill him in on whatever Kelly said. As it stood, they didn't know if Nickson was still in the building.

He kissed her again and headed for the door.

"Baer," Kelly said, just before he opened it. "Thank you for… being honest."

"I did it for Frey, not for you."

Okay, he didn't have to be that honest.

"Regardless," Kelly said. "Thank you."

He nodded and went out. So he got a thank you and she got accusations of being cheap? That was fine.

Baer had taken a burden for her, he'd been ready to be the bad guy, saving her the trouble.

"So…" Holly said, dragging Kelly to the bed to sit her down. "Is Nickson here? Is he gone? Are you together? Apart? What?"

Kelly exhaled. "He's in the shower, we're… coming to terms with it." The next appeal came her way. "It's a relief really to find out you and Baer are serious. How do you deal with it?"

"Mostly by pretending it doesn't exist." Kind of true. "When he's with me, we're together, he's mine."

"He does it for a reason, doesn't he? It's not like an addiction or—"

"He has his reasons." She went to join her cousins on the bed. "I won't get into that though, that's his business."

"And Nickson? What are his reasons for doing it?"

"He doesn't do it anymore," Kelly told her sister. "That part of his life is over." She inhaled, paused, then released the breath. "I can't judge him for what he did in the past. We all have histories, he got in trouble, had some debts and that's all gone now."

Better gone than still ongoing through their marriage. Still, the timing of that would be massively coincidental. He just happened to pay off all his debts and give up Squires in the same time bracket he met and fell for Kelly?

"All gone?" Holly asked. "Are you sure?"

"He says so."

"Yeah, but he also said he wasn't an escort so…"

"He didn't say that," Kelly leaped on the defensive. "I didn't ask that question and he never lied. He was ashamed, embarrassed. Think about it, if it was the other way around and I'd sold myself to cover debt, we'd crucify him for judging and dumping me."

Yes, maybe, though that sounded more like it came from Nickson's mouth than from Kelly's.

"All that matters is that you love him," Freya said, taking Kelly's hand. "If you love him, and you want to be with him, we'll support you."

She was speaking for Holly too, although the woman hadn't told her that explicitly. What choice did they have? They'd wanted Nickson to be honest, for Kelly to know the truth, and now she did. They could all relax and enjoy their vacation; tensions would die down. This was family time and Nickson was Kelly's choice. They had to give the guy a chance.

# THIRTY-TWO

"NOT SURE WHAT I'll do with myself now," Holly said, gazing at the car door that had just closed.

Back in the city, they'd dropped Donaghue off at a hotel. Because he lived there? Because he had another client? She didn't ask. Sometimes it was easy to forget Holly and Donaghue weren't really a thing. For all his confidence, and sometimes overbearingness, she'd gotten used to his presence.

"Enjoy the peace," Baer said. "I won't miss living with that guy."

"You only feel that way because you've never had sex with him," Holly declared. "And I know that for a fact, because I asked him."

"And you believed him?" Baer asked, sly enough to be playing with her.

Holly blanched. "He lied?"

Baer actually laughed. "Babe, there isn't enough money in the whole damn universe."

"I was just getting used to him," Freya said. "It will be quiet without him around."

"We should do it again," Holly said, sort of excited. "Double date. Hang out. It would be fun. We could ask Kelly and Nickson too, make it a triple."

Except that would mean paying Donoghue again. Just Donoghue? What would happen now they were back home? She and Baer had adhered to the rules, both his and hers. That meant no money talk. So what happened now? Did she wait for him to have a night off from Squires and hope he wanted to spend it with her? Frustratingly, him putting up the barrier about money talk effectively boxed them in.

When would they talk about the future? The future... In her private daydreams, she imagined the future with him, and the twins, and Abel, and Truman, everyone getting along.

Except in the private picture, she and Baer lived together, they did get married, they did have kids. Was he being obstinate about the money as an excuse? Maybe he didn't want those things. He raised the twins with Abel; it could be that he was done with surrogate fatherhood. Freedom had allure. Only one way to find out what was in his head: he had to tell her.

Except she couldn't ask.

That meant talking about money, which was against the rules. He'd specified for their vacation; she hadn't put an expiry date on her rules. Did that give her an in?

This was nuts. How long would they go on ignoring the obvious? Were they just wasting each other's time? Kidding themselves this flirtation had a chance. God, she hated reducing it to a "flirtation," even in her head.

She wanted that future. She was ready. Pushing could send him over the edge. Cornering him wouldn't get her anywhere... So what? They'd just go on pretending they had a chance together, with the kissing, and the touching, and the… She was too old for that kind of naïveté. If she had to get over him, if there was no future, better to rip off the Band-Aid and get out now. He needed to be honest with her. Desire for clarity churned her guts and raised her heart rate enough that she almost demanded an answer there and then.

Thankfully, saving her the embarrassment of the outburst, the car stopped again. Holly leaned in to kiss her cheek and say goodbye as the door opened and the driver helped her out.

Baer's kiss bounced against the side of her head. "Back in a minute."

He jumped out the other side, both doors slammed, and she was alone.

Only for a few minutes, Baer was quickly back with her.

"What was that about?"

"Just getting her settled."

She leaned against him to tease. "Are you going to come up to my apartment and get me settled?"

He checked his watch. "Technically I'm still on the clock for another ninety-eight minutes." Hooked by his arm, he held her against his side. "But I'm willing to forget that if you are."

Tempted though she was, it would be ridiculous of them to stick to the rules for two weeks straight only to break them in the last few minutes. If they were going to break them anyway, they might as well have done it two weeks ago.

"The boys will want to see you," she said, stroking his torso. "Holly thinks she'll miss living with Donoghue…" Which was nothing to how she'd miss him in the night. "My bed will be empty tonight."

"Mine won't."

The abrupt answer startled her. "You have a client tonight?"

From her straight to someone else? God, she didn't want to know that. Couldn't he at least give her a little time to adjust to losing him?

"No," he said, finger-combing her hair to raise her attention. "I'll be in my bed. Come over for dinner. The boys will want to see you too."

She didn't want to make assumptions. "And…?"

"I'll share my sheets with you."

Her exuberance was ridiculous. She'd spent the night with men before, with this actual one, yet she was a schoolgirl being asked to prom by her high school crush. There was no better prize.

"Really?"

"Yes, really. Why wouldn't you?" Because, oh, so many reasons. "We've been sleeping together for two weeks. Telling me you've got a problem with it now?"

No way, no how, and there would be no payment exchanged that night. Their rules would apply.

So… "Do you have a client tomorrow?"

"I'm not an idiot." Which meant what exactly? "No, no client. You think I wanted to deprive myself another damn day? You and your fucking rules, Little Skit, you drive me wild."

Stooping over her, he joined their mouths, giving her a taste of what would come. What they'd missed. What she needed. Giving in was overdue. He was right, they had deprived themselves for too long.

And if he didn't have a client tomorrow, maybe they could spend the whole day together. Easy for her to say when her responsibilities would wait. Plenty of people steered her ships, she never had to do anything that she didn't want to do. There was always someone she could call to take care of things.

Just because they couldn't spend the day in bed didn't mean they couldn't spend it together at all. They could do something with the boys. Even if Baer had duties in the building, maybe she could teach the twins something in the kitchen.

It didn't feel right that they planned to part, even for a few short hours. She didn't want to lose his kiss, his wandering hands, the delight of his fingertips trailing up her thigh. Stuff. They could do stuff… more stuff. God, stuff tormented her.

The rules were good. Roxie had been right… Oh, screw Roxie.

Climbing onto him, she pressed her body to his, writhing, desperate to hold him as long as she could. Only his grip on her ass, pinning her against his erection, prevented her hands getting to him. He kept them too close, locked together, he wouldn't let her—

"Easy, baby," he murmured, gathering her hair to pull just a little and put space between their lips.

"But I want to—"

"I do too."

Except the side door was open… to the street. Okay, so that was embarrassing. Please say Narmer and the driver, who'd opened the door, hadn't seen her wanton act. No act, it was the God's honest, raw, undeniable truth. This man intoxicated her, she was addicted.

Their eyes met. "I don't know if I can go."

The groove of his dimple distracted her. "I come upstairs with you, there are no rules. I'll be taking what I want."

She shivered and kissed him again. "Tonight." What else could she say? The truth. Would it change things between them? She'd been keeping it to herself for two weeks and it didn't feel right anymore. "I want to say something, and I don't want you to say anything back. I think I knew before we went…" This didn't require a rambling prologue, the words should be enough on their own. "I love you. I'm in love with you. Think about it, about maybe if you could ever feel the same way." When air passed his lips her fingertips leaped to them. "Don't say anything. I don't want a knee-jerk reaction or for you to be polite. Just think about it."

She climbed off him and he let her go. The smile on her face as she crossed the sidewalk to go into her building probably said it all to any onlookers. Maybe she'd been stupid. But however he felt, at least she could console herself knowing she told him the truth. No games or uncertainty, no drama, just the complete truth.

Of course by the time she got to her apartment, the adrenaline had worn off some. The doorman brought her things and shuttled her suitcase onto the stand in her closet. After tipping, she snatched her cell phone and called Roxie.

"Hey, honey! How was the flight? Any mile high action?"

"I told him I loved him." She kicked her shoes to the corner of the closet and silently growled at the heavens. "What was I thinking?"

"Did you mean it?" Roxie asked, her teasing ebbed. "Because if you meant it, you're supposed to say it. Some people will tell you that's rich coming from me, but there's no substitute for experience. If you meant it, it was the right thing to say. When did you say it? This morning…? On the flight…? What did he say? Did he say it back?"

"I told him not to say anything." It had only happened a few minutes ago, and already it was like an out of body experience. "Why would I do that? Why wouldn't I let him respond?"

"Because you want the truth. Guys have a habit of saying what sounds good in the moment, whether they mean it or not. You want the truth. When are you seeing him again?"

"Tonight. He asked me to go for dinner. Spend the night."

"Well that's a good sign. Did he say that before or after—"

"Before." A new kind of anxiety crested. "Oh, God, what if he regrets it? Maybe he doesn't want me to go over there now. He says there are women who use Squires like a dating service—what if it's all been a con and I'm one of those crazy people who—"

"You are not a crazy person. If he isn't insanely in love with you, he's the crazy person."

"What do I do? I shouldn't say anything, right?"

"You can't leave it out there forever unaddressed, but if he doesn't bring it up…"

That was the answer. If Baer didn't bring it up, if he didn't bring them, their future, their potential relationship up… that was an answer in itself.

"Why do I do this to myself? Why do we bother with men and relationships?"

"Because sex is fun. Because it's cool to have someone to eat dinner with and drive nuts every once in a while. And, mainly, because we can't help ourselves. Oh, honey…" Her friend sighed as she plopped herself down on the closet bench. "There's no way he doesn't love you, just no way. Do you want to come over? Have a few glasses of wine before…?"

"That's not a good idea. I said what I said when I was stone cold sober, imagine how my restraint will hold up if I'm drunk."

"You'd be surprised what truths come out when we lower our inhibitions."

And of everyone in the world, Roxie was one of the best placed to know that as fact. Second only to Zairn, Roxie's squeeze.

"That's what scares me."

"I can come over and—"

"No. I'm going to unpack and take a shower." And maybe a nap, maybe she was sleep deprived, that could be the reason for her spontaneous honesty. "But thank you, Rox. I don't know what I'd do without you."

# THIRTY-THREE

THE SHOWER AND nap revitalized her. Optimism reigned again and, grocery bag in hand, she arrived at the Claymores front door.

She knocked and waited. No answer. Strange. She knocked again and leaned in, listening for signs there were people inside. Maybe when Baer said come over, he meant his place upstairs.

Just as she backed off a step, a sound inside halted her. Maybe it was the door to the entryway being opened. Widening her smile, the click of the lock heralded the appearance of her guy. Her guy? Whether what she said earlier had an impact, the set of his brow stole her optimism.

"What's wrong? Did something happen when we were away? Why didn't you call me? Are the boys okay? Is it Abel? Your mom?"

"Change of plans. We've got something on tonight."

She didn't like cold, detached Baer. "We do? What?"

"Not us. Me and mine. It would be better if you didn't come around anymore. I've told Conrad we're through—"

"Through? We're—why? Us? Forget what I said in the car, it was stupid and impulsive, I was turned on—"

"You want to keep using Squires, go ahead. I'm just not on your menu anymore."

"I don't understand, I—I'm sorry. You said women were stupid falling for—I'm sorry."

"Conrad knows not to pair us again. Plenty of other guys there to pick from, guys who'll love to be controlled."

That startled her. "Controlled? What do you mean—I wasn't trying to control you. Whatever it is, we can talk about this, let's go upstairs and—"

"No, I have a client."

Oh, the twist of the knife split her open. Her love caused him to lash out? To rush home and immediately arrange to be intimate with another woman.

"I shouldn't have said—"

"This is nothing to do with what you said," he hissed, bowing a little. "And everything to do with what you did."

"What I did?"

"I said not to talk about it and you went behind my back. I don't know what the fuck kind of guy you're looking for, Princess, but it's not a guy like me. Did you expect me to be happy? How the fuck did you think I'd react?"

She had no earthly idea what he was talking about. "All I did was come home and take a shower, I haven't—"

"That's one of the shittiest things about it. You did it while we were away. You did it behind my back while we were off the board, and you just kept on smiling. I can't fucking believe—you have no idea who I am."

And she'd thought…

"Hound, I don't know what—"

"Money, it's all about money for you, isn't it? Am I supposed to be impressed? Grateful? You thought you'd pay off a few bills and I'd get in line? Not a chance. This family got along just fine without you."

"Paid—"

"Did you think I wouldn't figure it out?"

Stunned, her jaw relaxed, yet she struggled for air. "Baer, I didn't—"

"Stay out of my life, Freya. The Claymores are not one of your charity cases."

With that, he disappeared inside and slammed the door.

A charity case…?

On instinct, she almost knocked again. What would that achieve? She couldn't think straight, none of this made sense. She hadn't… Who had she talked to? Her cousins, Roxie, none of them knew enough about Baer to interfere. No one knew enough.

The groceries stayed with her on the ride across town. She didn't want to be alone but hadn't thought much about where she wanted to go.

Seconds passed in a flash, yet it felt like days before she arrived at Roxie's. She had the wherewithal at least to get in the right elevators. And thank God when the final one opened, there was Roxie, arms already open.

"Oh, honey…"

She dropped the grocery bag and went to accept the woman's comfort. They hadn't even talked… had they? She'd texted… maybe. God, she couldn't even remember the ride over.

"What happened?" her friend asked, guiding her to the couch. There were drinks and nibbles already laid out. Roxie was always a consummate hostess. Shame her guts felt too squeezed to function. "You went over there?"

"I went to… I was supposed to go for dinner. He wouldn't even let me in. Just said we were through and slammed the door in my face."

"I know it hurts, it's horrible…" Roxie guided a drink into her hand. "I can't believe he's such an asshole. I'm beginning to think K2 was the only exception in your dating history—though, I don't know him that well." Roxie's focus bounced to the side. "Is Kinloch Gramercy-Peake an asshole?"

"Sometimes."

That wasn't her voice. Zairn had joined them.

She turned to offer him a smile. "I'm sorry if I crashed a date night."

"Every night is date night," Roxie answered, urging the glass higher when she turned back. "Don't worry about him, he has some meeting thing anyway. Is it with Kinloch Gramercy-Peake?"

"No," Zairn said. "I can set something up if you want to hang out with him… Means no indoor plumb—"

Roxie's klaxon sound effect cut him off. "And that's why I don't know him better."

"I've spoiled you."

"Hey, I peed in actual toilets long before I met you, Skippy. I'm a worldly woman. I've never seen the allure of showering in an ice-cold waterfall. Hypothermia is not sexy. And while we're on the subject, why are men such assholes?"

"Were we on the subject?"

"We're on it now."

"You've asked me this before."

"And you are yet to come up with a satisfactory answer," Roxie declared and took her hand. "This Baer loser guy is threatened; he thinks your money, your independence, diminishes his manhood. You don't want to be with a weak-egoed man. Didn't Chapman teach you anything? You can do so much better. Here's what we're going to do, you're going to finish that drink, then were going to the spa. No, we'll bring it to us up here. We'll drink and beautify ourselves. After that we'll hit the Ruby Room to dance our troubles away. And don't worry, if you want casual, meaningless sex, Tripp's right downstairs. You know he's good for it."

Sex was the last thing on her mind. Baer... she'd never seen him like that. How could he think she wanted to control him? She wanted them to have a life together. No power struggle. Was that naïve?

"I don't know if I'm in the best headspace to be much of a dance partner tonight."

"What if you want casual, meaningless sex, Lola?"

"Aww, don't you worry your pretty head, Casanova, it's always meaningless with you. Meaningless but for the charge card."

"What a romantic," Zairn said, a smile in his voice. "I'm going downstairs, you two be good."

"Unlikely. I love you!" Roxie called out to him as the elevator closed.

She finally sipped the drink and was pleased it went down well. Maybe her friend was right, the alcohol might help.

"Roxie... will it always be like this? Am I meant to be alone forever? Why is it I keep thinking I've found it, only to have it taken away? I really thought... I really thought Baer could... Why does he care so much that I have money?"

"He's done you a favor, honey. Being with him would've been a nightmare, you shouldn't apologize for who you are any more than he should. Though, no, he should apologize for being him. Now you know he's small and threatened—"

"That's just it, he's not! Never was. I told him about Kinloch, about everything, he was never jealous, never threatened. The money shouldn't matter so much."

"They don't know how they'll feel about it until they live it. Trust that, it's coming from someone who knows. I didn't have any idea what this whole crazy existence would be until I was in it. I got through it because I loved Zairn, because he supported me, and always made sure my boundaries were respected... and that's not a sex thing—not only a sex thing."

"I was daydreaming about a future with Baer, and I liked what I saw. With Kinloch, it was mapped out, everything was anticipated for us." Which is why it would never have worked between them. Neither of them would've been happy in that existence. "With Baer, I thought... I imagined us in control, living a life that we chose... It was all in my head."

Roxie raised her glass. "You're not the first woman to have done that, and the only thing wrong with that is not looping the guy in. You wanted different things from the relationship."

She had no idea what he wanted from a relationship. "The way he made me feel, Rox..." She almost squirmed. "Was that all in my head too?"

With sympathy, Roxie's sorrow matched her mood. "I don't know, honey. I never saw you together."

"Holly said we had chemistry." She groaned and slugged another mouthful from the glass. "What is that? What's chemistry? He's a goddamn gigolo. It's literally his job to make women feel the way he made me feel."

"You wouldn't be the first woman to be played like that either."

"But he let me into his life, Rox. I met his family, his father; I went to his home. He doesn't do that with every client, and I know that because his father told me Baer never brought women around." Wouldn't take them long to figure out what he did if there was a constant parade of affluent women and a lot of cash coming in. "Why did he do that? To hurt me? And then…" Her glass met her lips again. "I tried to talk about it when we were away, and he made up his stupid rule…"

"His stupid rule?"

"I had a no sex while I was paying him rule—"

"Good rule."

Roxie inspired.

"And he said we couldn't talk about money."

"Because you'd fight about it."

"You know, it's worse than that. He didn't willingly let me into his life at all, I forced myself into it. I didn't think at the time that I—do you think it was all about the payday? The vacation—"

"Maybe. But if he's that kind of guy, you're well rid of him."

Roxie was being her friend, supporting her, and it was appreciated. She just couldn't believe Baer was that good an actor. Had it been fake all along?

"I think you're right…" Tipping the liquid into her mouth, she gulped until it was gone. "Let's call the spa."

# THIRTY-FOUR

PLENTY OF CHAMPAGNE later, with more than a few cocktails thrown in, the music and intoxication were doing their work. Baer…? Baer who…?

Sigh. If only…

The Ruby Room was a place of joy, oblivion, openness. For those granted the right to be there. It was the super-restricted playroom of Zairn and Roxie. Ensconced beyond the VIP area of the exclusive Crimson nightclub, it was an extension of the Lomonds' home, seventy-something floors above. Full of friends, safe, where anyone could get anything at any time. Hosting was what the resident couple did best. Publicly anyway, she wouldn't venture to guess what they did best in private.

Bar visits weren't necessary, unless someone particularly wanted to prop it up. Guests were taken care of there. Nestled in the corner of the couch perpendicular to the one reserved for Zairn Lomond, she was enjoying the latest full glass brought to her by a server.

Someone dropped onto the couch at her side. "Dere! You've been tucked up here all night. Time to hit the dance floor. Come on."

"Tripp Breckenridge, you're a secret sweetheart, aren't you?"

"Secret? No secret, everyone knows I'm a teddy bear."

"I know Roxie wants to take care of me…" Or more accurately, wanted him to take care of her. "But what would your mother say?"

"She'd have the church booked before breakfast. You're one of her favorites."

As they laughed, he threw an arm around her.

"You only get one shot with Roxie's girls. We have rules. Don't waste that shot on me. I'm not your forever girl."

"No such thing. No woman will tie me down."

They would if his mother had anything to say about it. Family was a big deal to the Breckenridges. A big, huge deal. While Deres were scarce, there was an abundance of Breckenridges. Alice Breckenridge, his mom, would always support her boys, no matter what, and the woman believed in the joy of love.

Did she believe in the joy of love anymore? Had she ever? Maybe once upon a time… to still believe would be sort of ridiculous.

A woman stepped up, out of the bodies dancing nearby to approach. Astrid. One of Roxie's assistants. Young, sometimes a little uncertain, but a beautiful person with a heart of gold.

Astrid crouched in front of them and Tripp leaned in to listen to the words whispered less than an inch from his ear. A young woman like Astrid could learn a lot from an experienced guy like Tripp Breckenridge. But he wouldn't teach, not Astrid… would he? Tripp liked women, that was for sure, but he wasn't indiscriminate, he had his own… parameters.

She bet everyone in that room had had sex of some sort in the last two weeks. Not her. No. She'd slept with the hottest man she'd ever met and somehow had been stubborn enough, ridiculous enough, to demand he keep certain body parts to himself. What had she been thinking? Stupid rules. Why couldn't she just let loose and have fun? What was wrong with her?

Maybe if she could figure that out, she wouldn't be facing a lifetime alone. Truman was all she had. And he wouldn't be around forever. Would she move into the house after he was gone? That big, echoey house. All alone. She loved living in it growing up, being there was a treat, and she'd rather have been there than at school most of the time.

Tripp laced his fingers between hers. "Come on."

"Come on where?"

He hoisted her to her feet and used their joined hands to hook her back against his chest. Weaving her through the dancers, they slipped into the elevator and then were going up.

"Roxie's got something for you upstairs."

"For me?" The hostess hadn't been at her side for a while. Roxie had a lot of people to entertain, so she hadn't thought anything of it. Now she learned the woman hadn't been in the room. "Upstairs where? What is it?"

"Just my job to get you there. I'll be around if there's trouble."

Trouble?

Why would there be trouble? Oh, what had Roxie got them into now? The tenacious woman was bold and unapologetic, whatever awaited her wouldn't be something subtle or benign.

They left the elevator on a floor of private suites. Not Roxie and Zairn's penthouse. Was that reassuring or not? Still with a hold of her hand and their bodies pressed together, Tripp guided her up the corridor and reached over her to shove open a door to send it rocking back, presenting the room to her. There was Roxie, not alone, with a couple dozen other people milling around. This was a private-private party of some kind.

There was music, alcohol, servers, canapés… Her friend spotted her and quickly rushed over.

"Okay, don't be mad," Roxie said, maintaining her smile though there was almost a wince in her eyes. "It was a spontaneous decision. Toria's suggestion actually…" Toria was another of Roxie's girls. "This is the best way to get answers. We're through letting them get away with it."

"Letting who get away with what?"

At that moment, the door in the far corner opened and Toria came out with two men. One of whom stopped her in her tracks. Okay, she hadn't actually been walking, but the whole world seemed to jar to a halt.

"Baer?" she hissed at Roxie, leaning in closer. "How did you get him here?"

"Honey, I get anything I want here. And if I phone for service, somewhere like Squires answers in a heartbeat. You know how much business we throw their way?" Roxie took her hand from Tripp. "We're going to give him a piece of our mind."

"Collectively?" Her friend led her across the room and her feet were too stunned to think about resisting. "Who are all these people?"

Roxie waved a dismissive hand over her shoulder. "People. Window dressing. A smokescreen, just like the half dozen other guys we requested from Squires."

Now that she mentioned it, the male faces were familiar. No Donoghue or Leon, but she got a flashback or two to the James Bond convention. Did they recognize her? What did it matter? The only person who mattered—oh, God, Roxie was taking her over there. She couldn't even bring herself to look up. Turned out she didn't need to, he made himself known.

"What the hell is this?"

"Oh, don't be so melodramatic, Baer," Roxie said and blocked his way, gesturing toward the door still open behind him. "Get in there."

He did as ordered, though his gait betrayed his reluctance, his anger.

"This how you get around what I said?" Baer asked, stopping next to the bed.

Yes, this was a bedroom. Great. Just where she needed to be holed up with him. The immaculate linens didn't bear a single crease. What a wonderful representation of their future. Pristine, perfect from afar but never to be touched.

"She knew nothing about this," Roxie said. "This was all me. Freya is one of the best, most kind, generous, incredible women not only in the city, but in the whole damn world. And men like you, who think just because you're pretty and women lineup, that you can treat kind, goodhearted people anyway you want. I say no. You don't get to treat her like dirt. Any woman like dirt. You don't pick them up, use them for their wealth—"

"Is that what she told you? Because the damn opposite is true. I don't want anything to do with her money. She's the one who chose to use it, to manipulate me and my family—"

Roxie laughed. "Not a chance I'll believe that. Of Freya Dere? No one would. You should do your research before slandering a woman like her. You're a creep, a letch, like all the other men who came before. You see her as a soft touch, a free ride. What you do allows you access to women with means, it doesn't follow that you can treat them like crap. Having money doesn't make them any less human. Did you think about that? What it's like to never know why people want to be in your life?"

"Yeah, she sold me that line too. Missed the part where she wanted every guy kowtowed. I sell sex, sure, that doesn't mean I'll give up my free will to the highest bidder."

She didn't get it. "I never wanted your free will. I wanted us to be together. What I said in the car—I told Roxie, before I came over to yours, I didn't want it to spook you. I could never have guessed it would make you do this. I don't understand how so much can change in so little time."

"You know exactly what you did. And it was nothing to do with what you said in the car." He scoffed in a sort of ironic laugh. "I was pissed then, sure. Not because you said it, but because you told me not to say it back. I thought we were there. I thought we had this and then you—"

"What?" she begged, cursing the alcohol for putting tears in her eyes. "What is it that you think I did? Conrad has the check, I wrote it before we left. And I told you the money was yours regardless of what happened on the vacation."

Except nothing had happened on vacation. As in, nothing bad. They'd been fine before they left, for the car rides, the flight. She couldn't understand where this was coming from.

"I don't give a shit about the money. You can keep your check. Conrad gave it to me, I put it in your mailbox on the way over here. I don't want it."

Now she was even more confused. "When did this change? The guy in the back of the car, when we were alone, the guy who invited me to dinner… How did we get from there to here?"

"You put us here. What? It wasn't enough that you paid all the past due bills—and my mom's tab, you put the damn account in credit like you were doing us a favor. Did you think I wouldn't figure it out? That I start dating a rich princess and it's a magical coincidence my rent's paid for the year, and the twins get accepted to some private school we never applied for, full tuition paid."

What was he talking about?

"Freya?" Roxie touched the groove of her back. "Are you okay, honey?"

No, the room was spinning. "I don't understand. How we got here… How we…"

Roxie guided her over to the bed practically barging Baer out the way. "Maybe this wasn't a good idea. You should lie down. I'll send the asshole away."

"I'm no asshole," Baer declared, offended. "She interfered. She went behind my back and tried to buy my family—"

"Oh, would you listen to yourself?" Roxie sneered. "You didn't know her at all if you think she's like that. She would never, ever go behind anyone's back. She would open her bank account to anyone in a heartbeat, but sneaking around, manipulating, being underhand, sly—"

"Roxie—"

"No, he doesn't get away with it. And you know what? I'm so damn pleased this has fallen apart now. God, do you have any idea what Zairn would do to this guy if he heard the way he's talking to you right now? So, asshole, if I were you, I'd get the hell out of here and never breathe Freya's name to anyone for the rest of your life. If you don't, you'll never work another day in the city, in this country. We'll make sure people wouldn't let you near enough to even shine their shoes."

"We're not like that. Roxie, we could never—"

"We don't have to be like anything. Just because you don't have a vindictive or scornful bone in your body doesn't mean I don't. I'm more than happy to ruin this asshole."

The door burst open, interrupting the moment. Astrid. Slightly out of breath, fixated on Roxie, and a few shades paler than she'd been downstairs. Uh oh.

# THIRTY-FIVE

"ASTRID?" Roxie's concern matched what she felt. "What happened? Where's Z?"

"On his way to wait for you in the car downstairs."

"Car? Where are we going?"

Remaining a little winded, Astrid managed a smile, though there was trepidation behind it. "It's Lilya."

"Oh my God, it's time? Time time?" Roxie's excitement was more enthusiastic. "Is Jane already—"

"At the hospital? Yes."

"I knew she'd get there first." Roxie bounded a step away, then paused to spin on the spot, wide eyes pinned to her. "Honey—"

"I'll be fine," she said, broadening a smile. "You go. Go."

"Want me to call Ballard to kick this asshole out?"

"No, we'll be fine."

"Okay, I love you." Roxie rushed back to hug her and kiss her cheek. "Tripp won't go far. And you already have Ballard on speed dial. If it's not him, one of his guys will be around."

"Now go, you don't want to miss the main event."

Roxie rushed out with Astrid, leaving her alone with Baer.

"No one has to kick me out, I'm leaving on my own."

"It wasn't me," she said before he could turn all the way around. "And Roxie's right, you didn't know me at all if you thought I was capable of that." He'd accused her of the same, the other way around. "I don't know what happened, but I can help you find out, if you want."

"It doesn't matter. I don't want any of it. Take it back."

"I can't take it back if I don't know where it came from. It's not mine to take back. There must be someone in your life with the means to—"

"If there was someone in my life with those means before you, who'd do this, I wouldn't be working at Squires, would I?"

Good point. She was the only variable, the only new person, and he was right that she had the means. Her grandfather—

And she almost groaned. The air left her body in a sort of slump. Man, she was slow on the uptake.

Truman. Of course Truman. How did he do it...? Found out things about the people in her life, she'd never asked for details. Yet, somehow, he always did. Hadn't she warned Baer of that? Shouldn't they be forearmed?

"It was Truman."

"Truman?" he asked. "Your grandfather?"

"Didn't I tell you he always interferes with my romantic relationships?" The question was rhetorical.

The only one who'd do this… "God, I'm so sick of this. In the past it was… It never mattered like this…"

Because Kinloch knew what to expect, and other men from her past weren't as important as this. As him. Baer was the most important one, and, what a surprise, she'd screwed it up.

"Why would he pay off my debts? What does that achieve?"

"Only he can answer that…"

She bounced to her feet and stalled in a wobble, and there Baer was at her side to hold her up. Because he cared, or was it human instinct?

Not so long ago, she'd woken to those eyes admiring her, adoring her, that was his description. He'd wanted to be with her then, he had, it couldn't have been an act all along. And if he wanted money, why wouldn't he be pleased that—

"Okay, time to go."

She hadn't heard anyone join them, but when Baer stepped aside, Tripp was there with one of Roxie's security guards at his back.

"Go?" Baer asked.

"Yeah, buddy, you've outstayed your welcome. You'll get your fee—"

"Fuck my fee," Baer said, putting himself in front of her. "You think I'm leaving her alone with Tripp Breckenridge? She's been drinking."

Tripp laughed. "Frey and I have known each other our whole lives—why am I justifying myself to you? If we want to fuck, we'll fuck. It's nothing to do with you."

"Yeah? You think I'll fucking walk away?"

Two new guys appeared, both security, advancing, with Baer the focus of their intent.

334 ~ SCARLETT FINN

"No one has to fight," she said, sneaking around him. "There's nothing to worry about. Tripp doesn't know how to hurt or pressure a woman, especially me."

With his jaw tight, Baer stooped closer. "If you think I'm leaving you alone with another guy—"

"What other guy?" she asked. "For there to be an 'other,' there has to be a first. You've made it perfectly clear you don't want that role." Because now with some of the confusion cleared up, her own hurt could manifest. "You were so quick to pin blame on me for overstepping, and you're doing the same thing now. Tripp is my friend. And didn't you say I could use other Squires guys?" There were a few in the next room. "You're free to see your clients, and I'm free to make my choices."

"Lil'—"

"Don't make a scene. If these guys have to put their hands on you, the press downstairs will take your picture when they throw you out."

Which could lead to reports online, to his family seeing him there, to them asking questions and possibly finding out what he did to keep the family afloat.

Still frowning, the glare left her to land on every other guy there. Then with a huff, Baer stalked on out. Security went after him, they wouldn't hurt him, they'd just make sure he really went.

"You okay?" Tripp asked after her next exhale.

"Truman's screwing up my life."

"He wouldn't know himself if he wasn't sticking his nose in."

"I have to confront him," she said, sinking back onto the bed again. "He screwed everything up."

"It's three in the morning, so I'd suggest doing it tomorrow."

She lay down and closed her eyes. "Tomorrow?"

"Tomorrow."

# THIRTY-SIX

HER GRANDFATHER. He was her agenda. She wasn't nervous.

After waking at Crimson, the previous night's events took a minute to come back. Boy, when they had, they'd hit her with purpose. On some things, she maybe hadn't learned her lesson.

There was no rush, she wanted to be reasonable about this. Emotion wasn't the best driver when it came to calling someone out. She wouldn't be emotional, she'd be calm, clear, and maybe he'd get the message to butt out.

Would Truman understand? She had to find out why. In the past, when investigating her romantic interests, she'd never heard of her grandfather going so far as to force the guy into the black. What odd comeuppance.

Did it matter?

Baer gave up on her. More than that he judged and ousted her without a fair trial. What did that mean? That he wasn't the stalwart she wanted him to be, that's what it meant. He'd given up on them too easy. Almost like he wanted the excuse to get rid of her.

Descending in the Crimson elevator, the truth was sinking in. Baer didn't want her, probably never had. She'd lost him. Was it even worth going to the house and demanding answers from Truman? What did she hope to achieve?

As expected, her car waited at the curb. What was unexpected? The man leaning against it talking to her driver. When they noticed her, both straightened and the driver went to open the back door.

She traversed a few steps toward Baer. "What are you doing here? How did you...? Why are you here?"

And why was he talking to her driver? How would he even know she was still there or when she'd be walking out?

"Truman," he said, approaching to meet her midway on the sidewalk. "You're going to talk to him."

And that mattered to him... "Yes. How long have you been waiting out here?"

"You're not the only one with connections."

Whatever that meant.

"Okay."

Weird kind of coincidence he'd be there at the same moment as her.

She got in the car, purse hooked around her forearm. It was ironic that Roxie was known for forgetting to charge her phone, yet there were charging docks on every nightstand. An addition Zairn introduced after getting with Roxie.

The car door didn't close, which wasn't a big deal until Baer got in to join her.

Only then was the door closed.

"Uh... what are you doing?"

"Coming with you."

"I didn't invite you."

"You're going to confront this guy about screwing with our relationship, you're not doing it alone."

"We don't have a relationship." This was unexpected and, these days, she didn't like unexpected. How was she supposed to stay cool and reasoned with an interloper in tow? "We'll drop you wherever—"

"No. Thanks for the offer, but I'm not going anywhere."

"Yes, you are," she said. "We are not doing this. I don't need a chaperone with my own grandfather. This is Dere family business, nothing to do with you."

"He came for me to get to you—"

"That's not what happened."

"So what did happen?"

Exactly the question. "That's what I'm going to find out."

"*We*. That's what *we're* going to find."

"Why would you want to be here? Yesterday you demanded I get out of your life. Now you're in my car. I'm sorry for Roxie hiring you last night. If it interrupted things with your other client, I'll call Conrad and apologize. Or was your client at the Crimson party?" Maybe Roxie got to him through the client. Few people would refuse an invitation from Roxie Kyst. She closed her eyes and shifted her purse. "Don't answer that. I don't want to know." She'd have to visit that building in future and did not want to carry the visual with her. "Would you like us to take you home or to Squires?"

"Neither. I'm coming to meet this Truman, find out why he got in my head."

"Oh, and you think that attitude will encourage me to take you along? No. This is between me and my grandfather."

"And me. I can talk to him alone—"

"This is none of your business. And you wouldn't even get through the gate without me. You want me to leave your family alone? You leave mine alone."

"We can fight about this from here until your grandfather's doorstep, I'm coming either way."

"No, you're not."

"What are you going to do? Wrestle me out of the car?"

Okay, what kind of gentleman was he? No, she couldn't wrestle him out of the car. Well, she could, not personally, of course, she'd have someone do it for her. Except she was not that person and wouldn't do that to him.

This wasn't a simple request for information.

"You want to know if it's true, don't you? You still doubt me. That's what this is, isn't it? You want to watch me ask him, because you still believe it was me."

"No, I want to stand next to you while you accuse him and ask him what the hell gives him the right to interfere with us. I almost lost you because of this. He's got to know he crossed the line."

Almost...? What was he saying? She was afraid to ask and fixed her eyes on the privacy screen between them and the driver. She couldn't hope, couldn't let her mind run away with daydreams again.

"What would Roxie do?" she whispered to herself.

"When we're through here, we're going back to yours."

Who did he think he was? "You can't dictate my day, you're not coming back to mine. I don't want you at mine."

Because it was the only place they'd made love, and that was the memory of him there that she wanted to keep.

He took her hand to his lap. "I'm not insecure about you being worth more than me. The money thing screws with my head because we've had no one to rely on for a long time. Makes it difficult to trust someone would stick around, that someone might want to get involved with my messed-up family."

Startled, she fixated on their united fingers. "Your family isn't messed up," she muttered before snapping from her daze and snatching back her hand. "And that doesn't explain why you'd accuse me of being duplicitous. I was only ever interested in an equal partnership and we always communicated, we've never hidden things from each other."

As far as she knew.

"That's what I thought too, then soon as I got back, there was Abel asking what was going on. There's a stack of mail showing every bill up to date, in credit, and I have no fucking idea what to tell him."

"And you went straight to me trying to control you?"

"I'm sorry, baby, what else was I supposed to think? You're the only one I know with that kind of power."

Money wasn't power, not if it took away the man she cared for most.

"Roxie thinks you're threatened by the money."

"I'm not."

"That it diminishes your manhood."

He actually smiled. "It doesn't."

"So why is it okay for a less affluent woman to be with a more affluent man? But it's not okay the other way around? You shut me down when I tried to talk about it, which I only did because I wanted to be with you. To be together, we'd have to join our lives. We needed a plan and—it doesn't matter."

"It does," he said, and grabbed her hand again. "It matters because I hurt you, and it matters because you're right. The money stuff… when we were away… I've spent a lot of time these last five years focused on where our next meal is coming from. Money has been my life because I had the kids, everyone, relying on me. There wasn't a day I woke up that I wasn't prioritizing bills in my head, which one had we skipped last month, which one was likely to bring collectors to my door… In the shower, I'd worry what would happen if I slipped and cracked my skull open. How would they survive? What would my dad do? Where would the twins end up?"

In care, probably. And she had no idea what would happen to his mom. She'd known it was a burden on him, all of it. Though he loved his family, they were solely reliant on him. Yet she hadn't been aware how it consumed every minute of his life. And he was right. Even a simple slip in the shower, on the stairs, on the sidewalk, could spiral everything out of control.

"I only ever wanted to be a part of your life," she murmured. "Never to take it over."

"And then there's you…" He scooped both hands around her jaw to cradle her head. "This beautiful, incredible woman who lands on me from nowhere." Not exactly accurate, but close. "And you're not just smart, and kind, and funny, but you see beyond the—my life was never a problem for you."

Not entirely true. "I was never wild about the other women, but I understand why you do what you do. That was never about control—"

"I know."

"I wanted to be patient, not to rush you, but the idea of you…"

"I know," he said again, his thumb moving in a slow caress. "I'd feel the same way. It was never about me wanting to go to them. But if I gave it up and we fell apart… When you're living on a knife edge, it's like the adrenaline's going all the time. And you don't want to let up because that's when there's a risk everything falls apart. And, come on, why would a woman like you want to be with me?"

"Money doesn't matter to me."

"Yeah, but I'm a—"

"Good, decent man, willing to do anything for the people he loves. Why wouldn't I want to be with you?"

"Do you think we can get past this last twenty-four hours?"

"I don't know."

Being together in such a concentrated setting then losing each other as fast was jarring. Could they know it wouldn't happen again? Could they trust?

"Lil' Skit, I would never—"

"I can't promise that Truman is done. We can go over there and talk to him, but that doesn't mean he'll accept us."

"I can handle it."

Of that she wasn't so sure. "Can you? Because you were quick to jump ship yesterday. I need an equal who'll fight these battles with me, not run away at the first sign of trouble."

"I can be that guy."

"There's no guarantee he won't push at you."

"Let him push."

When he tried to join their mouths, she pulled his hands away to lean back. "How do you see our future? If we were to have one, what would it look like?"

"How do you want it to look?"

"No, see, I don't want that, I don't want you deferring to me, putting the onus on me to develop a plan. I want an us future, not a me future with you as a passenger."

"I want what most people want, freedom, security, love."

"And you didn't think we could have that?" God, in so many ways, he infuriated her. "You can't be with me without dealing with my grandfather. Sometimes he's the kindest man in the world, but he can be ruthless. And he thinks it's his right to have an opinion on everything. I can't be with you if you'll be scared away at—"

"Then tell me this, will you support me?"

"Support you? In what? With Truman?"

"You know I come with the kids, my parents."

"That was never an issue for me." Maybe this was the moment to ask… "Though I have wondered…"

"Wondered what?"

"Would we live together?"

"Yes."

His certainty was encouraging.

"All of us? You know we could get a place big enough for everyone. Your mom too. We could have full-time staff for her, and the boys could see her every day…" Stop. Stop. Slow it down. Talk about getting carried away too quickly. Again. "This is what you didn't want, isn't it?"

"I didn't want to fall for you and lose you. I still don't. Though there's some part of me that… You bring so much to the relationship, what do I bring?"

"Your family," she said. "I've never had kids around, parents, life in a household."

"Well, we have that readymade."

"And I… You could…"

"Don't be hesitating."

"I know you've had more than your share of responsibility to deal with but…" The pounding of her heart didn't know whether it was nervous or excited. "Kids of our own, you could bring those."

The slow curl of his lips calmed her heart. A little. At least it wasn't trying to jump out of her chest anymore.

"That's one responsibility I'm happy to have."

The kids or the bringing of them?

"And I have a lot of work with the foundation. We have to make life or death decisions and work with families at the hardest times of their lives." He was uniquely qualified for that. "I'll share in your responsibility, but you have to share in mine too. It's something we can... Abel could help too. Work as much as he wants or doesn't want from home. We could do it together. Being with me means sharing in those heartaches and joys too. You're great with kids and understand the importance of family. Don't you want the chance to help others who could find themselves in situations like yours?"

"I do, actually."

"I don't want to do this on my own forever."

"You don't have to do anything alone, never again."

"And if Truman cuts me off or blackballs me, well..." She sighed. "We'll go into escorting together."

"I already told you," he said, cupping her jaw again. "Not a chance in hell."

She didn't resist his next kiss, she sank into it, into him. A weight of tension pressurized the air, forcing them close. They could lose this tomorrow; she could lose him. Through another misunderstanding or life tearing them apart, they'd both seen it.

Levying her weight back, she curled her lips into her mouth, steadying her breathing. "Any clients today?"

Though she wasn't so sure she cared about the rules right then.

"No," he said, unzipping her dress. "Only you, Little Skit."

"Good," she said, wriggling up her skirt to climb onto him. "Because I need something only my man can give."

# THIRTY-SEVEN

SHE'D NEVER FEARED her grandfather and still didn't. They rolled up the driveway and Baer ducked to look out the side window, taking in the view.

"This place is bigger than our vacation one." Yep, and it wasn't split into smaller apartments either. "Does he know we're coming?"

"No." Maybe. Sometimes, he just knew things. "He always works from the house on a Sunday."

The car stopped, and she immediately tugged his arm to get his attention. "Hound, you don't have to come in with me."

"I have to come in with you."

With a hold of her hand, he opened the door and led her out. No, she never feared her grandfather, but since Kinloch, she'd never been with a man so willing to confront him. Most wanted her grandfather's favor, and going in shouting the odds might not make the best first impression. Except Baer's potential actions weren't what preoccupied her.

Truman could say anything, do anything, threaten anything. This would be the real test of Baer's feelings for her, of whether their relationship could survive.

Inside, she took off her coat to hand it off to the valet while Baer ventured deeper into the foyer, absorbing it all.

He whistled. "This is some… We'll have to put trackers on the twins, we'll never find them in here."

Good. That was good. He was talking about their families merging, that was important… if her grandfather allowed it.

"Do you want to wait here? John can give you a tour or get you something to eat or… there's a billiards table downstairs. You can play some… Or there's my bedroom but…"

Might not be a good idea to hole him up in her room when her grandfather could be volatile.

Baer's focus came back as he did, and he held out a hand to the valet. "John?"

"Yes, sir," the valet said, looking to her for a smile of permission before he shook Baer's hand.

"Baer Claymore. You'll be seeing a lot of me. We'll teach the kids about loyalty to good staff, so your job's secure."

She laughed and took his arm, coiling hers around it. "I doubt he wants to be working here in fifty years."

"Never know, baby."

The wide corridors and thick carpets gave the place gravity, like God himself couldn't shake these foundations. Though, with her grandfather in charge, that was probably true.

They stopped at the closed door to Truman's office.

"Stay here a minute."

"Lil'—"

"Just a minute, okay? Let me… if we go in hard, he'll get defensive, no chance of him being reasonable then." And they needed at least a glimmer of that. Pushing to her tiptoes, she pulled him down for a quick kiss. "A minute, that's all."

"One minute."

He kissed her again and brows high, backed away a step.

This was her cue; it wasn't familiar to hold such trepidation. Still, shoulders back, she marched into her grandfather's office.

Always bold and proud, he was standing behind his broad desk.

"You did it again," she said, tossing her purse to the chesterfield.

"Gentlemen, excuse me," Truman said, though there was no one else in the room. "We'll reconvene later." He leaned over his chair to press a button on his phone. Right, the phone. "I didn't expect to see you today; this is a nice surprise. How was your vacation?"

"If you didn't expect to be seeing me today, you have no idea the severity of what you've done."

He smiled, resting his hands on the back of his chair. "What did I do?"

"What you always do, you interfered in my life. How many times do I have to tell you that I make my own choices? You can't get involved. This is my life. Mine."

"I do what I do to protect you."

"How does paying off my boyfriend's debts protect me?"

His mouth opened in a silent "ah." "The gigolo. With his debts paid off, he has no need to pursue you."

Well, at least the escort thing was a conversation she didn't have to instigate. "His name is Baer."

"His real name?" Truman asked with a smile that became mocking. "Or is that his stage name?"

"Why can't you let me run my own life?"

"You're far too old for teenage rebellion, and I can't, for the life of me, decide if this is fright or insanity."

"Fright? What are you—"

"The right man will come along when it's appropriate. If you would allow me to introduce—"

"I am not going to marry a man you choose; I'll marry a man I choose. You can't butt in and take over—what was it supposed to achieve? Throwing money at him like that? I suppose I should be grateful you didn't just wrap it in an envelope and mail it to him."

"A man in his profession likes money, craves money, and I did consider paying him off direct, but it wouldn't have been wise to give him another avenue to manipulate you. I assume that's what he did, given his parents' health issues, he manipulated your sympathies. He has what he wants and no longer needs you. I removed the problem."

"And you think by doing that, he'll drop me?"

"He's made his choice. I don't see him here, do you?"

That satisfaction was short-lived.

"Look harder," Baer's voice rose behind her.

Okay, so that wasn't a minute… maybe it was a minute, but she didn't expect him to time it to the second.

Her grandfather immediately hardened in concern. "You brought him to our house?"

Not exactly by choice, but she wouldn't say that. "We're together. Regardless of your interference, because we trust each other, we communicate." She didn't hear Baer approach but appreciated his hands sliding onto her shoulders. "Baer, this is Truman Dere. Truman, meet Baer Claymore."

"The man she's going to marry."

Okay, so they hadn't discussed that far, but she wouldn't object. In fact, the house might make a good venue for—and she was getting ahead of herself. What was with that?

"You're a tenacious man, but there's a time to leave the stage," her grandfather said and turned his chair to sit down and retrieve his checkbook. "Every man has a price."

"Not this man," Baer said. "You heard about my job and assumed I was with Freya for the money."

"You had considerable debt."

"That didn't need to be paid by you. Freya and I will make our own way, we don't need your money."

"Oh, really?" Truman asked, sinking back in his chair, spine still straight. "He wants you to cede your trust, your security, isolate you from those who—"

"I don't want to isolate her from anyone. You're her family, which means you're mine. And if you've done so much digging, you know that's why I did the work I did, to support my family." Discernment narrowed her grandfather's eyes just a fraction. "There's nothing I wouldn't do to keep my family safe. I don't have addictions or dangerous habits; I wasn't fueling anything that could hurt Freya. I made my money, I paid my bills. I wouldn't abandon my family, just as I wouldn't abandon Freya. She's my everything now."

"Is that so?"

"Yeah, you better get used to this face because it's gonna be around a lot, 'specially on birthdays, holidays, and not just mine, you'll get used to my little brothers' faces too because my family is now yours."

"And you'll expect us to support them—"

"Stop it," she said. "Listen to what he's saying. We could storm out of here and tell you to keep your money. It wouldn't change anything, Baer and I will still be together, tough times or not. You shouldn't want the people you care about to suffer, like Baer did in supporting his own. He gives his everything to his responsibilities, and all we need from you is acceptance."

Slowly, her grandfather examined them both. "He's the first man since Peake to face me direct."

"I know."

"You should've married Gramercy-Peake."

"Well, Granddaddy, if I'd done that, I'd be living in some log hut in oblivion with twenty kids and you'd never see me. With Baer, I stay in the city."

Come on, respond to the tease, he loved her, he had to see what this meant to her.

"Is that your plan?"

"Our plan is to get married," Baer said before she opened her mouth. "I love her, very deeply, and nothing will shake me from my conviction to be with her for the rest of our lives."

"You love her?" Oh, and her insides were doing a happy dance. "Yet you go out every night and sell—"

"I'm not selling anything," Baer said. "I quit."

Even she didn't expect that and glanced over her shoulder. "You quit?"

"This morning. I can't be with anyone else, it's not possible anymore. It's us, no one else." Oh, thank God, and she'd thought she was happy before that admission? "Freya and I are going to be together, Truman. You talk a big game about protecting her, what is it you're protecting her from? Heartache? Because you have enough dough that my financial troubles mean squat to you. It's a drop in the ocean, right?" Truman nodded once. "So it's not about money, and you have no reason to suspect me of being a physical threat to her."

"Baer—"

"All that's left is emotional pain," Baer said, intent on Truman. "You don't want her heart broken."

"It's an honorable purpose."

"No," Baer said, surprising them both. "It would be, if you weren't the cause of it." That startled her grandfather, not something that happened often. "You love her and you want her to be happy. I'm standing here telling you I will dedicate the rest of my life to that purpose. And if you refuse us your blessing, if you rail against our marriage, what happens to her heart then? You are her family, her history, her future, it's all wrapped up in you. She worships you."

"And I her."

"Then don't break her heart. She's picked me and I'm not going anywhere. Freya is warm and kind, she's open and vulnerable. Those qualities came from somewhere and you raised her. That tells me all I need to know about you as a man. I love her and I know you do too, troubles and celebrations, we're a part of each other's lives now. Trust her to choose. Trust her heart."

Trust her. Would he do that? Would Truman Dere acquiesce for her?

Her grandfather exhaled. "My blessing?" She could only hope. Truman looked at her. "This is your pick?" She nodded. "You're sure?"

"Roxie likes him."

Or she would when she got to know him.

"Then I suppose it's time to meet the rest of the family," Truman said. Her heart could've stopped. "Bring them here, and we'll see what we can do about that blessing."

Rushing around the desk, she threw her arms around her grandfather, tears already staining her cheeks. "Thank you."

"Yes, yes, now if we're having guests, I'll need peace to finish here."

She kissed his cheek and hurried to join Baer who guided her back into the hallway.

"Did you mean that?" she asked as he closed the office door. "What you said about getting married and giving up Squires?"

"I haven't been with anyone since you." He slung an arm around her. "Though I may need to pick up a few clients to buy you the kind of ring you deserve."

Smiling, her hand landed on his stomach. "There's always the sixty-thousand-dollar check."

"That should about cover it. Now you said something about a bedroom…"

Together. Families united. Who could have thought bumping into a guy while beating a retreat would lead to pure happiness? Faith… Hope… A lifetime of false starts brought her to that moment, to Baer, and she wouldn't trade him for anything.

# Read more from the Roxiverse in
# *Nothing to Beat...*

**Thank you for reading this tale!**
If you can, please take the time to review.

~

Ask your local library for more Scarlett Finn
novels!

~

For all things Scarlett Finn
check out:

www.scarlettfinn.com

# Next in the Roxiverse:

SCARLETT FINN

www.ingramcontent.com/pod-product-compliance
Lightning Source LLC
Chambersburg PA
CBHW030552170726
48283CB00002B/296